proximity

OTHER BOOKS AND AUDIO BOOKS
BY TRACI HUNTER ABRAMSON

UNDERCURRENTS SERIES

Undercurrents

Ripple Effect

The Deep End

ROYAL SERIES

Royal Target

Royal Secrets

Royal Brides

SAINT SQUAD SERIES

Freefall

Lockdown

Crossfire

Backlash

Smoke Screen

Code Word

Lock and Key

Drop Zone

Spotlight

Tripwire

GUARDIAN SERIES

Failsafe

Safe House

STAND-ALONES

Obsession

Deep Cover

Chances Are

Chance for Home

Kept Secrets

Twisted Fate

Proximity

proximity

A NOVEL

TRACI HUNTER ABRAMSON

Covenant Communications, Inc.

Cover image *Dry Roses* © Grape_vein, iStockphotography

Cover design by Christina Marcano

Cover design copyright © 2018 by Covenant Communications, Inc.

Published by Covenant Communications, Inc.

American Fork, Utah

This is a work of fiction. The characters, names, incidents, places, and dialogue are either products of the author's imagination, and are not to be construed as real, or are used fictitiously.

Printed in the United States of America

First Printing: October 2018

22 21 20 19 18   10 9 8 7 6 5 4 3 2 1

ISBN: 978-1-52440-682-0

For Tiffany and John

ACKNOWLEDGMENTS

RARELY DO I FIND so many pieces of real life making their way into a novel, but *Proximity* pulls from events that have occurred over the past several decades. Thank you to Tiffany Hunter for sharing your story and for living so many of the memories captured within these pages. I'll play hide-and-seek with you anytime. Thanks to my parents for the many summers in Pinewood and to Wanda Hunter for providing the upgraded backdrop of Grandma and Granddad's house.

My continued appreciation to the people at Covenant Communications who have helped guide my writing career, especially Samantha Millburn, Stephanie Lacey, Kathy Jenkins, and Robby Nichols. Thank you to my critique partners, Paige Edwards and Ellie Whitney. I don't know what I'd do without you.

Thanks to my husband, Jon, and to my children, Diana, Christina, Lara, Gabriel, and Luke for your continued support. I also want to thank Sarah Miller for the inspiration for Tia's career. It's been a joy watching you become the woman you are today.

Thanks to my fellow Mingus Marauders who made my years in Cottonwood such an adventure, especially Paula Robinson, Stephanie Futral, and Lora Feight.

Finally, thank you to the many readers who continue to support my writing. I hope you enjoy catching up with some old friends while making some new ones.

Chapter 1

SNOW-CAPPED MOUNTAINS. DEEP RAVINES. WATER flowing through the river below. Colby Farren stared at the ocean in the distance and breathed in the crisp Alaskan air.

He closed his eyes and let himself remember his days with Lexi before things went wrong. Three glorious years. She had been a bright spot in his otherwise dark world as he had completed his law enforcement training and suffered through his rookie year for the small police force in Valdez, Alaska.

A gust of wind tore along the ridge, and his breath caught in his chest. His broken dreams bubbled inside him. Lexi had always wanted a June wedding. He had desperately wanted to give it to her. Instead, everything had ended when department cutbacks had forced him to find other employment.

Why hadn't she agreed to go with him? Life would be different in the lower forty-eight, but they could have made a good life together there. *Together.* He let that word repeat in his mind before it shattered against the memories.

Lexi had made it clear they would never be together again. With another icy breath, he looked out over the ravine one last time. Then he turned and climbed into his SUV, not bothering to buckle the seat belt. In two more days, June 2 would be remembered only as the day he'd left Alaska. It most certainly would not be his wedding day.

* * *

Tia didn't take the time to glance at her watch. She was late. She was always late. Tonight, she had tried so hard to make sure she'd left the high school on time. How was she to know one of her football players would sustain a knee injury ten minutes before the end of practice? Experience. After three years as Mingus Union High School's athletic trainer, she should have known Murphy's Law was always in play when she had someplace to be, even when the only thing going on at practice was out-of-season weight lifting.

Her low heels clicking against the pavement, she rushed across the parking lot in the Arizona heat. She lifted her long hair off her neck to expose it to fresh air as she made her way from her car to the restaurant. Inside, several tables had been pushed together in order to seat the entire wedding party. Tia's eyes narrowed when she saw that only half the seats were occupied. Was it possible that a dozen people were even later than she was?

From her seat by the head of the table, the bride-to-be noticed her arrival and waved. Confused, Tia closed the distance between them and hugged her best friend. "Julie, where is everyone? I thought this was supposed to start twenty minutes ago."

"I lied," Julie said.

"What do you mean you lied?"

"Our rehearsal dinner doesn't start for ten more minutes."

Tia looked at her phone and read the note she had put in her calendar. "But you said six."

"Yeah, but you're always late, and I wanted you to be on time."

"Seriously?"

Standing by the head of the table, the groom coughed to cover what could only be his laughter. Tia looked from Julie to Drew and back again. "Do you guys have any idea what I went through trying to be on time? I'm lucky I didn't get a speeding ticket."

Drew slung his arm around her shoulders. "Tia, we love you, but it doesn't matter how hard you try. You're never on time, especially on a day when you have work."

"And you always have work," Julie added.

"Not this weekend." Tia eyed them suspiciously. "You didn't lie to me about the wedding too, did you?"

"We thought about printing a fake invitation for you, but we figured we wouldn't be able to pull the same stunt twice," Drew admitted.

The restaurant door burst open, and Tia turned to see a light-haired man rush in, his blue eyes scanning the room until his gaze landed on Drew.

As though replaying her entrance, he crossed to them and asked, "Where is everyone? I thought I was late."

Julie simply smiled. "You're right on time."

"But I thought . . ."

"Evan, have you met Tia?" Drew asked. When Evan shook his head, Drew continued with the introductions. "Evan Spence, Tia Parker."

"Ah, the missing groomsman," Tia said. "It's nice to meet you."

"Good to meet you too," Evan said, offering his hand. "Maid of honor, right?"

"Yeah."

When the rest of the wedding party streamed through the door, Drew and Julie moved to greet them.

Seeing the lingering confusion on Evan's face, Tia lowered her voice and asked, "Let me guess. No matter how hard you try, you're always late. Right?"

"How did you know that?" Suspicion replaced his previous confusion. "Has Drew been talking about me?"

"No, but I'm guessing Drew told you the rehearsal dinner started at six."

"Yeah." He pulled his phone from his pocket and checked the time. "At least, I thought he did."

"Julie told me the same thing." Tia motioned toward the door. "I only got here a minute before you."

"Wait a second." He whipped his head around to look at the bride and groom before turning back to her. "Are you saying Drew lied to me?"

"And Julie lied to me," Tia confirmed. "The reason we're both on time tonight is because our friends know us too well."

Evan's blue eyes flashed with mischief. "Do you think they know us well enough to expect retaliation?"

"Aren't the groomsmen in charge of decorating their car?" she asked, pleased to see they were standing on common ground.

"That happens to be one of my areas of expertise."

"If you need help, I'm available," Tia offered. "I happen to have a whole box of window paints I would be happy to donate to the cause."

"A new partner in crime. I like it." Evan held up his cell. "Sounds like I need your number so we can make plans."

Tia took his phone and entered her contact information. A moment later, her phone buzzed with a text message from Evan so she would have his number as well.

"Okay, everyone," Drew said, coming back to his place at the head of the table. "Grab a seat. Dinner is served."

Evan pulled out a chair for Tia before taking the seat beside her. After giving the waitress their drink orders, Evan said, "I gather you live around here."

"I live in Cottonwood. It's about twenty-five minutes away. What about you? Where are you from?"

"Michigan."

Her lips curved up immediately. "How are you doing with the Arizona heat so far?"

"I melted somewhere between the airport and the rental car lot."

"Be grateful Julie and Drew decided to get married in Sedona instead of Phoenix."

"I voted for Detroit," Evan said. "Much cooler this time of year."

"Sorry, but I'm not thinking Detroit sounds like the most romantic spot to get married."

"Have you ever been?"

"Does the airport count?" Tia asked.

"Not even close." He picked up his water glass and took a sip. "You'll have to come visit sometime, and I'll show you around."

Doubtful the offer was sincere, she lowered her voice and asked, "Would I have to be on time for anything?"

"Yeah." Evan leaned closer, as though sharing a secret. "The plane."

"Right."

"Don't worry. I'm sure I could lie to you about what time your flight leaves to make sure you don't miss it."

"That would make you as bad as them." Tia glanced in Julie and Drew's direction.

"Maybe, but if it got you there, it would be worth it."

Chapter 2

EVAN STARTLED AWAKE WHEN HIS phone rang. Was he late? He pushed aside the fog in his brain, remembering where he was. Drew's wedding wasn't until tomorrow. The only pre-wedding activity scheduled today was the combined bachelor/bachelorette parties, and those wouldn't start until this evening.

The phone stopped ringing only to start again five seconds later. Bleary-eyed, he read the bedside clock in his hotel room: 5:14. In the morning.

He snatched up the phone and answered it to stop the incessant noise. "Hello?"

"Evan, it's Wendell Harrison."

Wendell Harrison. The British intelligence officer Evan had worked with when redesigning the British security system for their public transportation. "What can I do for you?"

"There's been an attack on a train outside London. I need your help," the man said in his distinctive British accent.

Evan shot straight up in bed and forced himself to ask the dreaded question. "Casualties?"

"Four confirmed dead, and at least thirty injured."

"I'm so sorry, Wendell." Grief bubbled up inside Evan. He had spent months writing new computer code and upgrading the security monitoring systems for the British to prevent exactly this kind of terrorist attack. While logic told him no system was foolproof, that didn't stop the question from racing through his mind. How had this happened? "What can I do to help?"

"We're shut out of the security program. It looks like it reset. We need to access it so we can identify the people involved."

"Just a minute. Let me see if I can unlock it from here." Evan opened his laptop and keyed in several passwords to access the surveillance feed through a backdoor he had created in his program. "The programming reset because someone tried to hack into the system."

"The security video?" Wendell asked, panic in his voice.

Evan pressed a few more keys, a sigh of relief escaping him. "Still intact. I'm emailing you instructions on how to gain access again. If you have any problems, let me know."

"Thank you, Evan," Wendell said, his relief evident.

"Good luck to you." Evan hung up the phone and did an internet search for the latest news. His stomach roiled when an image popped up of the victims along the side of the tracks, their bodies bruised and broken.

He powered off his laptop and closed his eyes against the terrifying reality so many miles away. This weekend was supposed to be about the hope and future for one of his closest friends. Instead, dozens of people were living a nightmare. Struggling against the senseless loss, he contemplated how he could keep his job from interfering with what should only be a happy occasion.

Moving to the window, he stared out at the red rocks radiating beneath the early-morning sun and decided there was only one thing to do. He changed into his workout clothes and headed for the hotel stairs. Maybe a good run would help him push away the feeling that somehow he could have done more.

* * *

Tia pushed through the door to the hotel stairs, surprised to find someone two steps from the landing. "Sorry," she said automatically before she recognized the familiar face staring back at her. "Evan. What are you doing up so early?"

"I could ask you the same thing. It's three hours later where I live." He waited for her to enter the stairwell before he closed the distance between them. "Do you normally get up at 5:30 in the morning?"

"Pretty much. Like you said, I'm from here. No one in their right mind goes running in the middle of the day."

"I hadn't thought of that."

"I don't know how far you were planning to go, but you're welcome to join me," Tia said, continuing down the stairs.

"That would be great," Evan said. "How come you're staying here at the hotel? I thought your place wasn't far."

"It's not, but Julie wanted me close by this weekend. I think she's worried if I commute back and forth, I won't be where I'm supposed to be on time."

"Does it strike you as odd that two people who are always late are up at the crack of dawn?"

"Yeah, that is kind of weird, isn't it?" Tia glanced at him, her eyes the color of spun gold. "Could you imagine how late we would be if we didn't start our day this early?"

"That's a scary thought." They reached the first floor, and Evan opened the door leading outside.

Tia started forward. "Come on. I'll show you the Sedona that tourists don't always see."

"Sounds like an offer I can't refuse."

* * *

Sweat dripped down Evan's back as he slowed to a walk beside Tia. Their run had given him exactly what he'd needed: a way to get his body moving to clear his mind. He couldn't quite free himself of the images of the terrorist attack this morning, but at least he had managed to push them to the back of his mind for a while.

"Do you mind if we hike through the woods for our cooldown?" Tia motioned to a trail leading along the creek. "It's only about a mile."

"Sounds good." He followed her lead, letting himself enjoy the contrast of foliage and red rock. "I can use the shade."

"This isn't hot," Tia countered.

Evan's mood lightened when Tia stopped by the stream, leaned down, and splashed water on her arms, face, and neck. "I thought you said it wasn't hot."

"It's not," she said without missing a beat.

Evan watched the water trickle off her neck and into the fabric of her T-shirt. Deciding to follow her example, he leaned down beside her and splashed himself, only he didn't limit his efforts to his exposed skin. Water sluiced up over his head, down his back, and onto the waistband of his shorts. Refreshed, he repeated the process with more exuberance, this time including Tia in the drenching.

"Really?" Sarcasm dripped along with the water that now trickled down her right leg.

Evan caught the look on her face, an expression that fell somewhere between amusement and disbelief. "Oh, sorry," he lied.

"Don't forget that I'm your partner in crime for getting even with Drew and Julie," Tia reminded him. "I don't think you want to be on my bad side."

He straightened and debated briefly. "You may be right."

"Come on. It's this way."

Amused that Tia hadn't been fazed by getting soaked, he followed behind her. They picked their way up a narrow path for about a hundred yards. When it widened enough to allow them to walk side by side, Tia said, "Tell me everything I don't know about you."

"Like what?"

"Anything. Everything." She sidestepped an oak tree and looked back at him.

Evan thought of Brooklyn and the eighteen months they had been together, as well as the business partnership that had dissolved when they'd parted ways. He pushed her out of his mind and focused on safer topics. "Let's see. I was born in Ann Arbor, which is where my parents still live."

"Brothers and sisters?"

"One of each. An older sister and a younger brother," Evan said. "What about you?"

"An older sister. She's already married, with two daughters." Tia's expression brightened. "Kyla is already threatening to get even with me when I have kids because of the presents I sent her girls last Christmas."

"What did you send them?"

"I bought them new stockings." Tia's shoulders lifted. "I even filled them for her."

Evan caught the mischievous look in her eyes. "What aren't you telling me?"

"Musical instruments may have been involved."

"What kind of musical instruments?"

"Loud ones," Tia admitted. "My sister also isn't looking forward to filling the stockings this year. They were a bit larger than normal."

"How much larger?"

"My youngest niece fit inside hers." Tia held up a hand. "But she was only a year old, which isn't so bad."

Evan chuckled. "So, you and your sister are close."

"Yeah. Of course, any time we argued about anything, our mom would guilt us into behaving."

"How did she do that?"

"She'd tell us how she was always so proud of us for getting along. That was usually followed by some comment about how embarrassed she was that we were making her a liar. The conversation usually went downhill from there."

Evan thought of his own childhood and the clashes that had often occurred between him and his siblings. "I think I'd prefer that kind of conversation over my mom yelling every time a fight broke out."

"Did you fight much?"

"Mostly when my sister caught us spying on her." He gave her a sheepish grin. "I don't know what the big deal was."

"Let me guess. Slumber parties?"

"Dad didn't believe in those, but there was a huge tree in the front yard with a great view of the street and our front porch," Evan admitted. "Her boyfriends didn't seem to appreciate our presence, but my dad never seemed to mind."

"I'll bet."

The light played through the trees, catching the highlights in Tia's dark hair. She glanced in his direction, and not for the first time, Evan noticed the unique color of her eyes. "Your eyes really are gold."

"That's what it says on my driver's license."

"Do you have any idea how rare your eye color is?"

"What can I say?" Tia said. "I'm one of a kind."

"I'm starting to believe that." They came over a rise, and their hotel came into view. "How about we grab some breakfast after we get cleaned up?"

"Sounds good," Tia said. "Want to meet me at the hotel restaurant in about thirty minutes?"

"Perfect. I'll see you then."

* * *

Colby took his passport back from the border guard and put his SUV in gear. He pulled forward, an unexpected sense of excitement bubbling inside him. Canada. Not once in his twenty-nine years had he ever before ventured out of Alaska.

When he had used the internet to map his route, he had seriously considered having his car shipped so he could take a plane instead, but he wanted the chance to experience new things, to start fresh and leave the past behind.

The memory of Lexi surfaced, but he pushed it aside. He couldn't think about what should have been.

He took in the landscape, a little disappointed that the rugged mountains lined with trees in front of him looked very much like the ones in his rearview mirror. He wasn't sure what he'd expected, but more of the same wasn't it.

Four more days of driving, he reminded himself. Surely, by the time he reached the end of his journey, he would find the new adventure he was looking for.

* * *

Tia fastened her earrings and stepped into a pair of black heels. Her day had been a blur of running errands for Julie, but somehow, she had managed to have both breakfast and lunch with Evan.

A knock sounded on her door, and she opened it to find Evan standing on the other side.

"You're starting to scare me," Tia said. "This is three times today you've been on time."

"Don't look now, but you're on time too."

"Wow. You're right." She stepped into the hall and closed the door behind her. "Maybe this is like when you're multiplying numbers and two negatives equal a positive."

"Two late people joined together make an on-time couple?" Evan asked, amused.

"Something like that."

Evan motioned to her three-inch heels. "Do you want to take the elevator?"

"The stairs are fine."

"Are you sure? Those heels don't look like they're easy to walk in."

"I'm an athletic trainer. Believe me, I've learned to walk and run in just about every kind of shoe." She lowered her voice as they headed down the hall. "Do you know what we have planned tonight? Julie hasn't told me anything."

"That's probably because she doesn't know anything," Evan said. "Drew wanted it to be a surprise. He reserved a bunch of tables for a concert at some local restaurant."

Tia stopped walking and grabbed his arm. "The Sound Bites Grill?"

"Yeah, I think that's it."

Her grip on him tightened before she let go and waved a hand in the air. "Oh my gosh. Julie is going to die."

"Why?" Evan asked, drawing out the word.

"Kendra Blake is playing tonight," Tia explained. "She's Julie's all-time favorite singer. Jules was so disappointed when she found out Kendra was coming on a weekend she wouldn't get to see her. It's not very often Kendra performs in such an intimate setting."

"Well, Julie not only gets to see her. She also has backstage passes for after the show."

They reached the ground floor, and Tia looked at him with a serious expression. "I think we should be okay. I know CPR."

Evan shook his head and laughed. "I don't think meeting her favorite singer will be fatal."

"No, but maybe we should stop by the store to get some smelling salts."

"Come on." Evan took her by the elbow. "I'm sure it won't be that bad."

Chapter 3

EVAN DIDN'T KNOW JULIE COULD scream that loud. The moment Drew parked the car in front of The Sound Bites Grill, Julie let out a piercing shriek that was still bouncing off the interior of Drew's SUV.

Tia leaned close. "Told you."

They all climbed out of the vehicle, Julie's excited chatter overshadowing all else.

"Drew, I can't believe you got us tickets. This is so amazing."

Evan recognized the moment Drew opened his mouth to tell her about the backstage passes. Behind Julie, Evan and Tia motioned with their hands and shook their heads.

"Wait," Tia mouthed.

Apparently recognizing the wisdom of spacing out his fiancée's surprises, he nodded in agreement.

"That was close," Tia muttered under her breath.

"Is there a drugstore nearby?" Evan whispered back. "Maybe we should get those smelling salts."

"She made it through the initial shock okay," Tia whispered back. "I think she'll be fine."

"What about getting some earplugs for us? That's one heck of a scream she's got."

"I know. I think I still have hearing damage from when we went through the haunted house together when we were seven."

They walked into the restaurant. There were tables scattered throughout the open space and a stage on one end of the room. Five tables in front of the stage each had reserved signs posted in the center, the area dimly lit in anticipation of the stage lights turning on.

A few other members of the wedding party had already arrived, and Evan was searching for two seats together when a man in his forties approached.

"Hi, Joel," Tia greeted him. "This is Evan. He's one of Drew's groomsmen."

"Good to meet you." Joel shook his hand and turned back to Tia. "I need you to come with me. Evan, you should come too."

"Is everything okay?" Evan asked, curious.

Joel's only response was to lead them down a hall toward the backstage area. A tall, blond man stood outside the dressing room door. He focused on Tia. "Are you the maid of honor?"

"That's me."

"Great." He offered his hand. "I'm Charlie Whitmore. My wife wanted to talk to you before the show starts."

The dots connected the moment Evan heard Charlie's name. He would have needed to be hiding under a rock not to know of his marriage to Kendra Blake.

"I'm Tia Parker, and this is Evan Spence," Tia said, unfazed. Maybe Tia didn't realize she was talking to a superstar's husband.

"Good to meet you both." Charlie knocked twice on the door before pushing it open and motioning them inside.

Evan waited for Tia to go first, stepping into the surreal a second behind her. The stunning blonde standing by the dressing table turned to face them, a warm smile lighting her face.

"You must be the maid of honor." Kendra stepped forward and clasped both of Tia's hands with hers.

"It's so good to meet you," Tia said.

Evan was impressed that Tia was able to speak coherently when meeting a celebrity of Kendra's fame.

Charlie introduced Evan, and Evan opted for a simple nod in lieu of a greeting.

"When I heard about your friends' wedding party being here tonight, I wanted to do something memorable, but I didn't have any contact information," Kendra explained. "I hoped you might know their favorite song or help me pick something that would be special for them."

"Honestly, just mentioning them from on stage will make their night," Tia said.

"I can do that, but I have a couple other ideas I wanted to run by you."

Evan watched as the two women bent their heads close together over a paper on the makeup table.

"Does Kendra do small concerts like this often?" Evan asked Charlie when he managed to dislodge his tongue from the back of his throat.

"No, but we're vacationing nearby with her family, and Kendra knows Joel from when she was a kid." Charlie's gaze stayed on his wife as he spoke. "Personally, I think she prefers the small venues. She loves getting to talk to fans without feeling like she's going to get stampeded."

"The timing sure worked out," Evan said. "My ears are still ringing from when Julie found out we were coming tonight."

"I'll take that kind of scream any day."

"That's right. You're with the FBI, aren't you?"

"Yeah. I alternate between the Nashville and Phoenix offices," Charlie said. "I'm actually going to be working in Flagstaff for the rest of the year. Other than her performance tonight, Kendra will take the next few months off to rest and write."

"I can't imagine how crazy your lives must be," Evan said.

"Hey, when you find the right woman, any sacrifice is worth it."

Evan glanced at the two women. "I'll take your word for it."

* * *

Tia's ears were still aching from when Julie had found out she was meeting Kendra Blake in person. The whole situation didn't seem quite real.

Charlie had invited her and Evan to join the happy couple when they went backstage. When Julie came face-to-face with her idol, she was barely able to put together a coherent sentence. After ten minutes, Tia saw Charlie's subtle signal that it was time to move Julie and Drew along.

Tia put a hand on Julie's arm. "Kendra, thanks again for everything tonight. We'd better let you go. You must be exhausted."

"It was good meeting all of you," Kendra said. "Julie and Drew, enjoy tomorrow. I hope you have a wonderful marriage."

"Oh, thank you." Julie shook her hand, pumping it several times. "Thank you so much."

Tia tugged on Julie's arm and guided her toward the door. She glanced back and saw Charlie mouth "Thank you" as they continued forward.

Tia motioned with a thumbs-up and called out, "Thanks, Charlie."

"Can you believe this?" Julie asked, stepping into the cool night air. "We were talking to Kendra Blake. *The* Kendra Blake."

"Drew, you did good," Tia said, crossing to their car.

"Yeah, you're doomed now," Evan said. "You'll never be able to top that one."

Drew's eyes widened in horror. "You're right."

"Don't worry, Drew," Tia countered. "She was already in love with you."

"True," Julie confirmed, finally looking like she might be coming down out of the cloud she was flying on. As soon as they all climbed into the car, Tia realized she was wrong. Julie was still flying high, and Tia wondered if her friend would manage to sleep tonight.

They entered the hotel together and ran into Drew's youngest sister and parents in the lobby. To Tia's surprise, Evan took Tia's hand and said, "We'll see you guys later."

He led her toward the stairs. When they were out of earshot, he said, "Sorry, but if we'd stayed with them, we might have gotten stuck all night. Drew's sister never stops talking."

"She's eighteen. That's what teenagers do."

"I guess in your line of work, you would know." Evan pushed open the door to the stairwell. "What time are we supposed to leave for the ceremony?"

"Do you want me to tell you the truth, or should I lie?" Tia asked.

"Since we're both on a roll, let's go for the truth."

"We need to leave for the church at two."

"I'd offer to give you a ride over, but I guess I'm taking some of Drew's family in my car."

"It's fine. I have the window paints in my truck anyway."

Evan lowered his voice. "We still need to decide when we're going to decorate the car."

"I was thinking about that—"

Evan's phone rang, and he pulled it free of his pocket. His brow furrowed when he saw the screen. "I'm sorry. This is a work call. I need to take it. Can I call you in a few minutes?"

"Yeah, no problem." Tia watched him answer his call and head back toward the stairs. She let herself into her room, two questions on her mind: What did Evan do for a living? And why would someone call him at one o'clock in the morning?

* * *

"Sorry about that, Wendell," Evan said when he entered his hotel room. "I can talk now. What's the latest?"

"The police picked up the suspects an hour ago," Wendell told him. "Once we accessed the surveillance video, they were able to identify the culprits."

His earlier questions and doubts surfaced. "Any idea how they got past security?"

"They had an inside man working at the Gatwick train station. He had disabled a couple of the main security cameras. Luckily, he didn't know about the backup cameras you helped us install."

Relief flowed through him at the realization that his programming hadn't been at fault. "Do you think he's the one who tried to hack the security system?"

"Oh yeah. That's how we found him. The internet connection led us straight to him," Wendell said. "Glad you convinced us to add that tracker program."

"I'm glad it worked." Evan toed off his shoes and kicked them into the hotel room closet. "Let me know if there's anything else you need."

"I will. Thanks again for your help, Evan," Wendell said, raw emotion evident in his voice. "Today could have been a lot worse."

* * *

The lower forty-eight. Colby had seen pictures and watched movies, but now, driving through the open spaces of Montana, his reality came into focus. He was completely alone.

Been there before, he reminded himself.

Absently, he rubbed a hand over his stomach where a particularly nasty scar remained from his childhood, a gift from his father.

The beatings he had endured growing up now seemed like a bad dream that had happened to someone else, as did the fight that had ultimately caused him to leave home at eighteen and never look back. He shook the memories away. He wasn't his father's punching bag anymore, nor was he the lost teenager trying to make ends meet in Anchorage. He had a career and a future now, one he had fought hard to carve out for himself.

He rolled his shoulders to work out the stiffness that had settled there. Fifty-nine hours of driving in four and a half days hadn't seemed like that much when he'd planned his route, but the inactivity had combined with boredom, making him anxious to get to his final destination. The idea that he was more than halfway there didn't give him much consolation.

A highway patrolman waited on the median as he passed by, reminding Colby that for the moment, he was a civilian like everyone else. He didn't like the feeling. A couple more days. Once he reached Arizona, he would receive his new badge and police-issue weapon. After that first step was complete, he would find a way to make everything right in his new world.

* * *

Evan tugged at his tie as the lights dimmed and the first dance for the bride and groom was announced. After spending most of his time over the past few days with Tia, he had felt like he was calling an old friend earlier when he had dialed her number to work out the final details of when they were going to "decorate" the bride and groom's car. He waited until the song was halfway over before he slipped out the exit and headed for the parking lot.

Tia had arrived before him. He stared when he saw her standing beside a classic Chevy truck that looked straight out of the 1940s. She lowered the tailgate and lifted out a box nearly as big as she was. Her keys dangled from her right thumb, and her feet were bare. He moved forward and took the box from her. "What's all this?"

"Window paint." She waited for him to set it beside Drew's car and leaned down to open the box.

Evan eyed the tubes of paint and looked at her pale-pink gown. "You're going to ruin your dress."

"No, I won't." She riffled through the contents and pulled out some masking tape and several rolls of plastic sheeting. When she straightened, she asked, "Did you bring the cans?"

"Yeah." He held open a plastic bag filled with old soda cans, pieces of string piercing the center of each.

"This is great. I'm surprised you were able to find so many."

"Apparently today is recycling day in Drew's neighborhood."

Her laughter carried on the faint breeze. "You start on the cans. I'll get the car ready to paint."

Not sure exactly what she had in mind, Evan went about his task. After he finished tying the cans to the rear bumper, he stood to find Tia had taped plastic sheeting to the edges of the glass so Drew's classic Mercedes was protected, with the windows still exposed.

Evan glanced at his watch. "If we're out here much longer, they're going to know it was us."

"I'm done." Before he could question her further, she let out a low whistle. Thirty seconds later, three teenagers emerged from the nearby trees. Tia held her keys out and handed them to the only girl in the trio. "Beth, I'm trusting you to keep these guys in line."

"Don't worry, Park," one of the boys said. "We've got this."

Tia gave them a stern look. "If I hear about my truck being anywhere other than the road between here and the pizza place, I won't be happy."

"Yes, ma'am." Beth gave her a mock salute.

"Thanks guys. Pizza money is on the dash."

Surprise illuminated Beth's face. "Wait. You actually have cash?"

"Don't look so shocked. I may not like ATMs, but I do know how to use them." Tia turned to Evan and tucked her hand into the crook of his arm. "Shall we?"

"Wait." Evan turned to see the teens digging into the paint supplies. "They're going to paint the car?"

"Of course. We couldn't have you get your tux dirty."

"And you gave your car keys to a teenager."

"Beth was in my class for a few years. I trust her."

"Why don't they drive their own car?"

"Because you have to show your invitation to the parking attendant at the bottom of the hill," Tia explained. "The views are so great up here, there isn't enough parking during events if they let the tourists through."

Together they made their way back inside. "How are you planning to get home?"

"I'll get Julie's mom and dad to drop me off where the kids are leaving my truck."

"I can take you." Evan pushed the door open and added, "I have to make sure my partner in crime doesn't leave any evidence behind."

"If you put it that way, I'd love a ride."

"Great." He lowered his hand to take hers. The first notes of Kendra Blake's song "Proximity" filled the room. "Care to dance?"

"I'd love to."

Evan led her to the dance floor and turned her into his arms. With her feet bare, she was several inches shorter than he was, probably five seven. Her hand came up to rest on his shoulder, and a ripple of attraction shot through him.

Typical. This was the first time in over a year he'd come across someone he wanted to see again, and she lived across the country.

He let the words of the song wash over him, the lyrics resonating with him somehow.

I want to be with you
I need you here with me
We will cherish every moment
We're in close proximity.

Tia looked up. "How long are you in town?"

"Not long enough," he said without censure. "I leave tomorrow afternoon."

"That's too bad."

"It really is." Despite the knowledge that this was their last night together, Evan pulled her closer and held on.

Chapter 4

LIFE WASN'T FAIR. AT LEAST, her love life wasn't fair.

Every time Tia met a guy, within a week or two, she discovered some huge obstacle that made a real relationship impossible. Jesse and his penchant for taking off on his motorcycle for six months at a time. Dominic, who appeared to have everything going for him until Tia discovered his chosen profession was playing online poker in his parents' basement. Then there was Isaiah and his ex-wife who threatened to keep their two-year-old daughter from him if he kept seeing Tia. Or Shane and the wife he hadn't told her about. Separated or not, she wasn't sticking around a guy who said he was single when he wasn't.

Now Evan, who was geographically challenged. Why couldn't she meet a nice guy who lived around here?

She rolled over in bed, the light streaming through her bedroom window. She glanced at the digital clock on her bedside table: 7:54. She was debating whether she should go back to sleep when her phone chimed.

Her heart lifted when she saw Evan's name light up her screen, along with a photo the two of them had taken together at the reception. *Breakfast this morning?*

Love to. When and where?

His response came back within seconds. *Does nine work? You pick the place.*

She swung her legs over the side of the bed. Holding her phone, she headed for the bathroom. She considered briefly which local diner would be best for a Sunday morning breakfast. Not sure she wanted to deal with the speculation or the intrusion that would come from eating in town, she texted him her address.

Less than an hour later, she received another text. *I think I have the wrong place. The address you sent me is for a house.*

Tia slid the pancakes from the griddle onto a plate before she set aside her spatula and made her way to her front door. When she pulled it open, she discovered Evan still sitting in his car. She recognized the moment he saw her. Humor lit his face, and he climbed out. When he reached her, he said, "I thought I was taking you out."

"I'm not sure if you're ready for that adventure today. Whether it looks like it or not, Cottonwood is a small town."

"Not interested in being the talk of your small town?"

"Not particularly." She noticed Bob Peterson walk out his front door to retrieve his newspaper. "Although it will probably happen anyway."

Evan turned around and met the older man's speculative look with a wave.

Tia fought back a smile and motioned Evan inside. "I hope you like pancakes."

"I love pancakes, but you didn't have to cook for me."

"I don't mind."

He stepped inside, took a look around the wide living room, and let out a low whistle. "Nice place."

"Thanks. It actually belongs to my grandparents. When they decided to move to San Diego, they offered to let me stay here."

"What about your parents? Where do they live?"

"They're in San Diego too. They moved there during my senior year of high school."

His expression held surprise and compassion. "You had to switch schools your senior year?"

"Actually, no. They moved. I stayed." She ignored the little pang of resentment that could still pop up at odd moments. "Dad got offered a new job, and Mom wanted to be closer to the beach. I was going to be a casualty of that decision, so my grandparents let me stay with them."

"You and your grandparents must be close if they handed their house over to you." He crossed to the wide window that overlooked the distant red rocks of Sedona. "You sure can't beat the view."

"Yeah, this house has one of the best views in Cottonwood." She motioned him toward the hall leading to the back of the house. "Come on back to the kitchen."

She led the way, not surprised when his gaze was drawn to the equally stunning view the bank of kitchen windows framed, this time of the mountain rising from the land behind the orchard in her backyard. Even though the house had been built in the early 1900s, it had been modernized a number of years ago, and the large, open kitchen boasted beautiful granite countertops and new cabinets. Contrasting the updated appliances, an antique oak table occupied the space beneath the windows in the corner.

Tia moved to the long island in the center of the room and breathed in the scent of pancakes and chocolate. "What can I get you to drink? Milk? Orange juice? Water?"

"You have to have milk with pancakes."

"Glad to see we agree." Tia pulled two glasses out of the cabinet and poured their drinks. Evan carried the pancakes and syrup to the table, waiting for her to sit before he took the seat across from her.

Tia slid two pancakes onto her plate before nudging the platter toward Evan. "What time is your flight today?"

"Four o'clock. I figure if I leave here by eleven, I'll have time to return the rental car." He speared a piece of pancake and popped it in his mouth, then nodded in approval. "These are good."

"Glad you like them. It's my mom's recipe."

"Wait. You made these from scratch?"

"Me and Aunt Jemima." Her lips quirked. "Mom was the one who taught me about adding the chocolate chips."

"You have a smart mom."

"I think so."

They chatted companionably over breakfast, their time slipping away too quickly. When Evan went to leave, Tia walked him outside. He unlocked his car and turned to face her. "I was serious about having you come visit me in Detroit."

A spurt of hope surged inside her, and she pushed logic aside. "I do have some vacation time coming up in July."

"I'll check my work schedule, and we'll pick a good time for you to come out."

"I'd like that." She cocked her head to one side. "What do you do, anyway? I don't think you ever said." *Please don't say online poker. Please don't say online poker.*

"I'm a computer programmer." He glanced at his watch. "I'd better get going."

"Have a safe flight." She started to step back, but before she could, he reached out and cupped both of her elbows to hold her in place. Keeping his eyes on hers, he leaned forward and kissed her. The brief meeting of their lips sent her head buzzing, and she was suddenly grateful his hands continued to hold her steady.

She found herself trapped in his gaze for a long moment, his expression unreadable.

Finally, he released her and pulled open his door. "I'll see you later."

Not sure she trusted her voice, she nodded and watched him climb behind the wheel. When he pulled onto the road, he lifted a hand to wave. She returned the gesture and wondered how soon she would see him again.

* * *

Evan pulled his phone free of his pocket the instant the plane landed. Since the moment he had left Tia's house, she had occupied his thoughts, and he was already eager to see if he could clear a week off his schedule to have her visit next month. If she wasn't able to come to Detroit, maybe he would brave the Arizona heat for a second time this summer.

He rolled his shoulders, his neck cracking as he relieved some of the stiffness. Mechanical issues had delayed his flight from Phoenix for over an hour, but for once, he hadn't minded. Texting back and forth with Tia had occupied his time, her dry humor causing him to bite back his laughter on more than one occasion.

He smiled when he pulled up a selfie he and Tia had taken at the wedding reception. He wondered how long he should wait before he made it his screen saver. He supposed he should at least take her out on a real date first. The memory of their brief kiss was enough to shoot a sense of anticipation through him.

With Tia in mind, he switched his phone out of airplane mode. His mood brightened when he saw her latest text. He started to respond but was interrupted by the elderly woman seated next to him. "Excuse me, but do you have the time?"

"Yeah." He read the time on his phone. "It's five minutes before midnight."

"Oh, I hope my daughter knew our flight was delayed," she said with a flutter of her hands. "I feel bad we're so late. She has work tomorrow."

"I'm sure she checked before going to the airport," Evan assured her.

The plane rolled to a stop, and the seat-belt sign chimed as it turned off. Anticipating the chaos of deplaning, Evan pocketed his phone and stood. In a series of practiced movements, he opened the overhead bin, retrieved his suitcase, and set it behind him before shifting his computer bag on top of it.

A man in his thirties bumped into him, and Evan had to fight to keep his balance. When he felt pressure on his bag and saw the guy's impatient scowl, he shot the man an answering glare. Tired and not particularly pleased to be back in Detroit, Evan faced forward and waited for the scatter of passengers in front of him to collect their belongings and make their way down the aisle.

He glanced at the woman beside him. "Do you have a bag up top?"

"Yes." She pointed across from them. "The bright-blue one."

Evan waited for the line to start moving before lifting it down. He motioned for her to go before him in an effort to protect her from the impatient man crowding them from behind. When he saw the speed of the older woman, he wondered at the wisdom of his decision. Even though it was almost midnight in Detroit, in Arizona, it was only nine. Still time for a quick phone call, if it didn't take him all night to get off the plane.

The woman's bag caught on one of the seats, and Evan fought back his impatience. The man behind him bumped into him again, but this time, instead of feeling only pressure, moisture splashed onto him and soaked the right side of his jeans.

Evan turned to see the look of apology on the man's face, his oversized water bottle tipped forward, the wide cap resting on top of his computer bag.

"Sorry," the man muttered under his breath.

Irritated on principle, Evan held his tongue. His eyes dropped to determine the potential damage to his laptop, grateful to see that most of the moisture had missed his bag, instead soaking him. He swiped the few pooling drops of water off his bag and turned to move forward once more.

When they finally stepped off the plane, Evan moved to the woman's side as they started up the Jetway.

"Thank you again for your help," she said as he stepped past.

"No problem," he said. "Hope you enjoy your visit."

Before she could offer any further conversation, he increased his pace. His fingers slid into his damp pocket and curled around his phone only to freeze when he saw who was waiting for him in the airport. His heartbeat quickened when the petite blonde's gaze met his. Apparently, his past wasn't ready to let him go.

Chapter 5

COCONINO NATIONAL FOREST. COLBY READ the sign on the side of the road and did a double take. Sagebrush filled his view, and there wasn't a tree in sight. Did Arizonans not know that trees were a requirement for a forest?

He pondered the oddity as he made a turn at the stoplight. The ability to see such vast distances with no water in sight made him feel like he was on another planet, businesses crowding the main road and houses dotting the hillside to the west. He continued up a rise, and his eyes were drawn to the vibrant view of red rocks to the east. He turned onto Highway 89A and drove less than a mile before his gaze was drawn away from the scenery to the dark ponytail swinging behind a well-toned body. Clad in cropped yoga pants and a bright-blue T-shirt, the woman jogged at a good pace, probably not much slower than his own workout speed.

He eased off the gas as he approached her. The GPS told him to take a right turn, but there wasn't an intersection in sight.

"Make a U-turn," the female voice demanded.

Colby continued forward. Surely, the GPS would reroute him once he got far enough past the phantom turn.

The jogger changed direction and headed toward a convenience store. When his navigation app again told him to make a U-turn, he signaled and turned into the parking lot. He gave the jogger a wide berth and parked near the front doors.

He climbed out of his truck and turned to face the woman. She appeared to be in her midtwenties, and her face was every bit as attractive as the rest of her. Eyes that were more gold than brown stared back at him. She slowed her pace and gave him a friendly smile.

The smile did it. Instantly, she transformed from another nameless beauty into someone approachable, someone worth knowing.

"Are you new around here or passing through?" she asked when she reached him.

"I'm new." He extended his hand. "Colby Farren."

"Tia Parker." She placed her hand in his, and a tingle of pleasure shot through him. She took a step toward the door. "Colby, may I give you a piece of advice?"

"I guess."

"Buy some sunscreen." She motioned to his pasty, white arms. "With skin as pale as yours, you'll be sunburned by the end of the day just driving around town."

"Sounds like good advice." He reached out and opened the door, waiting for her to pass through.

"Where are you from anyway?" Tia asked.

"Alaska."

"Oh, you're the new deputy. Welcome."

"Thanks."

Tia waved to the clerk before crossing to pull a cup from the stack beside the soda dispenser. She filled the cup with water and took a long drink before pulling a quarter from a small pocket in the back of her athletic pants. "Here you go, Rob."

"Thanks, Tia."

"Before you leave," Colby began, stepping into her path, "can you tell me how to get to Mingus Avenue?"

"Oh, that's easy. Take a left out of the parking lot and then another right a bit down the road. You'll see the Country Bank on your left. If you pass the hospital, you went too far." Tia explained the series of turns to get to his new apartment using landmarks rather than street names to guide him. When she finished, confusing him completely, she motioned to Rob. "If you can't find it, circle back here. Rob can help you get to wherever you're going."

She shifted around him and pushed open the door. "Nice meeting you, Colby."

"Yeah, you too." He watched her take a last drink of her water before tossing the cup in the trash. When she broke into a jog, he decided living in Arizona might turn out to be even better than he expected.

* * *

Tia waited until after she showered to check her cell phone in the hopes that the extra time would produce her desired results. Disappointment bloomed. No new messages.

After texting with Evan while he was stuck in the airport Sunday night, she had sent one last message to him to make sure he'd gotten in okay. When she didn't hear from him, she figured he hadn't responded because of the late hour. She waited until after she finished work today before sending another. Again, nothing. So much for keeping in touch.

A sigh escaped her. As much as she had looked forward to the possibility of seeing Evan again, maybe it was better if she let things drop. After all, they lived over a thousand miles apart. With her work schedule, she was rarely able to take off more than a day or two at a time during the school year.

She wandered into her living room, grabbed her remote control, and plopped down on her couch. She couldn't remember the last time she had been faced with an evening with nothing to do. Julie wouldn't be back from her honeymoon for three weeks, and tryouts for the fall sports season didn't start until late July.

She scrolled through the channels until she found the Diamondbacks game. When she saw they were losing seven to one, she decided to watch a movie for a change of pace. She flipped through her favorite comedies and loaded *While You Were Sleeping* before settling back against the couch cushions.

Her cell phone chimed, and she snatched it up. She tried to fight back her disappointment when she saw it was Wesley asking if she wanted to sub on his softball team tomorrow night. Given her current evening plans, she immediately said yes. Sitting around watching a movie for one night was fine, but she didn't think she could do this for many nights in a row. She needed something to do and people to talk to. Too bad Evan wasn't going to be one of those people.

Chapter 6

Evan walked along the Seine, the Notre Dame cathedral visible across the water. He loved this view. He loved the scents and sounds of Paris. But he missed Tia.

He still couldn't believe the guy's water bottle on his flight to Detroit had managed to short out his cell phone. That single moment had not only cost him his phone but his most recent contacts as well. More specifically, Tia's contact information.

Finding Brooklyn waiting for him when he got off the plane only served to further aggravate him. Though he had hoped to break ties with her in every possible way, he suspected their professional paths would continue to cross until his new business grew large enough for him to hire a business manager.

As much as he didn't want to see his ex, he still needed her professionally. She had the ability to drum up new contracts, and he had the computer skills that were in high demand. Regardless, he hadn't expected Brooklyn to present him with a new business opportunity so soon after his return to Detroit, certainly not one this lucrative or with so little notice. He had barely had time to run home, pack another suitcase, and catch his flight to JFK on his way to Paris.

The boost to his income would be significant, enough that he wondered if he would be able to make this his last time working with Brooklyn. Though it would be taking a step backward in his career, if he needed to, he could hire on as an employee somewhere in the States until he was ready to expand. He would miss the travel, but if he could be closer to Tia, it might be worth it.

He glanced at his watch. Only another two hours before he could check into his hotel room. At least the front desk clerk had been kind enough to store his luggage while he waited. Two more hours and he could settle into his room, charge his laptop, and find a way to contact Tia. They might have several thousand miles between them, but he already suspected that one weekend together wasn't going to be enough.

* * *

Colby made his way into the Cottonwood Police Station and followed the receptionist's directions to the police chief's office. The dark-haired man in his forties behind the overburdened desk stood at Colby's entrance. "You must be Colby Farren." He extended his hand. "Chief Andrew Jarvis. Good to meet you."

"Good to meet you too, sir."

"Come on in and have a seat." He retrieved a file from a filing cabinet and sat across from Colby. He glanced at the papers in front of him. "I understand you served for three years in Valdez, Alaska. This will be quite a change for you."

"Yes, it will," Colby admitted. "It doesn't look like this area has a lot of trouble with getting snowed in."

"Not at all, although when we do get the occasional snowfall, it throws everyone for a loop."

"It actually snows here in Cottonwood?" Colby asked.

"We'll get an inch every few years or so."

Colby couldn't have heard him right. Certainly an inch wouldn't cause any problems for anyone. He remained silent.

"It's rather unusual for us to hire someone without an in-person interview, but your police chief sent us your last fitness report." Chief Jarvis stood. "We have our annual assessment in two weeks, so you'll need to go through testing at that time."

"Not a problem."

"Good." Chief Jarvis motioned to the nearest uniformed officer. "Let me introduce you around. Raul, come meet our new recruit."

Raul sauntered toward them, his broad shoulders filling out his uniform despite his being several inches shorter than Colby's six feet. He stuck out his hand. "Good to meet you."

"You too."

"Colby moved here from Alaska this week," Chief Jarvis said.

"That's quite a change," Raul said with a faint Hispanic accent.

"It is that," Colby agreed.

"During the school year, Raul is assigned as the security protection officer at the high school."

"You have an officer at the high school full-time?" Colby asked.

"We do." Chief Jarvis nodded. "Having Raul on campus during school hours ensures the students' safety and helps us keep a finger on the pulse of problems there before they escalate."

"Makes sense."

A lanky, sandy-haired man approached. "Hey, Chief. Parker's coming tonight."

"Good. We can use her bat." Chief Jarvis turned his attention back to Colby. "Colby, this is Wesley Pearce."

"Good to meet you." Wesley shook his hand. "I don't suppose you play softball. We have a game and could use another outfielder."

"I'm sure my glove is packed in my suitcase somewhere," Colby said. "I normally play shortstop though."

"That position is locked up for tonight, but it's good to know we have someone else who can fill in there." Wesley snagged a piece of paper and a pen off a nearby desk. He scribbled something down before handing it to Colby. "Here's the address, and I put my cell number on there in case you get lost."

"Thanks."

"Warm-ups are at six thirty."

"Wesley, have Colby ride with you today," Chief Jarvis said. "You can do a loop over by the ball field to help him get his bearings."

"Will do," Wesley agreed easily.

The four men fell into step and headed for the briefing room. Colby walked in to see a half dozen men inside. Though their appearances varied, Colby couldn't help but glance down at his arms. Compared to these Arizonans, he looked like Casper the Friendly Ghost. Tia was right. He needed to invest in some sunscreen.

* * *

Tia shifted her backpack on her shoulder as she approached the ball field. A police car had been parked facing the road as though an officer was watching for speeding. Tia knew better. The majority of Wesley's team was made up of police officers. A well-placed cruiser could do wonders in keeping people from speeding during the game.

The umpire already stood to the side of home plate in preparation of the game starting. Tia quickened her step and made her way through the dozen other cars already in the lot. When she reached the gate that led to the home-team bench, Wesley was waiting for her.

"Hey, Parker. Glad you made it." He tossed her a jersey.

"Thanks." She slipped it over her head.

The man beside Wesley turned and looked at her, eyes furrowed.

"Oh, hi, Colby. I see Wes and the chief didn't waste any time recruiting you."

"Wait," Wesley interrupted. "You two already know each other?"

"I ran into him when I was running yesterday," Tia said.

"I hope not literally."

"Very funny."

Chief Jarvis stepped forward, his ball cap on backward because he was playing catcher. "Okay, here's the lineup." He called out everyone's name in their batting order and confirmed their positions. Not surprisingly, Tia was playing shortstop and batting third.

She headed onto the field and took her position, then caught the odd look Colby gave her as he passed her on his way to left field.

"Park!" Raul called out before throwing a ball to her. She took the relay and sent it to Wesley at third base.

A minute later, the game started. A line drive to second took care of the first out. The second batter connected on the first pitch and sent it to deep left field. Tia watched Colby sprint across the field and make a diving catch, lifting his glove to show the ball snow coning in the tip of it. The man had some serious speed.

"Nice," Tia said to no one in particular. She held up her glove to take the cut off when Colby threw the ball in, surprised when he threw it to Wesley instead. The oddity that he would be able to play so well and not know who to throw the ball to on a relay struck her as odd, but she quickly turned her attention to the next batter.

After he struck out, she jogged in to the dugout and selected her bat. When Colby reached the bench, Tia said, "Nice play out there."

"Thanks."

She waited by the dugout entrance as their leadoff man lined a ball between the first and second basemen. Tia stepped into the on-deck circle, timing her practice swings with the pitches.

Wesley flied out, and she walked up to the plate. Taking her stance, she lifted her bat over her head and swung at the first pitch. It sailed nearly to the fence, hitting the ground in the left center gap. Using the speed she had developed on the soccer field, she rounded first base and headed for second. She saw the relay coming and slid. The second baseman's glove swiped across her leg an instant after her foot connected with the base.

She waited for the safe sign before she signaled for time and stood. She didn't bother to dust off her pants. They were just going to get dirty again.

* * *

Colby sat in the corner booth and watched the friendly interaction of Tia and three of his coworkers. In addition to Raul and Wesley, Gio, from the night shift, had joined them, as well as his wife, Sofia.

"The other team is convinced we're bringing in ringers, especially after they saw Colby make that diving catch in the first," Gio said.

"They complain every time they lose," Raul countered.

Colby lifted his glass and took a sip. "How many teams are in your league?"

"Eight." Wesley snagged a nacho from the plate in front of Tia. "Everyone was on best behavior tonight, but the games have been known to get pretty intense."

"Especially when Bill is around," Sofia muttered.

"Bill?" Colby asked.

"Bill Moser," Wesley said. "He's a good guy, but he can be a hothead when he's been drinking."

"He's not that bad," Tia insisted. "One fight last year, and you won't let him forget it."

"You're only defending him because you used to date the guy," Raul insisted.

"That was three years ago."

Raul rolled his eyes. "Whatever."

Wesley lifted a hand to signal the waitress. He held up his glass. "Can I get another?"

"Sure." She took his empty glass and asked, "Anyone else?"

"I could use more water," Tia said. She eyed Wesley's hand as he took another nacho.

The waitress gave Tia a look of amusement. "And another order of nachos?"

"I'm only taking one more," Wesley insisted.

Tia rolled her eyes. "That's what you always say."

Chapter 7

Colby sat beside Wesley as they cruised down Main Street. "What's the deal with Tia?"

Wesley shot him a sideways glance filled with confusion. "What do you mean?"

"Raul mentioned an old boyfriend last night," Colby said casually before fishing for what he really wanted to know. "Is she dating anyone now?"

"Not that I've heard, but if anyone knows, it would be Raul." Wesley slowed when he reached a sharp bend in the road.

"Why's that?"

"Because he sees her all the time at work."

Colby's eyebrows drew together. "Why would Raul see her at work?"

"He's assigned to the high school. Tia is the athletic trainer there. They spend a lot of time together during the school year."

"That makes sense." Colby let their conversation replay in his mind as they continued into old-town Cottonwood. He stared out at the old-fashioned storefronts, many of which looked like they were straight out of an old western. When a guy walked out of a store and settled a cowboy hat on his head, Colby wondered if he had been transported back in time.

After another sharp bend in the road, Wesley took a left. Once again, Colby tried to make sense of his new home. To his left, open land stretched out before him that consisted mostly of dirt dotted with desert brush. To his right, an oasis of green startled him. Automatic sprinklers watered the wide, grassy area.

He could admit now that he'd been annoyed when he'd discovered a woman had been chosen over him to play shortstop, but Tia had been more than adequate in her abilities. She'd even scored twice during the game.

He liked athletic women.

Lexi had always made a point of staying in shape, but she preferred hiking over organized sports.

He fought back the image of their last time together, grateful when Wesley broke into his thoughts. "Speak of the devil."

"What?" Colby straightened, his dark eyes scanning the area.

Wesley pointed at a classic red pickup circling through the round-about as they approached. "That truck is hers."

Colby caught a glimpse of Tia's profile as she passed. She continued through, taking the exit that would allow her to continue on Highway 89A. "I wonder where she's headed this time of day."

"Since she's already passed her street, she's probably on her way to Jerome." He pointed at the town a few miles up the side of Mingus Mountain. "I don't know what it is with her and Grapes, but I swear she would go there every day if the school would let her have a long enough lunch break."

"Grapes?"

"A little restaurant. Good food, but a little higher end than I can afford on a regular basis." Wesley began his loop back toward the retail section of town. "I don't know what your work shift is for the weekend, but we have another game on Saturday at ten."

Though Colby itched to know if the attractive shortstop would be present, he held his tongue. Instead, he said simply, "I'll be there."

* * *

Tia parked her car by the old jailhouse in Jerome and headed on foot past the dilapidated building up the steep road leading to her favorite restaurant.

Tourists crowded the streets, and she couldn't help but smile when she saw one walk by with a classic T-shirt that read *Jerome: A hard-drinking biker town with an artist problem.* That about summed up the ghost town built into the side of the mountain.

She crossed the street and rounded the bend to find a half dozen people standing outside of Grapes. She hoped they were going instead of coming. Not waiting to find out, she chose to enter the shop next door that adjoined the restaurant.

Before she managed to disappear inside, she heard her name being called. She turned to see Colby trotting up the steps behind her.

"Hey, Colby. What are you doing here?"

"It's my day off. I thought I would check out some of the local sights."

"If you're looking for souvenirs, you're in the right place." She continued into the gift shop, where T-shirts hung like wallpaper above shelves containing the folded versions.

"What are you doing here?" Colby asked, following her inside.

"Coming to get some lunch." Tia headed for the doorway into the restaurant. As she feared, the interior was packed with customers, and the line was out the door.

Colby stepped behind her. "Crowded."

"Yeah. It wasn't bad when I came up on Wednesday, but it can get crazy on the weekends. I was hoping I was early enough to beat the Friday crowd." She shifted to the side as the manager approached. "Hi, Dennis. I'm afraid to ask, but how long is the wait?"

"Your table should be ready."

"You knew I was coming?"

"Of course. Wednesdays and Fridays at eleven thirty. Just like clockwork." He looked at Colby and asked, "Will there be two of you?"

Colby gave her a questioning look. "Is it okay if I join you?"

"Yeah, sure," Tia answered instinctively.

Dennis grabbed a menu from the bar and handed it to Colby. "Tia, you're at your usual table."

"Thanks, Dennis." She glanced back at Colby. "It's this way."

Tia led the way past the bar and up a flight of stairs to a small round table beside a window. Colby waited for her to sit before he lowered into the seat across from her.

"Do you want to look at the menu first?" Colby asked.

"No, I already know what I want."

"Any suggestions?"

"Do you like mushrooms?"

"Not particularly," Colby said. "I'm more of a meat and potatoes kind of guy."

"If you like hamburgers, their Zin Burger is good."

Their waitress approached. She turned her attention to Colby first. "What can I get you?"

"I guess I'll try the Zin Burger."

"Good choice."

"And to drink?"

"A coke."

She scribbled on her pad and tucked it into her apron. "I'll get that right in for you."

Colby opened his mouth to say something, not managing to get any words out before their waitress headed for the stairs. "What about your order?"

"Oh, Debbie knows what I want."

"How do you do that?"

"What?"

"I've been at restaurants with you twice now, and both times, the waitresses not only knew you by name, but they knew your order without you telling them," Colby said. "I lived in a town that had less than three thousand people, and no one ever knew what I wanted before I told them."

"Yeah, but you probably changed up what you wanted on occasion."

"I guess."

"Usually, when I find something I like on a menu, I stick with it," Tia said. "Besides, it's not surprising everyone knows me. Working at the high school puts me in contact with a lot of people."

"But we aren't even in the same town as where you work."

"The kids from Jerome go to Mingus High School," Tia explained. "So, tell me about this little town you came from."

"Valdez, Alaska."

"Like the Exxon Valdez?"

"One and the same. Of course, the oil was cleaned up a long time ago."

"What made you decide to move here?"

"The police department had to make some cutbacks. Since I was the newest guy on the force, I was the one left without a job."

"That's tough," Tia said. "It must be a pretty big change going from Alaska to Arizona."

"That's the truth."

"Did you leave any family behind up there?"

His jaw clenched for a brief moment. "Just an ex-fiancée."

"Sorry."

"It is what it is." Colby's face clouded. "I thought Lexi would come with me. She had other plans."

"At least you won't have to worry about running into the ex here in Arizona."

"True."

The waitress approached with their drinks. Tia took a sip of her water and settled back to get to know the new guy in town.

Chapter 8

"Hey, guys." Tia dropped her bag on the bench beside Raul. She scanned the half dozen men sitting nearby and then held up her cell phone. "I want everyone to take note that I am on time."

"Warm-ups ended five minutes ago," Raul told her.

She looked out at the other team warming up on the field. "I thought we were the home team today."

"Nope."

She held up her phone again. "Let the record show that I thought I was on time today."

Colby approached them, glove in hand. "Hey, at least she's here before game time."

"Exactly." Her eyes narrowed. "Have these guys been telling you that I'm always late?"

"Lucky guess."

From the spot on the other side of Raul, Wesley riffled through his bag until he came up with a paper and pen. He held them out to her. "I have something I need you to sign."

Tia took the paper from him. "What's this?"

"Your registration form so you'll officially be on our team."

"I already told you, I'm not sure I'll be able to make all the games."

"Doesn't matter," Wesley countered.

Raul looked up from where he had been retying his cleats. "Wesley wants to make sure none of the other teams can get you to play with them."

"Really?" Tia held the paper out.

"Hey, you know it's going to happen," Wesley insisted. "And technically, we're not supposed to have guest players come for more than two games without signing them up."

"Fine." Tia took the pen and scribbled her signature across the bottom. "But don't get mad when I'm not here."

"We have games on Tuesday and Thursday next week, but as long as you're here at next Thursday's game, we're good."

"Who do we play Thursday?" Tia asked.

"Bill Moser's team."

"I'll be here."

"Good." Wesley took the pen and paper back from Tia. "But will you be on time?"

* * *

Colby stood a few spaces from Tia's car. The rest of their team had already left the field, but Tia had remained behind to treat one of their opponents when he sprained his ankle sliding into second.

The players from the game after them had already started their warmups, and the parking lot was busy with people coming and going. He straightened when he saw Tia approaching, her shirt tails hanging loose over dirt-stained white softball pants.

"Colby, what are you still doing here?"

"I thought maybe you'd let me take you out to lunch." Colby saw the flash of awareness on her face and the tension that came into her shoulders. "That is, if you don't already have plans."

"Actually, I do have a pretty crazy day," she said, grabbing the lifeline he had thrown her. "Thanks anyway."

"No problem. Maybe another time."

Her eyes dropped to the ground, and she fished for her car keys. "Yeah, maybe."

Colby's grip tightened on his keys, and he shifted aside to let her pass. Fighting back disappointment, he fell in step with her toward her car. "Good game today."

"You too. See you later." Tia's steps came to a sudden stop when her tires came into view. "Shoot."

"Oh man." Colby's gaze swept down. Two flat tires at the same time. What luck. "What can I do to help?"

"Thanks, but I'll be fine. I have Triple A." She pulled her cell phone from her bag and scrolled through her contacts. "I'll have them give me a tow."

"How long are they going to be?" Colby asked after she finished her call.

"About forty-five minutes." She opened the door to her truck and tossed her backpack inside. She pocketed her cell phone and keys before fishing her wallet out of her bag.

"Do you need a ride anywhere?"

"No, that's okay. It'll be easier if I wait and take care of this now."

"I can wait with you," Colby said.

"Oh, you don't have to do that." She slammed the door closed.

"I don't mind."

He caught the familiar look on her face, the one that said, "I want to say no, but I don't want to be rude." He had seen that expression on Lexi's face often enough before they'd started dating. "Do you want to watch the next game for a while?"

"Yeah, I guess I can do that. Tony will call me when he gets here." She retrieved her keys from her pocket and locked her truck. When she started back toward the field, Colby walked beside her.

"Shall we scout out the competition, then?" he asked.

"I guess so."

* * *

Tia slowed to a walk when she reached the garage. She knew she could have called any number of friends to give her a ride there, but she needed to run off the annoyance about having to buy two new tires. So much for a vacation this summer.

Colby had been nice enough to drop her off at her house after the tow truck had arrived at the ball field, but she felt bad he had stayed with her after she had turned him down. He was nice enough, but she wasn't looking for someone to date, at least not until she could stop thinking about Evan.

Julie's wedding had been a week ago. At lunch on Wednesday, she had broken down and texted him one more time. Again, he hadn't responded. She wished she could get him out of her mind.

The smell of oil and exhaust assaulted her senses as she passed by the three open bays of the garage. When she entered the office, the owner looked up. "Hey, Tia. How's the football team looking this year?"

"We got all our starters back but four." She crossed to him and leaned an elbow on the counter. "Break it to me gently, Frank. What's the damage?"

"It's the oddest thing." His brow furrowed. "My guys checked for punctures on both tires. There isn't anything wrong with either of them."

"Seriously?" Relief washed over her. "What caused them to go flat, then?"

"Best guess, someone was playing a practical joke on you. Looks like someone let the air out."

"Not a very funny joke."

"I'll agree with you on that one." He retrieved a large plastic envelope off the counter and dumped out her car key. "Here you go."

"Don't I owe you something for your time?"

"I'm not going to charge you for putting air in your tires."

"Frank, you're the best." She scooped up the keys. "While I'm here, can I schedule a tune-up for next week? I want to get it done before I head to Flagstaff for the girls' volleyball camp."

"No problem." He pulled up his schedule. "Tuesday work for you?"

"Yeah. I can drop it off on my way into work."

"I'll put you down for eight."

She held up her keys. "Thanks again, Frank. Enjoy the rest of your weekend."

"You too."

Tia left the office, her mind pondering who would have messed with her tires. Probably some high school kids who saw her truck and decided it would be a funny way to let her know they had seen her at the softball field. She climbed into her truck, and another thought surfaced. Would kids be daring enough to mess with a car when three police cruisers were parked in the lot? Regardless, whoever had let the air out of her tires was either very brave or very stupid.

* * *

Colby approached the ball field, his eyes scanning for Tia. Her truck wasn't in the lot, but after having two flat tires at Saturday's game, he supposed it was possible she had called someone for a ride. He hoped there would be a day when he would become that trusted friend she would call.

"Sorry, Raul," Wesley said as Colby approached. "I'm already covering a shift for Lance that day."

"What's up?" Colby asked.

Raul turned to face him. "I'm looking for someone to cover my shift tomorrow. Interested?"

A refusal started to form before he remembered Raul worked at the high school. Colby weighed his options: trying to catch Tia at lunch and hoping for another invitation to join her or working at the high school and having access to where she would be the rest of the day.

The second option won out. "Yeah, I can do that for you."

"Thanks a lot," Raul said. "During the summer, it's kind of like a split shift. You'll need to be at the school at 9:30 when the volleyball team shows up for their weekly practice. Then you move to a regular patrol until 4 when the admin staff leaves for the day."

"Is it your responsibility to check locks and secure the building?"

"The custodian takes care of the main entrance, but you'll need to check the rest of the doors, especially those for the gym and the weight room. The kids are always trying to block them open," Raul said. "Tia normally catches those, but if she's dealing with any injuries, sometimes one will get past her."

"Sounds straightforward enough."

"Speak of the devil," Wesley said with a nod toward the parking lot.

Colby turned and lifted both eyebrows. Instead of wearing her usual white softball pants, Tia had paired her jersey with yoga pants that looked like pink, blue, and purple paint had splattered all over them. Talk about bright.

"What are you wearing?" Wesley asked as soon as she was in earshot.

"I didn't have time to finish my laundry this weekend."

"You forgot to put your stuff in the dryer again, didn't you?" Raul asked.

"Shut up." Tia gave Raul's arm a playful punch.

"Why? Because I'm right?" Raul countered.

"I'm not telling Gabrielle anything anymore," Tia said.

"Who's Gabrielle?" Colby asked.

"My wife," Raul told him. "She works at the school as their finance clerk."

"And used to be one of my best friends until she married this guy and started telling him all my secrets." Tia jerked a thumb at Raul.

"Hey, at least she didn't tell me about the time you—"

Tia slapped a hand over his mouth. "Don't make me hurt you."

The chief approached from the far side of the bench. "Tia, what have I told you about assaulting my police officers?"

"Don't hurt them in public?" Tia said, keeping her hand in place.

Colby watched the easy back and forth between Tia and his coworkers, a touch of envy rising within him.

She dropped her hand and gave Raul a stern look. "How did you ever get Gabrielle to marry you?"

"Must have been my good looks and my charm."

"I have no comment to that," Wesley said before Tia could respond.

Tia shifted her attention to Wesley. "Hey, I wanted to ask you guys if any of you saw someone messing with my tires after the last game."

Wesley shot her a confused look. "No, why?"

"Someone let the air out of two of them."

"That's weird." Raul's eyebrows drew together. "I was parked right next to you, and I didn't notice anything wrong with your tires when I left."

"How long were you here after everyone else took off?" Wesley asked.

"I don't know?" She turned to Colby. "What do you think, Colby? About twenty minutes?"

"Something like that." Colby shrugged. "Sounds like it must have happened after everyone else took off and before I got to the parking lot."

"Probably just some kids messing around," Wesley said.

"I guess."

"Come on guys." Raul took a step toward the field. "Let's go warm up."

Colby grabbed his mitt and made his way onto the grass. When he turned to toss the ball with Raul, Tia passed by, her neon-bright pants catching his attention once more. No doubt about it. This girl was born to stand out.

Chapter 9

WHAT A PERFECT SATURDAY. A breeze stirred the otherwise warm day, and Colby was about to see Tia for the third day in one week. His day working at the high school would have been boring except that he had seen Tia eleven times. He had even managed to stand by her during most of volleyball practice.

Colby heard the rumble of Tia's truck, and a ripple of excitement surfaced. He watched Tia approach the field, easily identifying the man who had once dated her. The tall, dark-haired man wearing number thirty stood at first base, but when Tia walked by, he couldn't stop staring at her. Not that Colby could blame him.

A protective surge bubbled inside him, and he moved toward her. With a nod at number thirty, he said, "So, that's the ex?"

Tia looked at the other team warming up. "Actually, I don't see Bill here yet. Believe it or not, he's worse about getting places on time than I am."

"Oh." Colby shot a look at number thirty. "The way that guy was staring at you, I figured you had dated him."

Tia glanced over her shoulder. Her eyes met the other man's gaze. "Nope." She lifted a hand and waved. "He's cute though."

The wave of jealousy swept over him, through him. He choked it back. After all, the man on the other side of the field wasn't the one standing by Tia's side right now.

Certainly, once she spent more time with him, she would realize they could build a future together.

"Hey, Tia," someone shouted from behind them.

They both turned. "Hi, Bill."

"Ready to lose today?" Bill flashed a cocky grin, his dark eyes dancing with equal parts humor and ego.

"What do you think, Colby?" Tia asked instead of responding to her ex. "Are we ready to lose today?"

"I wasn't planning on it," Colby said, pleased to see she didn't appear to have any interest in the broad-shouldered man approaching.

"Yeah, me neither." Tia held both hands out. "Sorry, I guess it may be your team that ends up on the losing end today."

Bill's eyes flashed in challenge. "I doubt that."

"Okay, everyone," Chief Jarvis called out. "Time to warm up." He slowed when he reached Colby and Tia. "Hey, Colby. Raul couldn't make it tonight. Can you play second base?"

"Sure. No problem."

"Great." Chief Jarvis slapped a hand on his shoulder. "Let's play ball."

* * *

Tia probed Bill's hand and wrist, noting the quick intake of breath when she touched a particularly sensitive spot. What was it with people sliding into second this year? Today's injury had resulted from a headfirst slide. "I hate to tell you this, but you need to go get it checked out. Looks like you broke at least one metacarpal bone, possibly more."

"I'm fine," Bill insisted through gritted teeth.

Tia looked up at one of his teammates. "He needs to go to urgent care."

"Come on, slugger." The teammate slapped Bill on the back. "Let's go. I'll give you a ride."

Bill let out a frustrated sigh. He waited for Tia to release his hand before he said, "Your boyfriend over there is lucky I already broke my hand, or I'd be seriously tempted to break it on his pretty face."

"Who are you talking about?" Tia asked. "I don't have a boyfriend."

Bill lifted his chin, indicating someone behind her. "Does he know that?"

Tia glanced over her shoulder at Colby, who was waiting behind the backstop. "He's just a friend."

"Well, your friend broke my hand on purpose."

"It was an accident," Tia said.

"Right," Bill huffed out. "He accidentally ground his heel into my hand, even though I was clearly already safe."

His teammate lifted his bag as well as Bill's. "Come on, Bill. Let's get that hand X-rayed."

Tia stood as well. "Let me know what the doctor says."

Bill jutted his chin out as an acknowledgment and continued forward.

Colby waited for them to pass before he approached. "Is he going to be okay?"

"Looks like it's broken."

"Oh man. I feel bad."

"These things happen." Tia pulled off her examination gloves. "Did everyone else already leave?"

"Yeah. I think they were going to The Chaparral to grab a drink. Did you want to go?"

"I'll probably stop by for a few minutes." Tia tossed her gloves in the trash can as she passed.

"Great. I'll see you there."

She watched him veer off to where he had parked a few spaces away. Where did Bill get the idea that she and Colby were dating? Sure, Colby had asked her out last Saturday, but since then, everything had seemed normal enough between them. Could she have misread the situation? A seed of concern planted in her mind, but when she saw that Colby climbed into his car without so much as a second glance at her, she decided Bill must have had an extra dose of testosterone flaring up tonight.

* * *

Colby rose from his seat in the corner and waved at Tia when she walked in. Her eyebrows drew together, causing that adorable crease on her forehead. She looked around the bar area before crossing to their table. "Where is everyone?"

"I'm not sure." Colby held a chair out for her and waited for her to sit before reclaiming his seat. "I thought this was where everyone was coming tonight."

"Maybe they went to the 10-12 Lounge instead. They go there sometimes too."

"Well, we're already here. Can I get you something?" He watched her debate her options and added, "By the time we get over to the other place, everyone will probably be leaving. We left a good twenty or thirty minutes after they did."

"I guess you're right."

The waitress approached and set a water glass in front of Tia. "Are you still waiting on someone else?"

"It looks like it's just us tonight," Colby said. He put in his order, not surprised when the waitress didn't bother to ask Tia for hers. He settled back in his chair. "How did you get interested in becoming an athletic trainer?"

"I don't know." She wrapped her fingers around her water glass but didn't drink. "I helped out my trainer when I was in high school, and I always enjoyed it. When I realized Northern Arizona University had a program there, I decided to try it."

"And the rest is history," Colby finished for her.

"Something like that." She took a sip. "What about you? What made you decide to become a cop?"

"Not a lot of options in Valdez. It was mostly by process of elimination."

"What do most people do there?"

"Fishing and the oil industry. The tourists create some jobs too, but I preferred a more stable income." He gave her a wry smile. "That didn't quite work out the way I planned."

Her voice held compassion when she asked, "How do you like it here in Arizona?"

Colby stared at her for a moment, long enough to see her cheeks flush. He found her reaction endearing. He leaned forward and lowered his voice. "Much better than I thought I would."

Chapter 10

TIA LEANED DOWN AT THE edge of the stream and used her hands to splash cool water onto her face. She needed this, this chance to get away from everyone and everything. Between wondering why Evan had gone from texting her constantly to ignoring her completely and having Colby ask her out on a regular basis, a girls' day was a welcome reprieve.

"Tia, wait up," Julie puffed out from behind her.

Tia straightened and turned to see her friend struggling the rest of the way up the trail. Dappled sunlight filtered through the sycamore trees that dominated the canyon, a light breeze helping to combat the ninety-degree heat.

"Need a break?" Tia asked.

"Yeah." Julie followed Tia's lead and splashed water on her face before lowering herself onto a large boulder. "How did I let you talk me into this again?"

"You didn't want me to hike alone. Besides, you said you want to be more active this summer," Tia reminded her.

"Yeah, but I was thinking something more like wading in the pool, not spending four hours hiking behind the Energizer Bunny," Julie countered. "This is Arizona, for heaven's sake."

"Which is why we started at six this morning." Tia opened the drawstring pack she had carried on her back and pulled out a plastic baggie filled with red grapes. "Besides, you know you missed me while you were on your honeymoon."

"And yet, somehow, we both survived." Julie lifted her water bottle and took a long drink. "By the way, Drew and I are heading up to my folks' cabin in Pinewood this weekend. Do you want to join us?"

"Going on a romantic getaway with a newly married couple? Hmm. Let me think about that." Tia tapped one finger on the side of her cheek. "I think I'll pass."

"Oh, come on. It will be fun," Julie insisted. "We're heading up Thursday, but Drew has to telework on Thursday and Friday."

"I don't know . . ." Tia popped a grape into her mouth and held out the bag. "Do you want some?"

"Yeah, thanks." Julie accepted the offering and pulled out a cluster. "Is there any particular reason you don't want to come with us this weekend? Besides not wanting to feel like a third wheel?"

"No. Why?"

"Because I can tell something is bugging you."

"Nothing's bugging me."

"This is me, remember?" Julie waved her hand in a circle around her face. "I can tell when you're stewing over something."

Tia sighed, then let the truth spill out. "It's Evan."

"Evan Spence?" Julie asked. "Drew's friend?"

"Yeah." She lowered herself onto a large rock beside Julie. "He came over for breakfast the day after your wedding. I thought things were good. He even texted me back and forth for a few hours when he was at the airport."

"And?"

"And nothing. I sent him a couple texts to make sure he got home okay, and he hasn't responded to any of them."

"That's weird." Julie chewed a grape thoughtfully. "From what Drew's told me about him, Evan doesn't seem like the kind to ghost someone like that."

"Well, that's exactly what he did to me." Tia let her gaze linger on the stream, the water swirling with every obstacle in its path. "Why is it that the guys I want to date never stick around, and the ones I'm not interested in won't leave me alone?"

"Uh-oh. Is Bill trying to come around again?"

"No, nothing like that." Tia hesitated, not sure how to express the uneasy feeling she'd had since Colby had asked her out the first time.

"Then who is it?"

"His name is Colby Farren."

"Wait. Isn't he the new guy on the police force?" Julie asked. "The one who moved here from Alaska?"

"Yeah."

"I heard he was cute."

"He's good-looking, athletic." Tia reached down and splashed some water from the stream onto her arms. "He seems nice enough."

"Have you gone out with him?"

"He's asked a couple times, but I don't know . . ." Tia trailed off, trying to put it in words. "I think at first, I was hoping I would hear from Evan, and I didn't want to start something with someone else until I knew where things stood."

"And now?"

Tia contrasted the time she had spent with Evan with her various encounters with Colby. "Evan makes me laugh. Colby doesn't."

"I'm sure you were laughing plenty when you were decorating Drew's car."

Tia gave her an innocent look. "I didn't decorate your car."

"I'm your best friend. I know you were behind it."

Tia avoided the accusation by packing her remaining grapes in her bag and taking another drink of water. "Are you ready to go?"

Julie groaned. "How much farther?"

"Two more miles. Piece of cake."

"Mmm. Cake."

Tia laughed. "Come on. I don't want to be late for work."

Julie's laughter joined hers. "You—on time? Now, that is funny."

* * *

Evan looked out the window of his hotel and took in the view of the Eiffel Tower in the distance. The view never ceased to captivate him, but after three weeks in Paris, he was ready to get back to the States. And he was ready to get a new cell phone.

The company he was currently working for had provided him a phone for his use while in France, but it didn't give him access to international calling outside of Europe. Skype had given him the ability to communicate with his family and friends back home. Except for Tia. Though he had searched for a way to contact her, none of the Tia Parkers he had found on social media and Skype matched her profile. Drew had been noticeably absent online as well, so Evan couldn't even get her number from him. Newlyweds.

He paced away from the French balcony and circled the bed. The room was barely big enough to hold the full-sized bed. He collected his wallet and room key off the tiny dresser, slid them into his front pocket, and headed out the door.

When he reached the lobby, he offered a discreet nod of greeting to the desk clerk and made his way through the revolving door. He debated briefly if he should walk the dozen blocks to his destination, but a glance at his watch made the decision for him. He crossed the street and entered the subway using his prepaid pass.

Three minutes later, he entered his train and let his gaze sweep over the other occupants. Three American tourists to his right spoke in English at a volume louder than Europeans would consider acceptable. Even if their behavior hadn't given them away, their backpacks and tennis shoes would have. He wasn't sure where the two men to his left were from, but their inability to open the door when they reached their stop announced loudly that they weren't from around here. One of the locals took pity on them and lifted the latch to open the door for them.

Summer in Paris. While it sounded great in a movie script, reality was that the city was full of tourists. The recent terrorist attack outside London had heightened security in all major cities around the world. For once, Evan wished he could have found work somewhere lower profile. Phoenix, perhaps?

Only another two days, he assured himself.

He reached his stop and tried to ignore the smell of urine as he walked through the corridors of the station and out onto the main road.

Two blocks later, he entered the main entrance of the local offices for his current employer. Brooklyn stood by the reception desk, her perfectly manicured nails tapping impatiently. After she closed the distance between them, she motioned toward the elevators and lowered her voice. "We've had some developments."

His stomach curled. Developments typically meant one of two things: another terrorist attack or a glitch in their security software. Neither boded well for him making his flight on Thursday.

The elevator doors slid open, and Evan waited for Brooklyn to enter first. Two other men joined them, forcing him to hold his questions. The moment they reached his temporary office, Brooklyn closed the door behind her.

Evan crossed his arms over his chest. "Well?"

"The local government approved emergency funding last night to expand surveillance in their train and subway stations." She took a breath before delivering the next blow. "We want you to oversee the first phase of the installation."

Evan absorbed the implications and did the mental math. If he accepted, he would nearly double his income for the year. He would also be stuck in Paris for at least another four weeks. "When would they want me to start?"

"Immediately."

He blew out a breath and circled behind his desk. "Okay . . ."

"Excellent. I'll have the contracts drawn up."

"You didn't let me finish," Evan said. "Once I put in the order for the equipment, it will take at least a week for everything to arrive. I want to take those days for a visit back to the States."

"But why? By the time you get there, you would only have five or six days before you would have to return."

"Yes, but I only had enough time when I found out about this job to throw my clothes in a suitcase and grab a cab back to the airport," Evan said. "I have some loose ends I need to tie up before I spend another four weeks here."

"Can't you tie them up from here?"

"No. I can't," Evan said. "And there's one more thing."

"What's that?"

"I have a couple of stipulations I need put in the contract before I sign."

"What kind of stipulations?"

"A modification of my travel allowance," Evan said. "And the contract goes through my company, not yours."

She huffed out a sigh. "Fine. Write it up and get it to contracts. We'll see if they agree."

"I'll have it to them by this afternoon." Evan didn't know if he would be lucky enough to need the extra accommodations, but it never hurt to be prepared.

Chapter 11

TIA LEANED FORWARD IN HER office chair and scrolled through airline tickets, debating. She needed to get away. Really get away. With Fridays off during the summer and no softball game on Saturday, this was the perfect weekend for a short trip, but she still wanted to take a week for herself sometime later this month.

When nothing popped out at her on the travel sites, she signed off and looked forward to tomorrow. She still hadn't decided if she should drive to Phoenix for the weekend to stay with her sister or if she should take Julie up on her offer to spend the weekend in Pinewood. The girls' volleyball team would show up for camp on Monday in Flagstaff, which was only twenty minutes from Julie's family cabin, and Tia had agreed to chaperone. Going up early would give her some time to relax before spending the entire week living in the dorms. At least she would have a private room.

Glancing at the clock on the wall, she stood and gathered the first-aid kits she had assembled to take with her next week. "Can't hurt to be prepared," she muttered to herself.

She locked away her files and shut down her computer. Lifting the two toolbox-sized kits, she headed out the door and made her way to the parking lot.

The moment she saw the familiar figure leaning against her truck, her steps stuttered. "Evan?" She shook her head, not trusting the vision in front of her. "What are you doing here?"

"Would you believe I lost your phone number?"

An eyebrow lifted. "You don't seriously expect me to believe you flew all the way from Detroit to get my number, do you?"

"I didn't fly in from Detroit." Evan pushed away from the truck and started forward. "I flew in from Paris."

"Paris?" she asked. "What were you doing in Paris?"

"Work. I got roped into a job and left only a few hours after I got home," Evan explained. "I am so sorry I haven't called or texted you since I left. My phone got ruined when I was on the plane."

A weight dropped off her shoulders, and she set down the first-aid kits. With some effort, she pushed aside the hurt his silence had caused. "I was wondering what happened."

"I tried finding you online—Facebook, Skype, Instagram, even your school email."

"You wouldn't find me on social media. Because I work at the school, I don't use my real name online," Tia said. "And they changed to a new email service, so my email address changed. I guess they haven't updated the school website yet."

"That explains a lot." He edged closer. "I know you probably have plans this weekend, but any chance you'd have some time we can spend together? I'm only in town for a few days."

"Believe it or not, you picked the perfect weekend to visit," Tia said. "I was toying with going to Phoenix or Flagstaff for a few days because I don't have any plans."

"Flagstaff is in the mountains, right?"

"Yeah."

"When do we leave?" Evan asked. "And where do you want to stay?"

"Actually, Julie invited me to spend the weekend with her and Drew in her family's cabin in Pinewood."

"Do you think they would have room for one more?" Evan asked.

"Maybe we should make a phone call."

"And you should pack." Evan took her hand. "It's really good to see you."

"It's good to see you too."

* * *

"I still can't believe you're here," Tia said from the passenger seat of his rental car. "Or that we managed to arrange a trip to the mountains in less than an hour."

Evan glanced over at her. "I can't believe you're still talking to me after I dropped off the face of the planet like that."

He could hear the smile in her voice when she said, "Yeah, well, you make me laugh."

"That's all it takes for a guy to convince you to go out with him?"

"Apparently so." She toed off her shoes and put one foot on the dash. "That and the ability to decorate a car."

"I can't say I ever thought that skill would come in so handy." He had second-guessed himself all the way across the Atlantic, trying to determine whether he was making a ridiculous mistake in coming to Arizona. The idea that she might have started dating someone else had reared its ugly head more times than he cared to admit, and he wasn't quite sure what to think about the flood of relief he had experienced when he had received a warm welcome.

She tapped her foot in time with the radio. "Have you really been in Paris all this time?"

"Yeah. I was in Detroit for less than six hours before I got on the next plane."

"That's crazy. Do you travel for work often?"

"This is the first time in a while." Evan thought of Brooklyn and his desire to make this his last job with her. The idea of soliciting work in Arizona slipped into his mind. "Usually, I'm able to do a lot of my work from home. Then I travel to wherever I'm installing or upgrading software systems."

They chatted as they made their way up the freeway, the open spaces of the desert giving way to pine and juniper trees dotting the landscape.

Tia motioned to the upcoming sign. "You're going to take the Munds Park exit. It's the next one."

"How far is Flagstaff from Pinewood?"

"About twenty or thirty minutes. Why?"

"At some point, I thought we could go into town so I can buy a new cell phone."

"I like that idea."

Evan took the exit and followed Tia's directions until they reached a two-story cabin with a wide front porch running the full length of the structure.

Evan parked next to Drew's car on the gravel driveway. He was barely out of the car when Drew stepped outside.

"If I had known all I had to do to get you to come visit was to introduce you to Tia, I would have done it years ago."

"Maybe you should have," Evan countered. He opened the trunk and retrieved their suitcases.

"Let me help you with the luggage." Drew jogged down the six steps and picked up Tia's suitcase. "Come on in. Make yourselves at home."

Drew led the way up the steps. Evan waited for Tia to go first before following them onto the porch. He glanced behind him and couldn't help but stop to take in the view. In the fading light, the sea of pine trees appeared as mere shadows beneath the blue-and-orange-streaked sky.

Tia put a hand on his arm. "Gorgeous, isn't it?"

"Now, that's a sunset." He remained rooted to his spot for a moment before forcing himself to turn away from the view to follow Drew inside.

To his delight, the glass-fronted living room faced west and invited the view inside. A sectional couch faced the window, and he didn't see any kind of electronic screens anywhere. A free-standing fireplace occupied the corner, the hearth consisting of a square of red brick.

"Hey, there." Julie rounded the corner from the kitchen on the far side of the room and greeted Tia with a hug. "Glad you made it."

When Julie turned to greet him in kind, Evan said, "Thanks for letting me crash the party."

"The more the merrier." She motioned toward the hallway behind her. "Evan, I was planning on you taking the downstairs guest room. First door on the left."

"I assume I'm in the bunk room," Tia said.

"Yeah. I'm not sure Evan would be able to get comfortable in one of those twin beds."

Tia looked over at him as though measuring his height. "Yeah, I don't think so."

"Hey, I can sleep anywhere," Evan said. "Anything that isn't an airplane seat sounds great to me."

"You must be exhausted," Julie said. "Drew told me you flew in from Paris today."

"Yeah, but I actually did sleep on all my flights."

"We'll all understand if you need to turn in early," Tia said.

"I'm fine. Really."

Drew set Tia's suitcase at the base of the stairs. "I assume you two ate dinner on your way up."

"We made some sandwiches at my house before we left."

"I don't know if you're interested in dessert, but there's a fire pit out back, and Julie brought marshmallows," Drew said.

"S'mores?" Tia asked hopefully.

"I may have seen graham crackers and chocolate bars in there somewhere."

"I thought as an athletic trainer, you wouldn't eat all that sugary stuff," Evan said.

"Only on special occasions." Tia stepped through the door and turned back to face him. "Like any time marshmallows, chocolate, and graham crackers are in the same room."

"She has amazing willpower," Drew told him.

"So it seems."

* * *

Tia leaned back in her chair, her fingers adequately sticky from the remnants of her s'more, the scent of citronella competing with the wood smoke rising into the night air.

Across from her, Julie stood. "I'm heading to bed. You guys help yourselves to anything in the kitchen."

"Thanks, Julie," Tia said.

"Yeah, thanks," Evan added. "And thanks again for letting me join you this weekend."

"No problem."

Drew stood as well. "Good night, guys."

"Night." Tia watched them leave, the night sounds washing over her. Crickets chirped. A toad croaked. Overhead, stars twinkled, framed by the tall pines. "I really love it here."

"It's beautiful," Evan agreed. He reached for her hand and shifted forward in his chair. "I thought about you a lot while I was gone."

"I thought about you too," Tia admitted. "Even though I was trying not to."

"Would it be out of line for me to ask if you're dating anyone else?"

"No."

His eyebrows furrowed. "No, I wouldn't be out of line? Or no, you aren't dating anyone else?"

"No to both."

His voice lowered, and he leaned forward until she could feel his breath mingle with hers. "Good."

One hand rested on her knee as he closed the distance between them. The moment his lips touched hers, her stomach leapt into her throat and a shiver worked through her. She could taste the promise in his kiss, and she struggled to fight back the regret. His life was across the country, his future in another world than her own. Yet, beneath the shadows of the pines, under the twinkling stars, she couldn't help but yearn for what they could be together.

Evan pulled back, his face still close, his eyes intense. He muttered something in a foreign tongue, and she wondered if he was as affected by the kiss as she was. Before she could ponder the question, his lips were on hers again. Her thoughts scattered; her emotions exploded. This. This was what she wanted.

Evan's hand lifted to cup the back of her neck, his fingers working into her hair. A new set of chills shot through her as she let herself sink into the heady sensation of feeling treasured.

When he pulled back, his hand slid down to take her hand. Silence hung between them for several seconds before he asked, "Have you ever been to Paris?"

"No, I haven't. Why?"

"We talked at Julie and Drew's wedding about you coming to visit me in July," Evan reminded her. "It's July."

"We talked about me visiting you in Detroit."

In the flickering light, she saw his eyebrows lift. "You would rather visit Detroit than Paris?"

"No, but it was more likely to be in my price range." She held up a finger when she added, "And don't even think I'm going to let you pay for a ticket for me. Last-minute flights are rarely cheap."

"They are when you have a free ticket on standby."

"What?"

Evan rubbed his thumb over the back of her hand. "Did I mention that my current contract just got extended?"

"No, I don't think so. Why?"

"I may have negotiated an airline ticket and a hotel room so you could visit me this month."

Tia pulled back. "Seriously?"

A cloud of doubt flickered over his face. "I hope I wasn't being too presumptuous, but it sounded like your schedule is crazy once school starts. I thought you might consider making the trip." He leaned forward to press his lips to hers once more. "Worst case, you get a week or two in Paris to see the sights."

"And best case?"

"We get the chance to see where this thing between us is going."

Tia let the possibilities spin through her head, and she let hope bloom inside her. Throwing caution aside, she said, "I like the best-case scenario. Let's go for that one."

She watched his surprise melt into delight. "Deal."

Chapter 12

THE FIRST RAYS OF SUNLIGHT filtered through the gauzy white curtains of Tia's room. She had stayed in this room on many of her previous visits to Julie's family cabin. With its two sets of bunk beds, this was the first time she hadn't had roommates.

She propped herself up on her elbow, enjoying her view from the top bunk nearest the window. Pine trees dominated the landscape, and she watched a pair of squirrels scamper up a particularly thick trunk, causing a robin to take flight.

A sense of peace washed over her.

She hadn't realized how much she had craved time away. The thought of Evan sent a bevy of butterflies fluttering in her stomach. A good-looking guy with a great sense of humor and a real job. She wondered if he liked to hike.

She headed downstairs, assuming she would be the first one up. She was surprised to find Evan standing at the stove, a spoon in hand. "What are you doing up so early? Aren't you on a completely different time zone?"

"I try not to think about that. If I only pay attention to my watch, my body adjusts quickly enough," Evan said. "Besides, we weren't up that late last night."

"True." She slid onto a stool at the kitchen counter. "What are you making?"

"Oatmeal."

"I like oatmeal."

"Good, because there aren't a lot of options here."

"Maybe we should make a trip to the store today."

"I already started a list," Evan said.

"Do you want to go after breakfast, before things start getting crazy, or would you rather wait until we head into Flagstaff?"

"Probably best to buy groceries closer to home."

"True." She glanced at the clock on the stove. "The store opens in about an hour."

"Did you want to go for a run first?"

"We could do that, or we could go for a hike afterward."

"I bet there are some great trails around here." Evan lifted the pot off the stove and dished up two bowls of oatmeal.

"Thanks."

"You're welcome." Evan took the seat beside her. "Should we wait for Drew and Julie to get up before we go?"

"We could go to Flagstaff and back before Julie gets up." Tia patted his leg. "I think we can manage without them."

"I'm sure you're right."

* * *

Evan followed Tia into the general store and looked around at the eclectic selection of household items and groceries. It was as though someone had shrunk a Walmart and stuffed it into a rustic version of a convenience store. The older woman sitting beside the cash register looked up from her paperback novel and slid her reading glasses down her nose.

"Good morning. Is there anything I can help you find?"

"We're just after groceries this morning," Evan said.

Someone approached from the center aisle. "Hey, Mrs. Burgess, do you have any more apricot jelly?"

"Bottom shelf."

"Found it."

Evan glanced over as the man emerged, surprised when he recognized him. What were the chances that he would run into Charlie Whitmore both times he came to Arizona? A greeting hung on the tip of his tongue. Not sure if Charlie would remember him, he hesitated.

Tia apparently didn't have such reservations. "Hey, Charlie. What are you doing here?"

Charlie looked over at them, recognition lighting his eyes. "Looks like the same thing you are." He extended his hand to Evan. "Evan, good to see you again."

"You too."

"How long are you guys staying in Munds Park?" Charlie asked.

"I'm here through the weekend," Tia said. "I head up to Flagstaff on Monday."

"What about you, Evan?" Charlie asked.

"I'm here until Wednesday," Evan said, amazed the man remembered his name after a brief encounter a month ago.

"Hey, what are you guys doing for dinner tomorrow night?" Charlie asked. "Kendra is trying a new recipe. We'd love for you to join us."

"Really?" Evan gave him a speculative look. "I thought Kendra was trying to hide away for a while."

"We miss having people our age to hang out with when we're up here." Charlie shot a look at the store clerk. "No offense, Mrs. Burgess."

She lifted her paperback. "None taken."

"That sounds like a lot of fun, but we're here with Julie and Drew," Tia said. "As much as I love Julie, she would totally fangirl Kendra all night."

"You're probably right." Charlie pulled his wallet from his pocket and slid a business card free. "If you do find you two are free, give me a call. My cell phone number is on there."

"Thanks."

"And if tonight doesn't work, maybe we can have you come for lunch or something," Charlie said. "Every time Kendra starts writing music, she cooks when she gets stuck. I swear I have to double my workouts when we're here."

"We were going on a hike after we drop off our groceries. I don't know what your schedule is like this morning, but . . ." Evan let the unspoken invitation hang in the air.

"Actually, I don't think we do have anything planned." He glanced at his watch. "When were you heading out?"

Evan gave Tia a questioning look. "What do you think? Around eight thirty?"

"Yeah." She spoke to Charlie when she added, "I was planning to start at the Janice Trailhead."

"Perfect. Our place isn't far from there." Charlie pulled his phone from his pocket. "Shoot me a text so I have your number. After I talk to Kendra, I'll let you know if we're joining you."

"Sounds great." Tia added Charlie to her contacts and texted him.

"I'd better finish up here, or Kendra's going to wonder what happened to me." Charlie set the basket he held on the counter.

"Hopefully, we'll see you later," Evan said, picking up a basket from near the checkout counter.

"You can count on it."

"Where do you want to start?" Evan asked Tia.

Mrs. Burgess pointed to a display behind her. "Trail mix is over there."

Tia's lips quirked. "Let's start with trail mix."

"We can do that."

* * *

Tia and Kendra followed Charlie and Evan up the trail. She glanced at the woman beside her, a dusting of freckles visible on Kendra's nose. "Can I ask you something?"

"Yeah, I guess," Kendra said, a hint of caution in her voice.

"Does it get annoying being famous?"

Her laughter rang out. "Sometimes. Yes."

"I thought so." Tia circled past two pine trees on her left. "You were so nice to my friend Julie. I thought she was going to die when she met you."

"She was sweet."

"She is sweet, but the night of your concert, psychotic may have been a better description." Tia lifted the water bottle she held and took a sip. "Of course, you're probably used to that."

"Kind of." She swatted at an insect and continued forward. "I've had some security issues in the past, so I keep my interactions with fans pretty limited."

"I remember reading about when you had a stalker. I had nightmares just thinking about it. I can't imagine going through something like that."

"I try not to think about it myself," Kendra said. "Days like today when I can get out and feel normal make all of that feel like a bad dream that happened to someone else."

"Marrying an FBI agent may have been a wise choice."

"I thought so."

"Hey, Tia. Come here," Evan called to her. "Look at this view. It's incredible."

Tia caught up to him and looked out over the landscape dotted with pine trees, the terrain sloping downward into a deep canyon. "You should see it at sunset."

Evan slipped his hand around her waist. "Is that an invitation?"

"Maybe next trip. I think Drew and Julie are going to want to spend some time with us this weekend."

"Are you kidding? Those two are in their own world."

Tia glanced over to where Charlie stood behind Kendra, both of his hands resting on her shoulders. "They aren't the only ones."

"Newlyweds," Evan whispered so only she could hear.

"Yeah. Everyone should be that happy."

The humor dropped out of Evan's voice. "Yeah. They should."

* * *

Evan sat at the dinner table and watched Drew demolish Tia in a game of chess. For the third time.

He had to give it to her. She never gave up.

Their morning plans with Charlie and Kendra had stretched beyond their hike and into the afternoon. Lunch at their cabin, followed by another hour of visiting. Seeing Kendra Blake with her hair tucked through the back of her ball cap made him almost able to pretend she was like everyone else. By the time he and Tia had returned to Julie's cabin, Drew and Julie had already been to the pool at the country club. The newlyweds didn't ask any details about Tia and Evan's hike, and Evan suspected Tia was wise not to mention that they had spent the day with Charlie and Kendra. As a result, a quiet evening had ensued.

Tia made another unwise move.

Three moves later, Drew announced, "Checkmate."

Evan put his hand on Tia's shoulder. "I think it may be time to try a new game."

"How about gin rummy?" Tia asked, unfazed by yet another loss.

"No," Drew and Julie said in unison.

Evan looked from one to the other. "What's wrong with gin rummy?"

"Tia's like a card shark with that game."

"Poker?" Evan suggested.

"Even worse," Julie said. "If it's anything that's a game of chance, she wins. The girl is seriously lucky."

"It's not luck," Tia insisted. "It's skill."

"Right." Julie opened a cabinet in the corner and pulled out several games.

Tia stood and peered over her shoulder. "How about Boggle? You're an English teacher. You should relate to that one."

"I'm up for that," Evan said, not because he particularly favored the game but because he wanted to encourage a decision.

"I'll get the paper and pens," Drew said.

Three minutes later, Drew turned over the timer, and everyone started furiously scribbling words. Everyone except Tia.

Every few seconds, she would write something, but with the speed of everyone else, Evan suspected this really wasn't her game.

"Okay, I'll go first," Julie said when the timer ran out. She read through her words, groans erupting when everyone canceled each other out.

When it was Tia's turn to go, she said, "I only have five words left."

"I don't have many more than that," Evan said, hoping to make her feel better, even though he still had nine points.

"What have you got?" Julie asked.

"*Tun.*" She spelled it out to distinguish it from the other version that had already been said.

"Good one," Julie said.

"Then I also have *deter, determine, determined,* and *undetermined.*" She looked up innocently.

"What?" Julie leaned forward as Tia pointed out the spelling of her words.

"How many points do you get for a nine-letter word?" Tia asked.

Julie leaned back in her chair. "Unbelievable."

"Um, I think she won," Evan said.

"Like I said." Julie snapped the lid back on top of the game. "Lucky."

"Not luck." Tia lifted one finger in the air. "Skill."

Chapter 13

"I CAN'T BELIEVE THE WEEKEND went by so fast." Tia set the bowl of popcorn on the end table and sat beside Evan.

"I know." He stretched his arm across the back of the couch, his hand resting on her shoulder. "I wish I could stay longer."

"Me too." She tucked her feet underneath her.

"What is your schedule like tomorrow?" Evan asked. "Would you have time for me to take you out to dinner?"

"Yeah, I should be done by six. As soon as the girls are finished with their physical activities for the day, I can slip away for a couple hours. The drama won't start until day three."

"How do you know there will be drama on Wednesday?" Evan asked.

"They're teenage girls. There's always drama on day three."

"Since I've never been a teenage girl, I'll trust you know what you're talking about." Evan gave her a sideways glance. "Where do you want me to meet you?"

"Probably by the dorms. I'd say I'd text you when I'm done, but you still don't have a phone."

"I know it was selfish of me, but I didn't want to get a new one while I was with you," he said. "Is it bad that I didn't want any interruptions while I'm here?"

Touched by the sentiment, she reached up and patted the hand resting on her shoulder. "It's not bad. It's sweet."

"Glad you think so. I thought I would swing by and pick one up tomorrow after I drop you off at NAU."

"That will make things easier."

"It will," he agreed, his fingers toying with her hair. "You still need to give me what dates you can take off from work to come visit me."

Excitement at the prospect of seeing him again so soon, as well as visiting Paris, rushed through her but was also tampered by wariness. "Are you sure about this? You said you would be working, and I don't want you spending a bunch of money on me to visit."

"Like I already told you, your flight and hotel will be covered. The only thing you have to worry about is bringing money for any souvenirs you want to buy."

"If you're sure . . ."

"I'm sure." Evan shifted to face her. "How many days are you able to take off? And when's the soonest you could come?"

"The soonest I could leave would be a week from Monday, and I'd have to be back by the first of August."

"That would give you at least two weeks," Evan said. "I might have to shift the dates a bit based on what's available, but once I replace my phone, I'll see what I can do."

"You're pretty amazing, you know that?"

Evan reached down and gave her hand a squeeze. "You keep thinking that, okay?"

"Okay."

* * *

Evan loaded Tia's suitcase into the trunk of his rental car with a twinge of regret. Every day he spent with her, the more he dreaded leaving. Though he didn't look forward to getting back into the swing of working, he was eager to contact his office so he could arrange Tia's travel. A week apart wouldn't be so bad. He hoped.

In order to ride up to Pinewood with him last week, she had left her truck at home and arranged to travel back to Cottonwood with the volleyball team on Friday.

Tia stepped onto the front deck, carrying her purse and cell phone, her dark hair swinging loosely over her shoulders. Those amazing golden eyes met his, and visions danced in his head.

She descended the stairs. "Are the first-aid kits still in your trunk?"

"Yeah." He tried to memorize her features—the high cheekbones set in an oval face, the sprinkle of freckles on her straight nose, and the humor that always seemed to dance in her voice. The scent of her shampoo—strawberries and vanilla—mixed with the pine trees surrounding the cabin. He swallowed and managed to ask, "Are you all set?"

"Yeah." She started toward the passenger side door, but Evan took her hand and held her in place.

He saw her confusion when she looked at him, followed by her awareness when he moved closer. He lowered his head, preparing for the eruption of sensations when their lips met. He knew what to expect now, but that didn't diminish the impact when the ground tilted and his insides exploded. His mind hazed as her flavor poured into him until there was nothing left but what they created together.

Mine. The single word, the possessiveness of it, startled him. Never before could he remember being so consumed with one person. What was it about her that made him want to alter his future to align his with hers? He was just getting to know her, yet he couldn't remember feeling like this with anyone before.

"I wasn't sure how soon I'd be able to do that again," Evan said, stealing one more quick kiss. "Hope you don't mind."

Her cheeks flushed, but her gaze remained on him. "I don't mind."

"Good." He opened her door and waited for her to climb inside. As his mind jumped ahead to white gowns and diamond rings, he wondered how long he needed to wait before he would be able to make Tia his.

* * *

Colby typed his report into the computer console in his police cruiser for his latest call. Besides circling through town on his usual route today, he had already responded to two fender benders, a domestic dispute, and a theft at the local grocery store. What made the guy think he could walk in, pick up a twelve pack of beer, and walk out without paying was beyond him. The store clerk had chased the guy more than a quarter mile before Colby had arrived to take him into custody.

At least Colby hadn't been assigned to the speed trap on Highway 89A all day. After writing four tickets before eight o'clock this morning, he'd had his fill of cranky motorists. He checked the clock on his dash, deciding he had enough time to circle through town before ending his shift.

He cruised past the high school first to find only a few of the usual cars in the lot. He was disappointed that Tia wasn't there. A couple of times, he had been fortunate enough to be passing by when she'd left work. His timing had been off for days.

After ensuring the area was secure, he continued down the hill to the main road and turned toward the small airport on the edge of town, choosing to use Airport Road to circle back to the highway instead of turning around in the airport parking lot.

He slowed instinctively when he approached Tia's house on the corner. Though her house was along his route, he hadn't seen any activity there for a couple days, not even when he had taken his daily runs, which now included a loop that brought him down her street. He missed seeing her. Not having a game on Saturday had made him realize how much he had come to depend on her friendship.

Making his way back to the station, he parked his cruiser in his usual spot and headed inside.

"Hey, Colby," Raul greeted him when he walked inside. "Are you going to be at the game tomorrow night?"

"I was planning on it. Why?"

"Wesley said you could play shortstop. We need someone to stand in for Parker."

His heart sank. "Where's she going to be?"

"She's at some sports camp at NAU with the volleyball team." Raul headed for the door. "I'll let Wes know you can take her place tomorrow."

Colby let the disappointment seep through. He would happily forgo playing his favorite position on the ball field if it meant having Tia sitting beside him on the bench.

He managed only a few steps before his name was called again. This time, he turned to see Chief Jarvis heading his way. "I know this is last-minute, but is there any way you can cover the first few hours of Gio's shift tonight? He got caught in traffic coming home from dropping his daughter off at volleyball camp in Flagstaff."

"Is that where NAU is?" Colby asked.

"Yeah. It's about an hour's drive from here, but there was an accident on the switchbacks in Oak Creek Canyon, and he stopped to help," the chief explained. "He should be back in about an hour, but he wanted to have some time to eat and say good night to his kids before he came in."

"Tell him to take his time. I can cover for as long as he needs."

"Thanks."

"No problem," Colby said. At least this way, he wouldn't have to spend his evening sitting at home alone.

* * *

More than two hundred volleyball players crowded through the exits of NAU's practice gym. The last training session had gone over by nearly a half hour, so the extra fifteen minutes Tia had built into her schedule had already come and gone.

She fell in behind the teenagers until she finally exited the building and reached daylight.

Her mood immediately brightened when she saw Evan leaning against the wall, waiting for her. He straightened when she approached. "How was the first day of volleyball camp?"

"Busy." She noticed two of the girls from her school standing nearby and resisted greeting Evan with a kiss. "Sorry we ran late."

"No problem." He motioned toward the parking lot. "Are you ready?"

"Yeah." She walked with him to his car. "Did you get your cell phone taken care of today?"

"I did." He pulled it out of his pocket and handed it to her. "Here. Put in your phone number for me and then text yourself so you have my new number."

"Why did you change your number?"

"I'm considering new business options, and I wanted a different number in case anything came of them."

"That makes sense." Tia took it from him only to find the screen locked. "You need to unlock it before I can give you my number."

"The code is your birthday."

"How do you know when my birthday is?"

"I asked Julie," Evan said.

"And why did you make my birthday your passcode?"

"Because that way I won't forget it."

Touched, she glanced over at him, appreciating his strong jawline and expressive eyes. "You are too cute."

"Guys don't like to be cute. I'd prefer to go for ruggedly handsome."

"You're that too." She entered her phone number, texted herself, and handed it back. "When is your birthday?"

"July 14."

"That's only a couple weeks away." She stopped beside his car. "What do you want for your birthday?"

"How about you come out with me for a nice dinner? There's this great little restaurant I like in Le Marais." He unlocked the car and opened her door for her. Instead of pulling it wide to wait for her to get in, he reached inside and grabbed a handful of papers. "Speaking of which, I have your travel arrangements."

"What?" Tia took the papers and read the first page; her name was listed on an airline itinerary. To Paris. "You seriously got me a ticket to Paris?"

"I told you I was going to."

"I know, but it didn't seem real until right now." She skimmed through the details. A week from tomorrow night, she would be boarding a plane in Phoenix and flying through New York on her way to Paris. "First class?"

"Only on the way there." Evan pointed to where her return flight was listed. "The only seat available outbound was first class so they upgraded you. I'm afraid you're coach on the way back."

"Evan, I don't know what to say. This is unbelievable."

"Believe it."

She reached up and kissed his cheek. "Thank you."

"You're welcome, but this is as much for me as it is for you."

"Then I guess we'll both have to have a great time in Paris," Tia said. "But you avoided my question. What do you want for your birthday?"

He slid his arms around her waist. "I have everything I want right here."

Chapter 14

COLBY SCANNED THE WIDE, GRASSY area outside the women's dorms until he saw Tia appear through the main entrance. Instantly, his mood brightened. He hadn't seen her since last week at Wednesday night's game. Seven days was much too long.

He pushed open his car door and headed toward her. He saw the confusion on her face when she spotted him. Her steps slowed, and she angled toward him.

"Colby, what are you doing here?"

"I have a couple things I needed to pick up in Flagstaff, and Raul mentioned you were up here," Colby said. "I thought I would stop by and see how things are going."

"Going good so far," Tia said. "Our setter suffered a mild ankle sprain yesterday, but she was able to walk on it today."

"That's a good sign."

"Yeah." She took a step toward the building to their left, and Colby fell in beside her.

"Did you come up here last weekend?"

"Yeah. A friend of mine has a cabin nearby. I stayed with her for a few days before volleyball camp started."

"Sounds relaxing." Colby lifted the white paper bag he held. "I remembered you liked those chocolate chip cookies from the bakery downtown. I brought some for you."

Surprise reflected on her face. "That was nice of you." She took the bag from him and peeked inside. "Did you want one?"

"No." He patted his stomach. "I had one already."

"Well, thank you for dropping by. I should get back to the girls," Tia said. "They have a mini-tournament starting in a few minutes."

"Is it okay if I tag along for a while? I'd love to see how the hometown kids are doing."

"I guess . . ." She broke off when someone behind them shouted her name.

"Tia!" the man shouted a second time.

The man approached, and Colby instinctively sized him up. Maybe six one, one seventy-five, dark-blond hair, blue eyes. He jogged toward them with ease, and Colby guessed his athletic physique was from regular work-outs rather than physical labor.

"Hey, Evan." Tia motioned to Colby. "This is Colby Farren. He just started on the police force in Cottonwood last month."

"Good to meet you." Evan stuck out his hand.

Colby gripped it a little firmer than usual. "You too."

As though oblivious to what was going on right in front of him, Evan asked, "How do you like living in Arizona?"

"It has its moments."

"I bet. The heat in Phoenix is insane."

"Do you live here in Flagstaff?" Colby asked.

"Detroit, actually."

"Oh, so you're only visiting."

"For now," Evan said, and Colby saw the glint in his eye. For all the easy-going vibes flowing off Evan, Colby suspected there was a steel core running through him. Evan shifted his attention to Tia. "I'm leaving for the airport."

"Can you let me know when you get there?" Tia asked.

"I will." A private look passed between them. "I backed up my contacts, just in case."

"Good."

Evan leaned in and kissed Tia's cheek.

Colby's jaw clenched at the naturalness of the gesture. Where had this guy come from? Was he the reason Tia had yet to agree to a real date? He fought the surge of jealousy.

"See you later." Evan stepped away and gave Colby a measured look. "Good to meet you, Colby."

With a lift of his chin, Colby watched the other man leave. Reminding himself that Evan lived in Detroit, he waited for Tia's attention to shift back to him.

"Sorry about that." Tia's cheeks flushed slightly. "Evan's flying out this afternoon."

"No problem," Colby lied. "Now, where is our volleyball team?"

Tia stared at him for a moment as though trying to gauge his mood. Keeping his calm facade in place, he waited, wondering how long it would take her to understand that he was here to stay.

Finally, Tia motioned to the large building to their left that appeared to house the gym. "It's this way."

* * *

Evan fingered his wallet in his front pocket with his left hand and gripped his new cell phone in his right. The stream of text messages from Tia continued to amuse him and left him looking forward to when she would arrive next week.

He entered the office building, relieved when he didn't find Brooklyn waiting for him in the lobby. Three minutes later, he walked into his office and immediately heard his name called.

"Why didn't you call me when you got back?" Brooklyn asked. "I didn't know when to set up the installation meetings for you."

"I spoke to Claude a couple days ago," Evan countered. He began sorting through the mail that had been left on his desk.

"I'm the one who handles all the scheduling," Brooklyn reminded him. "When we dissolved our partnership, we both agreed to have my company handle all the business side of things and for yours to be strictly security development. I can't do my job properly if you don't keep me in the loop."

Evan didn't admit that he called Claude directly because he didn't want Brooklyn to have his new phone number.

His phone chimed, and the photo of Tia and him filled his screen.

Brooklyn snatched it up. "Who is this?"

"My girlfriend."

"Wait. Did you go all the way back to the States for a woman?" Brooklyn asked, her tone shrill.

"That's right."

"Why would you do that?"

One eyebrow lifted. "I'm not discussing my personal life with you."

"In case you've forgotten, I used to be your personal life."

"And this is why we stopped working together," Evan reminded her. Eighteen months had been more than enough to prove their lifestyles and their ethics weren't compatible. He stared at her with a new resolve. "This is it, Brooklyn. After we finish this job, I'm not working with you again."

"Evan, we both know better than that," Brooklyn insisted. "I have the connections. You have the computer skills. Together, we make the perfect team."

"I suggest you find someone else to be part of your perfect team." Evan reached out and took his phone from her. "In three more weeks, I'm going home, and my company will operate without your assistance. Now, if you'll excuse me, I have work to do."

* * *

Evan looked for the telltale signs of American tourists as he scanned the early-morning crowd at the airport. At only seven in the morning, many of the passengers were deplaning from transatlantic flights—weary families arriving on their European vacations, Parisians returning home from their holidays in the States, businessmen and women of multiple nationalities.

He admired the woman heading toward him, her sleek, dark hair falling over a tan blazer. A chunky necklace offset her white blouse, and her fitted jeans showed off a slender figure.

He scanned the crowd again, his eyes drawn once more to the approaching brunette. Then he focused on the face and stared. Tia continued forward, greeting him with a kiss on his cheek.

"I almost didn't recognize you," Evan said in a lowered voice. "You look like you're French."

"That's the idea." She shifted the oversized purse on her shoulder. "Never a good idea to stand out as a tourist."

"But I thought you'd never been to France."

"I haven't, but I know how to use the internet."

Evan chuckled and reached for her rolling suitcase. He put a hand on her back to guide her forward. "Baggage claim is this way."

"I didn't check any luggage." She motioned to the bag he was pulling. "This is it."

"Oh." Evan didn't know a woman could travel for more than a week without at least two suitcases. "In that case, let's go to the train station. It's here in the airport."

"Lead the way."

He guided her to the correct terminal and retrieved the passes he had already purchased out of his wallet and handed one to her. "Here's your transit pass. It's good for any of the trains and subways within the city."

"Thanks." Their train pulled in, and they boarded, luckily managing to find two seats together. Her voice low, she asked, "What time do you have to be at work?"

"I have time to show you our hotel before I head in," Evan told her. "Your room probably won't be ready this early, but the concierge will hold your bag for you. Did you get any sleep on the plane?"

"I did. The noise-canceling headphones were a great idea. Thanks for mentioning them." She patted her purse. "I'm sure I'll crash early tonight, but I thought I could do some sightseeing today while you're at work."

"If you want, we can meet for lunch."

"That sounds great." She fell into silence, and her eyes swept the train as though she was absorbing everything around her.

He did his own analysis, only his focus came from a security standpoint.

When they reached their stop, he led her across the street to their hotel. Once they were out of the fray of other passengers, he asked, "Do you have any idea what you want to see today?"

"It depends on you."

"Why does it depend on me?"

"Because you've already been here for a few weeks. I thought I would go to the places you've already been to that you don't care about seeing again."

"If you want to go up the Eiffel Tower, that would be a good thing to do today. The lines usually aren't as long early in the day, especially on a weekday." He pulled open the door and waited for her to walk through. "You also might be able to jump on one of the walking tours in the city. I really liked the one in Montmartre, but you have to sign up for those a day in advance."

"Is that something you would want to do again?"

"Probably not. I prefer to explore on my own, especially since I've already been on the tour before."

Evan spoke to the desk clerk, automatically switching into French. After he handed over Tia's bag, he thanked the clerk and gave Tia her claim ticket. "Ready?"

"I didn't know you spoke French."

"It's come in handy with all the traveling I've done for work the last few years."

"How did you learn?"

"I took both French and German in high school and kept going with German in college," Evan told her. "Living in Brussels for three months gave me pretty good control of my French."

"And your German?"

"Two months in Vienna followed by six weeks in Zurich did the trick on that one," Evan said. "I think that's why I keep accepting jobs in Europe. I know if I'm not using my language skills, I'll lose them."

"It's so true." Tia considered for a moment before adding, "Too bad Spanish isn't one of your languages. You'd fit right in in Arizona."

"Not surprising since you're on the Mexican border." They crossed the street to the train, and he gave her the address to the restaurant for lunch.

Her train arrived first, and he watched her get on with a wave of her hand. As she disappeared from sight, he found himself looking forward to hearing about her adventures when they met for lunch. Tia Parker in Paris. This should be good.

Chapter 15

SHE SHOULD HAVE BEEN BACK by now. Colby had yet to see Tia at all this week, even though he'd driven by her house and the high school on a regular basis. He hadn't even seen her truck.

Maybe she was sick. That might explain her extended absence. But she had seemed fine when he'd seen her last Wednesday and again on Friday morning when he had made a special trip to Flagstaff to see her before his afternoon shift.

He circled by the high school yet again and saw Raul walk out the front door. Raul immediately waved a hand. Colby pulled up beside his coworker's cruiser. He waited until Raul was within a few feet before he rolled down his window. This Arizona heat was stifling.

"Looks pretty dead around here today," Colby said conversationally.

"Yeah. A lot of the year-round staff are on vacation this week."

"That would explain the lack of cars," Colby said. "I thought Tia would be in since she was out of town last week."

"She was here Monday, but she left early." Raul said. "I'm not sure where she went."

She left early. That would explain why he had missed her. He had been on a late shift for the past two weeks.

"What are you doing up this way?" Raul asked.

"I was on my way to Verde Village. The chief said he wanted more of a police presence there during summer vacation."

"Good luck." Raul stepped toward his cruiser. "I'm heading home. I'll see you at the game tonight."

"Yeah. See you then."

Colby watched him go, a seed of envy planted. Not only did Raul get to avoid the irritation of traffic duty and cruising neighborhoods, but he also had a regular schedule—a schedule that included daily interaction with Tia.

Too bad his job hadn't been the one that had opened up when Colby had come to town.

* * *

Tia walked along the streets of Paris and tried to look like she knew where she was going. She peeked at the GPS on her phone, a single earbud in her left ear allowing her to hear the directions she had plugged in.

She had spent her morning at the Eiffel Tower, amused when she had gotten in line and the gate attendants had assumed she was a local. Though she had bought a ticket to go to the top, when she reached the first level, she had decided she was plenty high enough. Apparently, she had a fear of ridiculously high places. Who knew?

That hadn't stopped her from spending an hour staring out at the city, moving from one side of the platform to another, taking pictures of Paris from every angle.

An older couple from Baltimore had been nice enough to take a picture of her with the Seine River in the background. When she had wandered down along Champ de Mars so she could take photos of the Eiffel Tower from the ground, she had offered to take a photo of a young family from Germany. Through hand signals, the mother had offered to return the favor. Much better than a selfie.

The voice in her ear told her to turn left. She rounded the corner and approached a restaurant with tables pushed against the exterior wall, each table allowing enough space for a chair on either side. Pedestrians crowded past patrons who had chosen to enjoy the beautiful weather. Sixty-eight degrees in July. This was the life.

She was nearly to the entrance when she saw Evan approaching from the other direction. He met her at the door, kissing her cheek when he reached her. "How was your morning?"

"I officially love Paris. The view from the Eiffel Tower is beyond description."

"Did you take the lift up or did you walk?"

"I took the lift. I figured I would get plenty of exercise this afternoon walking around."

"Very true." He guided her inside and spoke to the waiter in French. As soon as they were seated and their drink order were taken, Evan said, "I'm planning to leave work at four today. I thought we could get an early dinner since I know you've got to be exhausted."

"I'm surprised it hasn't really hit me yet," Tia admitted. "Of course, flying first class made sleeping on the plane a lot easier."

"I imagine."

"Where do you want me to meet you for dinner?"

"Let's meet back at the hotel. That way you can get settled before we eat."

"Sounds good. Of course, once I sit still for too long, I'll probably crash for the night."

"That's what I always do my first night in Europe."

Tia opened her menu and glanced up at Evan, surprised. "My menu is in English."

"Yeah. I asked for an English version for you. I thought you might want to know what you're ordering."

"Thank you." She glanced over the options. "Okay, I know this may sound boring, but I think I'm going to get the French onion soup."

"That's one of my favorite things here."

Tia's phone chimed, and she looked down to see a text from Wesley.

"Is Julie checking to see if you got here okay?"

"Actually, it's from my friend Wesley. He wanted to make sure I was going to be at our softball game tomorrow."

"I don't think you're going to make it."

"You may be right." Tia debated for a moment on how to tell Wesley why she wasn't going to be at the game. Deciding her friends would think she was crazy for flying to Paris to spend time with a guy she had only known for a month, she opted to keep it simple. *Went out of town for a last-minute vacation. Be back in a couple weeks.*

"I gather you didn't tell your friends you were coming to meet me here."

Tia shook her head. "Is it selfish of me to want to keep our relationship private for now?"

"Not at all." He put his hand over hers. "I kind of like having you all to myself."

"I know what you mean," Tia said. "Right now, it almost feels like we don't have a long-distance relationship."

He gave her hand a squeeze. "We'd better enjoy it while we can."

* * *

Evan glanced at his watch. Only fifteen minutes late coming back from lunch. Not bad, considering. In fact, he probably deserved an award for not taking the whole day off to spend with Tia for her first day in town.

"Evan."

Claude Thomas was approaching from the other end of the hall, near his office. The older man's gray hair made him look older than his fifty-seven years, but like Evan, he liked to stay active. That decision had boded well for him, keeping him looking lean in his Savile Row. "Monsieur Thomas," Evan said, automatically slipping into French. "What can I do for you?"

"I believe the better question may be what I can do for you. Do you have a minute? I'd like to meet with you."

"Of course." Evan nodded toward his office door. "My office or yours?"

"Yours will do." Claude followed him inside, closed the door, and took a seat.

Evan circled behind his desk and lowered himself into his chair, his palms sweating. He couldn't remember Claude ever coming to his office before, and rarely did they speak unless Brooklyn set up a progress meeting for them. Of course, she always made sure she was present so she wouldn't miss anything.

"Is there a problem?" Evan asked.

"No, no problem at all." Claude shook his head. "Quite the contrary, in fact."

Evan fought back the urge to question further.

"I understand the installation on the upgraded security software is expected to take another three weeks."

"That's right."

"And this is the third time you have worked with our company."

"Yes. I worked once in the Marseille office and twice now here in Paris."

"The contract this time was significantly less costly than the last time we hired you."

Evan shifted in his seat. After discovering Brooklyn was overcharging clients on previous jobs, he had insisted on pushing the contract through his company rather than hers. With the trust between them broken, he had read every line. He swallowed and chose his words carefully. "A few months ago, Brooklyn and I dissolved our partnership. This contract was written through my new company, which has significantly less overhead."

"In other words, your company doesn't overcharge us."

Evan stiffened. "I believe the amount I am being paid is fair compensation for the services I provide."

"And Brooklyn?"

"She brokered the deal between us."

"Besides costing this company her portion of compensation and the extra two months of hotel bills, what exactly does she do here?"

"In the past, she has handled the business side of things."

"And in the future?"

Evan hesitated, only to remember he didn't owe Brooklyn anything. She would find out soon enough he was serious about not brokering future deals through her. "This will be our last time working together."

"Excellent." Claude leaned forward. "In that case, I have a business proposition for you."

"I'm listening."

"I would like to put you on retainer," Claude said. "Terrorism is on the rise, and we both know it's necessary to consistently monitor, change, and upgrade our computer systems, particularly in the summer months."

"Wait. Are you asking me to move here permanently?"

"That's exactly what I'm asking." Claude stood. "Think about it. I have our legal department working out a proposal I feel will be more than adequate. Besides a living stipend and a travel allowance, the compensation recognizes your extraordinary computer skills."

"I appreciate the consideration, but I will have to think about it." Evan stood and offered his hand.

"You have a few more weeks left on your current contract. Plenty of time to look for apartments as you consider." He moved to the door. "We'll talk again soon."

Evan stared as Claude opened the door and walked into the hall. Two months ago, he wouldn't have hesitated to snatch up the offer. A chance to live full-time in Europe, paid travel to visit his family, independence for his company without further interference from Brooklyn. Now, the only thing he could think of was the one downside he wasn't sure he could overcome: Tia.

He had already started looking into possible contracts that would bring him closer to Arizona. Now he had a great offer that would take him even farther away.

Chapter 16

TIA STROLLED THROUGH THE PARK, her hand in Evan's. Lush green foliage surrounded her, reminding her again that she really was in a different world. Three days in Paris, and the wonder hadn't worn off in the slightest.

She had been debating how to spend her Friday afternoon when Evan had texted to tell her he was getting off work early. After meeting at the subway station, they had wandered through the 19th arrondissement of Paris until they'd reached their destination.

The mature trees surrounding the huge grassy area made it seem like they were cut off from the rest of the city.

Evan led her to the shade of one of those large trees and sat on the grass, tugging on her hand so she would sit beside him. "I should have packed a picnic," he said, glancing at a young family sitting on a blanket a short distance away.

"That would have been hard to do since you didn't know you'd be able to take off early until an hour ago."

"True." Evan leaned back on his elbow, his gaze now focused on her.

"Is everything okay?" Tia asked. "You've been awfully quiet the last couple days."

"There's a lot going on at work. That's all."

The breeze ruffled his hair, and she stared into the depth of his blue eyes. His voice may have been casual, but she sensed something was troubling him. She hoped it wasn't her. "What happens when you finish your job here?" she asked. "Do you have something else waiting for you in Detroit?"

"I have a couple of clients in Michigan who have expressed interest in having me work for them again." He paused and rubbed his thumb over the back of her hand. "I was hoping to find something that would bring me to your side of the country."

The pressure that had been building inside her eased. "I'd like that."

"Are you doing what you want with your life?" Evan asked.

"That's a profound question."

He released her hand and raked his fingers through his hair. "I guess it can be. I mean, is being a high school athletic trainer what you want to do for the rest of your career?"

"I don't know." Tia hesitated, not sure she was ready to share her private hopes and dreams. She saw the uneasiness in Evan's gaze again and edged her way onto the bridge of trust. "I always figured I might change eventually, especially if I get married and want to start a family."

"Is that something you want for yourself?" he asked. "Marriage and family?"

"I do. I'm a traditionalist, I guess." She noticed the way his shoulders relaxed slightly. Not sure where this conversation was heading or how often she would even see Evan after this trip, she threw caution to the wind. "My plan when I took this job was to work for a few years and then try to work in a rehab clinic. My pie-in-the-sky dream is to open a residential clinic, one where athletes come for intensive rehab."

"That's a lofty goal."

"I know." She lowered her gaze and fought back the disappointment that his reaction was very much like the rest of her family's. Everyone could see the possibilities, but the obstacles were always too large to tackle.

"You know, Munds Park might be a good place to locate something like that."

"What?" Her eyes lifted to meet his again.

"I was thinking if you did something in the mountains, you could build your own miniature resort, complete with the rehab facilities you would need," Evan said.

"I never thought of that area before," Tia said. "My first choice was Sedona, but I'd never be able to afford land there."

"I've heard Sedona is pricey."

"Very much so."

"I guess if you opened your own place, you wouldn't have much time for travel."

"Maybe not the first year or two, but if I had the right staff, I would be able to adjust the number of clients to create natural vacation times."

A soccer ball rolled in their direction, and Tia shifted to block it before it bounced into Evan. She stood and kicked it back to the man who had started toward them to collect it.

"Merci!"

Tia lifted a hand in acknowledgment, then lowered herself to the ground again. "I don't know why so many people say Parisians aren't friendly. Everyone I've interacted with has been really nice."

"Maybe it's because they don't realize you're an American."

"Trust me. The lady at the bakery in Montmartre on Wednesday totally knew I was from the States," Tia said. "It was pretty comical, actually. I don't speak French. She didn't speak English. It's amazing how much you can communicate through hand gestures."

"What exactly were you trying to communicate?"

"That I wanted the chocolate tart in the display case." Tia pressed her lips together. "It was so good. If we go back to that part of the city, we need to go there again."

Evan leaned forward for a brief kiss. "I think that can be arranged."

* * *

Evan showered and dressed for the day, determined not to think of the date. Today was simply Saturday, his first full day to spend with Tia in Paris. With a few minutes to spare, he sat at the desk in his hotel room and read through the first page of the proposed contract. And read it again. And again.

Legal clauses in English were tough enough, but reading them in French was beyond him. He needed a business manager. Why couldn't Tia have been an accountant or a lawyer, preferably one who spoke French, instead of an athletic trainer? That would have been too easy.

Maybe he should have been a doctor instead of an engineer so he could have gone into business with her. The fact that the sight of blood made him queasy probably would have derailed that idea before he'd even gotten started. He thought of the frog he had dissected in high school biology class and shuddered.

Giving up on the fine print, he flipped to the performance clause in the contract and the summary of payment schedule. Claude hadn't been exaggerating. The offer was extremely generous. Though he hadn't said the words, Evan suspected he was being rewarded for putting a stop to the over-billing Brooklyn had put forward on their first two contracts.

Throughout the weekend, he had contemplated what he should do. Idealistically, he wanted to find a job in Arizona to be near Tia. Even if he found something somewhere else in the U.S., he might have a chance to convince her to change jobs and move near him. Sure, they would need to spend time making sure this relationship had a real future, but every time he thought about being without her in his life, his stomach went hollow and turned to stone.

He pushed away from his desk and stalked to the window, the contract still in hand. Tia loved Paris. Would she be willing and able to spend her summers here? From everything she'd told him, her work during the summer was mostly voluntary. The rest of the year would be the problem.

His phone rang, startling him. Only his friends and family in the States had his new number, and rarely did anyone want to pay the fees to make an overseas call. He picked it up and saw his dad requesting a FaceTime session with him. He hit the button to accept the call. A moment later, his father's face filled the screen, his office visible in the background. "Hey, Dad. How are you doing?"

"I'm fine. I thought I would call and wish my long-lost son a happy birthday."

"Thanks."

"I haven't heard from you lately. What have you been up to?"

"Things have been a bit crazy," Evan said. "I've been offered a contract extension here in Paris."

"For how long?" his dad asked.

Evan took a deep breath before speaking it out loud. "Indefinitely."

"Sounds like I may need to brush up on my French."

"I haven't decided for sure if I'm taking it," Evan said quickly.

"I thought you loved it over there."

"I do, but . . ." His voice trailed off, and his father instantly picked up on the problem.

"Are you going to tell me who she is?"

"What?"

"You love living in Europe, and you enjoy the work you do there. The only reason I can figure you would hesitate to take the job is because of a woman."

Evan leaned against the window frame, his gaze on the scatter of pedestrians below. "Her name is Tia."

"Tell me about her."

"I met her at Drew's wedding. She's beautiful, athletic, and has a great sense of humor."

"And . . ."

Evan let out a sigh. "She lives in Arizona."

"Any chance she would consider a move?"

"She's an athletic trainer for a high school. That's not exactly the kind of job that can transfer over here."

"If it's meant to be, you two will work things out," his dad said. "What does she think about this job offer of yours?"

"I haven't told her yet."

"Let me tell you, son—if you care enough about her to consider turning down a big job offer, you owe it to both of you to have an open and honest conversation about your future." He hesitated briefly before adding, "That's what love is all about."

Evan opened his mouth to dispute his father's assumption only to snap it shut an instant later. Love? Was it possible to fall in love with someone after only six weeks?

"Any big plans for today?" his dad asked.

A knock sounded on his hotel room door. "I'm about to find out. Tia's here."

"I'll let you go, then. I look forward to meeting her."

After he said goodbye, Evan glanced at his watch. Tia was only twenty minutes later than she had planned. Not bad, considering. He pulled open the door. She stood on the other side of the threshold, a reminder of his thirtieth birthday in her hand.

"Happy birthday." She leaned forward for a kiss before holding up a paper bag with "Happy Birthday" scrawled across the front. The scent of croissants tickled his senses. "I looked for birthday candles, but no one at the market could figure out what I wanted."

"I don't think I need a reminder of my age today."

Her eyes narrowed. "I thought only women stressed about hitting thirty."

"Where did you hear that?"

"I don't know. Probably read it online somewhere." She took his hand. "Come on. It's a gorgeous day. Let's go up on the roof to eat breakfast."

Faced with Tia's cheery disposition, he could hardly refuse. He stepped into the hall and pulled the door closed. Following her to the stairwell, he asked, "Are any of those chocolate croissants?"

"Of course." She flashed him a grin. "I know how to order those in French now."

"What else do you have in there?"

"I'm not sure. I just pointed at whatever looked good." She continued to the top floor, using her hotel key card to access the roof.

Together, they made their way to one of the rooftop tables. Tia set the bag down, turning to wrap her arms around his neck. "What would you like to do for your birthday? I keep asking, but you never give me an answer."

"I'm spending it with you. That's all I want."

He watched as her expression went from disbelief to surprise to acceptance. Reaching up on her toes, she brushed her lips over his. He drew her closer, the breeze flowing over them, mixing the scents of her shampoo, his aftershave, and the rooftop roses. His pulse hammered, and he changed the angle of the kiss, the sensations crashing over him until he thought he might drown and be swept away.

His hands caressed her shoulders, trailing down her arms. He fought back the knowledge that their days together were limited. He wanted to hold her like this for days, weeks, months, years.

As though she sensed where his thoughts had gone, she pulled back, her eyes meeting his. Before either of them had the chance to think, he captured her mouth again and let himself fall.

Chapter 17

TIA SAT IN THE PASSENGER seat as Evan navigated his way back into Paris. When he hadn't given her any ideas of what he wanted to do for his birthday, she had reserved a car and planned for a day trip to one of the nearby villages—a picnic in the park, an hour in a rented row boat on the lake, and a walk along the quaint roads.

"I still can't believe you arranged all of this without being able to speak French."

"I had to do something," Tia said. "If I waited for you to decide what to do for your birthday, you would have settled for croissants in the hotel restaurant and Indian food for dinner."

"I like Indian food."

"I know. That's why we have reservations for dinner at a restaurant I heard about."

Evan put his hand on hers and glanced sideways. "You didn't have to do all of this for me. It's too much."

"Seems to me that after you flew me to Paris—first class, no less—that you should enjoy your birthday surprise and not worry about me doing too much."

"Like I already told you, bringing you to Paris was as much for my benefit as yours."

She hoped he meant it, because she couldn't think of another time she had felt so comfortable with herself. No one she had ever dated compared to Evan. "Well, I have thoroughly enjoyed myself."

"You've crammed a lot into your first four days."

"I thought maybe tomorrow we could go exploring somewhere off the beaten path."

"Anywhere in particular?" Evan asked.

"No. I hoped you might have some ideas."

"I might." He made his way to the rental car agency, and together, they went into the office to turn in the car.

When they walked back outside, she slipped her hand into his. "The Indian restaurant is about a mile from here. Did you want to walk or take the subway?"

Evan looked up at the overcast sky. "It's not raining yet. I'm willing to risk it if you are."

They started down the street in silence. Tia looked up at the various buildings, absorbing the atmosphere the French architecture created and the way the old blended with the new. She motioned with her free hand to an apartment building that looked to be at least a hundred years old and had wrought-iron French balconies on each window. "Can you imagine living in one of these buildings?"

"What do you mean?"

"I bet a hundred people live in that building," Tia said. "They get up each morning, go down to the bakery for their bread each day. The subway is around the corner if they want to go beyond their neighborhood, and the beauty of the city is at their disposal any time they want to take advantage of it."

"Pretty different from where you live."

"Very different."

Evan seemed to ponder for a moment. "Do you think you would like living in a city?"

"I don't know. I think I might, but this is the first time I've really spent much time in a traditional city like this." She shrugged. "Phoenix is so spread out it still has an open feel to it. It's the same with San Diego."

"I hadn't really thought of it that way, but you're right."

Tia fell silent for a moment before she asked, "Are you going to tell me what's going on with you?"

"What do you mean?"

"I don't know," Tia began, annoyed that she had let herself say anything. After all, it was his birthday. She didn't want to upset him, but she could tell something was bothering him. Never a fan of stewing over the unknown, she pressed on. "You've seemed distracted lately. I hope it's not because I'm here."

"No, not at all."

"Work, then?"

"Yeah." He rubbed the back of his neck with his free hand. "The company I'm working for right now offered me an extended contract."

"That's good, isn't it?"

"It is good." Evan stopped walking and looked down at her. "At least it would be good if Paris weren't so far from Arizona."

"Wait." Two and two slowly equaled four. "You're saying they want you to live in Paris? Permanently?"

"Yeah. Not exactly the ideal for us, is it?"

Disappointment flowed through her. Stealing a week at Christmas and spring break might have made it possible to see Evan if he had been able to visit during her busy season, but travel to Paris took the better part of a day each way. "This is definitely taking long distance to a new level."

"Look, I realize we haven't known each other for long, but I want to give us a shot."

Tia stared at him, torn. She loved being with him, but could they last if they hardly ever saw each other? "How would we even do this?"

"I don't know," Evan admitted. "I'm still looking for jobs in Arizona, but the truth is that my old business partner used to solicit new business. I'm a bit out of my league with this right now."

Tia keyed in on the business side of things to give her emotions and logic time to battle. "What happened with your old business partner?"

"She was overbilling our clients." Evan tugged on Tia's hand, and they started down the street again. "I should probably tell you that Brooklyn and I also used to date."

A little stab of jealousy pricked her, and she did her best to ignore it. "Did you strike out on your own because of the overbilling or because the relationship ended?"

"Both," Evan said. "This offer in Paris is generous enough that if I take it for the next year or two, it would give me enough of a cushion to hire a business manager to line up jobs close to you."

"Two years," Tia repeated. She supposed it could be worse. At least he was already thinking about an end date.

"I was kind of hoping you would consider living here next summer."

"I could never afford that."

"I wouldn't ask you to." He brushed back a strand of her hair, tucking it behind her ear. "I can rent you a flat for a few months." He brushed a kiss across her lips. "Or maybe I'll convince you to marry me before then."

The mere mention of marriage caused butterflies to flutter in her stomach. A fat raindrop splattered on her arm. "We're heading into uncharted water here."

"I know." He stopped, ignoring the sprinkles coming down. "But I'm asking you to wade into those waters with me."

Tia forced herself to lift her gaze to his. She thought of her life before she met Evan. She had friends and a busy, fulfilling career. And since their first days together, she couldn't get Evan out of her mind. If she hadn't already been in over her head, maybe she would have been tempted when Colby had started asking her out. "I don't think I have much of a choice. I don't want to be with anyone besides you."

Relief washed over his features. He drew her to him and leaned down to capture her mouth in a blood-pumping, mind-numbing kiss.

Tia's heart bounced high in her chest only to drop to her toes. The sprinkles turned to a steady rain, droplets catching in her hair, moisture seeping into her shirt. She didn't care.

She let herself lean into him, into what they were together. Their limited time together had her savoring the kiss, memorizing the sensations for the many nights they would spend apart in the future. As much as she wanted to settle into a routine, she didn't want it unless it consisted of the two of them together.

Evan's lips trailed down to the curve of her neck, and a new shiver worked through her. He straightened, his eyes staring into hers again. "Thank you for giving me exactly what I wanted for my birthday present."

"But I didn't give you your present yet."

"I was serious when I said you're all I wanted."

Warmth seeped through her, and she leaned in for another kiss. "Somehow, I feel like I'm the one getting all the presents for your birthday this year." She pushed her damp hair back from her face. "Any chance I can ask for the same present for my birthday?" Tia dared to ask. "I won't have time to come to Paris to see you, but if you could take a couple days off at the end of October . . ."

"I'll be there," Evan promised. "Come on. Let's get out of the rain."

Chapter 18

COLBY'S STOMACH JUMPED WHEN HE heard the call over the radio. *Car accident near the high school* and *officer needs assistance* in the same sentence.

Cruising through Verde Village, Colby made an immediate U-turn before checking in with dispatch. Less than a minute later, the demand for an ambulance was reiterated over the radio.

Colby rounded the corner and stared. The damage in front of him was worse than he had imagined. The police cruiser had apparently been coming down the hill from the high school and had been T-boned by a two-ton pickup truck. A second police car had parked behind the accident, lights flashing. He left his own lights on and angled his car perpendicular to the incident. After checking in with dispatch to alert them to his arrival, he jumped out of the car. Wesley straightened from where he stood beside the damaged cruiser and pointed to the pickup. "Colby, check the other driver."

Colby rushed to the driver side of the truck, to where a boy no older than eighteen sat white-faced, his hands still gripping the wheel. His body trembled.

"Hey, it's going to be okay," Colby said in his most soothing tone. "Can you tell me your name?"

A breath shuddered, and he forced out the words. "Nolan McCoy." The boy turned his head to look at Colby now. A good sign.

"Are you injured?" Colby asked.

Nolan relaxed his fingers on the wheel, lifting his hands as though seeing them for the first time. He looked down at his chest and legs before answering. "I don't think so."

The screaming sirens of the ambulance made further conversation impossible.

Colby waited until the ambulance driver parked and turned off the sirens before he continued. "The paramedics will be over in a minute to check you out. In the meantime, can you tell me what happened?"

"I don't know." He stared at the crumpled cruiser, and tears formed in his eyes. Based on the streaks already on the boy's cheeks, Colby guessed these weren't the first tears he'd shed since the accident.

"Where were you going?" Colby prompted, attempting to take him back to the moments before the accident.

"I was going to work." He gulped in air and let it out with a whoosh.

Colby took in the scene and the skid marks behind the truck. "You were driving in the right lane?"

"Yeah. I was going to turn at the light."

"When did you first see the police car?"

"I caught a glimpse of it when it was approaching the stop sign. I expected it to stop, but it didn't. It kept speeding up."

"Did it have its lights or sirens on?"

Nolan's brow furrowed. "Not at first." He shook his head. "They turned on right before he hit me. That's why I hit my brakes."

"I'll need your driver's license and registration."

Nolan handed over his license and began digging through the glove box for his registration. Colby read the license. The kid was only seventeen.

"Do you have your cell phone with you?" Colby asked as soon as Nolan handed over the registration.

"Yeah."

"Have you called your parents yet?"

"I called my dad. He's on his way."

"Sit tight," Colby said. "I'll be right back."

He turned toward the other vehicle, the paramedics standing by while several firemen worked on the car. One of them was in the process of using the Jaws of Life to cut into the roof of the cruiser.

Colby could see blood on the dash. He moved forward to where Wesley was standing by helplessly.

"Who?" Colby asked.

"It's Raul," Wesley managed to say, his voice tight. "I saw his hand move when I first got here, but he hasn't said anything, not a single word."

"I'll call for a second ambulance to check out the other driver," Colby said. He motioned toward the police car. "You'll let me know how he is when they get him out of there?"

"Yeah. I will."

Colby turned his back to the accident. Only time would give him the information he needed about the extent of Raul's injuries.

* * *

"Wow. This is incredible. It's like the outside world doesn't exist." Tia absorbed the atmosphere: white linen tablecloths, dripping chandeliers, coffered ceilings. Live palm trees created privacy between the tables, and tall windows let in the last of the evening light. Waiters dressed in black tended to their tables, efficient and discreet.

She had never been in such a place. Nice restaurants, yes, but this establishment was in a class of its own. It was the sort of place where the business deals brokered were of the seven-figure variety and women walked away with new diamond rings on their left hands. Tia pushed that thought aside.

She followed the maître d' to their table, appreciative of Evan's manners when he pulled out her chair for her. As soon as she lowered into her seat, he circled to sit across from her.

She accepted the menu from the maître d' but lowered it onto the table as she looked around the room again. She brought her focus back to Evan. He looked every bit as handsome as the first time she had met him, but now she knew him well enough to appreciate his kindness, sense of humor, and even some of his insecurities. What surprised her more than anything was her ability to share so much of her own hopes and dreams with him. "I can't believe this is my last night."

"I'm trying not to think about that."

"I know what you mean." She took a sip of water and grasped for a positive attitude. Wallowing in reality wouldn't change it, and she didn't want to start the habit of wasting her time with him, wishing for more. She straightened her shoulders and announced, "I've decided to start being on time."

Evan nearly choked on his water. "On time for what?"

"Breakfast, lunch, and dinner. And maybe French class."

"You lost me."

"I normally go into school late and eat around nine or nine thirty. You're usually heading to dinner around that same time."

She could see Evan doing the mental math. "And when you have lunch, I'm usually hanging out at my apartment, especially if I work early hours."

"Exactly. If we FaceTime during our meals, it will be like we're still together," Tia said. "Technically, I only have to be on time twice each day since my breakfast and your dinner are at the same time."

"I like the way you think."

"Good. Maybe this will help us pretend we don't have a nine-hour time difference."

He took her hand. "You know, if you stay up late, you can always call me while I'm eating breakfast."

"I think if we're talking twice a day, you'll want a break from me."

"I don't know about that." He leaned forward for a kiss.

Tia let herself fall, wishing this moment could go on forever.

When she leaned back, she grasped for another glimmer of optimism. "Does France have daylight saving time?"

"Yeah. I think it changes around Halloween."

"Good, because when daylight saving ends, there will only be eight hours between us. Arizona doesn't ever change their time."

"I forgot about that." He paused as though thinking something through. "What's this about French class?"

"Turns out there's a conversational French class at the community college behind my house. If I'm going to spend next summer in Paris, I ought to learn how to communicate."

"Tia, that's a great idea, but how would you have time for that?"

"It's on Monday night. We don't have games on Mondays."

"Sounds like you have it all figured out."

"I do, except for one thing."

"What's that?" Evan asked.

"Can you be on time with me?"

"If there's anyone or anything worth making that happen, it's you." He leaned forward for another kiss.

Though it was only a brief meeting of lips, Tia's skin tingled and her heart rose high in her chest before landing with a thud. She had fallen for him. Completely, absolutely, fallen for him. Was this what love felt like? This overwhelming desire to create one life out of two?

She stared at him as he settled back in his chair, trying to memorize every feature. Unable to speak through her rising emotions, she squeezed his hand. She saw the way the muscle twitched in his jaw and suspected he too was struggling against the war of reality and dreams.

Their waiter approached, and Evan spoke to him in French. When the man agreed to whatever Evan had asked, Evan retrieved his phone and handed it to the man. Realizing the waiter was going to take a picture of them, she moved closer. After they both smiled for the camera, their waiter handed the phone back, waiting for Evan's approval before leaving them alone once more.

"What do you think?" Evan held out his cell so she could see the new image.

Though they had both smiled, the sadness was clearly visible in their eyes. "I think we need to take a picture like this when we see each other in October. It will be a much happier one."

"You couldn't be more right," he said. "For tonight, though, let's pretend it's our first day together instead of our last."

"Like reality doesn't exist." Tia laced her fingers with his. "I can do that."

* * *

Colby rushed into the emergency room and used his badge to gain access to the treatment area. Clearing the accident had taken over two hours. Colby had also been tasked with securing the wrecked squad car at the police station so it could be inspected by a forensics team.

He wasn't surprised that the lack of skid marks by the cruiser had resulted in Chief Jarvis making that request. The witness report further confirmed the possibility of foul play.

As soon as Colby had made sure the vehicle was ready for forensics, he had driven to the hospital.

He rounded the corner to find Chief Jarvis leaning against a wall, his concern palpable, a doctor standing nearby.

"Any news?" Colby asked.

"Not yet." The chief ran a hand over his face. "I don't understand how this happened."

"I'm sure the forensics team will piece it together."

"They'd better." Chief Jarvis straightened when a doctor approached. "What's the prognosis?"

"He's alive. We're doing everything we can to keep him that way." The doctor motioned them into a conference area nearby. As soon as he closed the door, he continued. "Raul suffered severe trauma to the head and spine as well as multiple broken bones."

The chief's jaw tensed several times before he managed to ask, "Is he going to make it?"

"We should know in the next twenty-four to forty-eight hours." The doctor laid a hand on the chief's arm. "I know that's not what you want to hear, but it's the best I can do for now."

"Thank you, Doctor," Colby said, seeing the chief struggling for control of his emotions.

He nodded and exited the room. Colby gave the chief a minute to regain his composure. "If there is anything I can do to help . . ."

"I appreciate that, Colby."

"I know sports are starting up at the high school soon," Colby said. "I subbed for Raul a couple weeks ago. I'd be happy to take his spot until he's up and around."

The chief looked at him with a dazed stare for several seconds. Finally, he nodded. "Yeah. I'd appreciate that."

"I'll talk to the shift manager to work out the details," Colby said. He started for the door.

"And, Colby?"

"Yeah?"

"Go back to the station and make sure that cruiser is under lock and key. I don't want anyone near it until forensics gets here."

Colby nodded. "Understood."

Chapter 19

Notre Dame. The Louvre. Arc de Triomphe, Sacré Coeur. Tia had crammed in every piece of culture she could during her days in Paris, but her favorite moments were those spent with Evan. Taking lazy walks along the Seine and in the park, exploring the shops in Le Marais, sampling baguettes and croissants at the bakeries in Montmartre, eating late lunches and even later dinners at sidewalk cafés.

She sat at such a café now, a croissant in her hand, and watched the pedestrians walk by. Her last day in Paris. Her stomach clenched at the thought.

I will be back, she promised herself. She doubted she and Evan would really consider marriage before next summer, but the idea that they would build their future together had been planted. Now to survive the next ten months.

"Hey, beautiful." The sound of Evan's voice chased away the doubts trying to form.

Her eyes lifted to meet his. "I thought you had a conference call this morning."

"I managed to reschedule it for this afternoon." He slid into the seat across from her. "I told them I had a pressing engagement that couldn't be changed."

Tia lifted the paper bag that lay on the table. "Here. I bought you breakfast."

"Chocolate croissant?"

"Of course." She smiled. "I've decided that if there were a bakery next to the high school that made these for me every morning, I would be on time every day."

"And knowing you, you'd run to work every day to burn off the calories."

"What's wrong with that?"

"Nothing, except that then you wouldn't have a car to use to get home safely."

Tia reached out and took his chin in her hand. "You're so cute when you get all overprotective."

Evan wrapped his fingers around her wrist and pulled free. The concerned expression on his face wasn't one Tia saw often. "I'm serious. I hate knowing I live too far away to help you if you need it."

"You're sweet, but I'll be fine," she said. "I only run on main roads, and I never go hiking alone. Besides, I have half the police department in my phone."

"Why do you have half the police department in your phone?"

"I told you about my softball team, didn't I?"

"You mentioned that you've been playing this summer. Are you playing with the police?"

"Except for me, everyone on the team is with the department."

"Then I guess I'll have to trust them to watch over you." He took a bite of his croissant before adding, "As long as they don't watch you too closely."

"As much as we plan to talk after I leave, you'll probably meet all my friends within two weeks."

"That's probably true." He broke off a piece of his croissant. "Is there any chance you might be able to get away for a weekend in September?"

"Maybe." Tia thought for a moment "I'm sure the football team will have an away game for at least one weekend. I could probably take off right after school on Friday and maybe take Monday off. I'd have to check volleyball's schedule to see if I might be able to squeeze another day beyond that."

"That could work," Evan said.

"Work for what?"

"I thought we could meet in Michigan for a weekend. I'd love for you to meet my family."

Tia let the implications of that roll over her. She swallowed hard and managed to nod. "I'd like that."

* * *

Colby sensed her the moment the high school office door opened. Tia entered, her hair pulled back in a ponytail, her bright-blue, cropped leggings paired with a neon-pink workout shirt.

"Tia. Welcome back," the secretary, Sharla, said in greeting. "How was your vacation?"

Tia's face lit up. "Amazing."

Sharla pointed at the clock on the wall. "You're even later than usual. It must have been amazing."

"It was."

Colby stepped out from behind his desk in the security office and approached them.

"Did you have a nice visit with your folks in San Diego?" Sharla asked.

"Hi, Tia," Colby said before the women's conversation could continue.

Tia turned. "Colby. What are you doing here?"

"I'm taking Raul's place."

Confusion lit her features. "Where's Raul?"

"Didn't you hear?" Sharla asked. "He was in a horrible car accident. Heard his brakes failed."

"What?" Tia looked from Sharla to Colby and reached out to take Colby's hand. "Is he okay?"

"He's still in critical condition." Colby put his free hand over their combined ones. He had missed this human contact, the feeling of a woman's hand in his.

Tia pulled her hand free much too soon. "When did it happen?"

"Monday," Colby said. "The doctors seem hopeful that he will pull through, but it sounds like it's going to be a long road."

"Oh my gosh. Poor Gabrielle. She must be beside herself."

"From what I understand, she's been by his side this whole time," Sharla said.

"I'm going to see if Principal Butler minds if I run over there to check on her."

"Do you think he'll let you?" Colby asked. "You just got back."

"Gabrielle and my sister were best friends growing up. I have to at least let Kyla know what happened."

"I can call and get an update for you. If you don't mind waiting until lunch time, I can take you over to see Gabrielle," Colby suggested. "You may have a hard time getting in to see her on your own. They only let one or two visitors in the ICU at a time."

He could see Tia's internal battle by the expression on her face. Instinct versus logic. Finally, she nodded.

"I'm going to head back to my office to make a phone call." She took a step toward the door and said over her shoulder, "Colby, you'll let me know what you find out?"

"Yeah. I will." He watched her walk out the door and disappear down the hall.

A family with two teenage boys walked into the office and occupied Sharla's attention. Colby moved back into his new office and picked up the phone. He hoped the hospital had good news.

* * *

Tears filled Tia's eyes the moment she rounded the corner. The thought of what Gabrielle must be going through right now crippled her, making her heart ache as she considered the possibilities. What would Gabrielle do if Raul didn't make it? They had been together for as long as Tia could remember. Their little daughter wasn't even three yet. Would she even have memories of her father if . . . ?

Her cell phone interrupted that thought. She pulled it out of her pocket to see the FaceTime request from Evan. She nearly declined before she thought better of it. For better or worse, she swiped at her eyes and accepted the video chat.

Instantly, Evan's normal greeting dissolved into concern. "Hey. What's wrong?"

Tia drew a deep breath and blew it out. When that didn't work, she pressed her lips together and tried again. "My friend was in a car accident." A sob broke out, and once again, she fought for control. "He's in critical condition."

"I am so sorry."

She hurried into her office and closed the door. Another deep breath. "This is so unreal. I saw him the day I left."

"Are you talking about that Colby guy?"

"No. His name is Raul. He was the resource officer here at the high school." She dropped onto one of the treatment benches. "He married one of my sister's best friends right after he graduated from college."

"How is the wife doing?"

"I don't know. I was going to go over there this morning, but Colby said he would call and get an update on Raul's condition. He said he could take me over at lunchtime."

"When did you see Colby?"

"Just a minute ago. I guess he's taking Raul's place." Tia's concern for Gabrielle surfaced again, another tear spilling over.

"Hey, it's going to be okay," Evan said. "Stay positive. Worrying doesn't do anyone any good."

Another bout of tears trickled down her cheeks.

"If the worst happens, you'll deal with it, but sometimes hope is the best medicine," he said.

"How do you know so much?"

"I survived my mom's cancer scare in high school," Evan said. "I know what it's like to worry. It will eat you alive if you don't try to keep your life in balance. If you focus on helping your friend's family, it'll distract you from the things you can't control."

She sniffled and reached for a tissue on her desk. "You're right."

"Did you run to school this morning?"

"Yeah. I thought it would help me adjust to this time zone again." Her brow furrowed. "How did you know?"

"Lucky guess." He scooted forward in his chair, so his face filled the screen. "After we hang up, why don't you see if you can take an hour to check on your friends? I'll text Julie and Drew and see if one of them can swing by to pick you up."

"You don't have to do that. I can text Julie."

"I know you can, but let me do this for you. We both know you aren't going to be able to concentrate on work until you see for yourself what's really going on."

"You're right."

"I'll talk to you in a few hours."

"Okay."

"And, Tia?"

She wiped her cheeks again and focused on the screen once more. "Yeah?"

His eyes connected with hers. "I love you."

Warmth flooded through her. "I love you too."

Chapter 20

COLBY KNOCKED ON TIA'S LOCKED office door a second time, looking down at the darkness of the room showing between the door and the ground. Where was she?

Thinking perhaps he had missed her in the front office when he had done his morning rounds, he headed back to the other end of the school. The news from the hospital remained the same. No change. At least Raul was still breathing. It could have been much worse.

When he reached the office, he approached the front desk. "Have you seen Tia? We were going to go to the hospital together during our lunch break."

"I haven't," Sharla said. "Sorry."

The principal poked his head out from his office. "Are you looking for Tia?"

"Yeah."

"I talked to her this morning. She's already at the hospital."

"Oh. I thought she wanted me to drive her."

"Julie picked her up," Principal Butler said. "Tia was so flustered, she probably forgot to tell you. I told her she could take another day off."

"Maybe I'll head over to the hospital too. I'd like to see how Raul is doing."

"Don't forget to grab some lunch for yourself," he said. "I know this has been a rough time for everyone in the police department."

"That it has."

* * *

Tia sat beside Gabrielle in the ICU waiting room, the scent of fresh biscuits lingering in the air. A call to her sister, Kyla, had given her insight as to what food to bring Gabrielle. Thankfully, a single phone call to the local diner had produced the desired items by the time she and Julie had stopped by on their way to the hospital. Now there was nothing to do but wait. And wait. And wait.

Tia had been at Gabrielle's side for only two hours, and the anxiety of not knowing Raul's fate was already driving her crazy.

"I don't know how you're able to stay so calm," Tia said, giving her friend's hand a squeeze.

"I think you're confusing numb for calm." She dragged a hand through her hair. "Tia, I don't know what I'll do if . . ."

"Hey, we already talked about this. We're going to plan for the best," Tia said, adopting the positive attitude Evan had encouraged. "I think after we see the doctor next, you should go home and spend some time with your daughter. I'm sure Olivia is missing her mama, and a bit of cuddle time will do you both a world of good."

"You're right. I'm just afraid that the minute I leave . . ."

"Maybe your mom can bring Olivia here to the hospital so you can have dinner with her tonight. That way you don't have to leave."

Gabrielle nodded and swallowed hard. "That might work."

"It's going to be okay," Tia promised, praying her words were true.

Gabrielle's only response was to stand and walk to the nurse's station. "Can you tell me how much longer until I can see my husband?"

"The doctor is with him now."

A new energy sounded in Gabrielle's voice. "He is?"

"Yes. As soon as he is finished, we'll change his dressing and let you come back to see him," the nurse said. "I'm sure you'll want to talk to the doctor first anyway."

Gabrielle nodded. She took a step toward her seat as the waiting room door opened. Kyla burst through, a huge wicker basket hanging from her arm. "Gabrielle." Kyla wrapped her in a hug and held on for a full minute before she asked, "How are you holding up?"

Tears welled up in Gabrielle's eyes. She wiped at some of the moisture on her cheeks. "I've had better weeks, actually."

"I bet you have." Kyla set the basket down on the coffee table in front of Tia. "I brought you some snacks. Knowing you, you won't leave the hospital until Raul is coming home with you."

"What is it with you two?" Gabrielle asked with a watery smile. "Tia brought me food too."

"I thought she might." Kyla turned to give Tia a hug. Lowering her voice to a whisper, she said, "Thanks for letting me know what was going on."

Tia simply nodded. Comforted by her sister's presence, she sat in her chair, waiting for the other women to sit beside her before she asked, "Who's watching the kids?"

"One of my neighbors is keeping them until Brandon gets home," Kyla said. She reached into her purse and handed Tia a protein bar. "Here. I figured you didn't think to get anything for yourself to eat."

"Thanks."

Movement by the nurse's desk caught everyone's attention, and Gabrielle quickly stood. The doctor approached, his expression unreadable.

Tia and Kyla also stood as Gabrielle asked, "Any news?"

"Your husband is alert and asking for you."

"He's going to be okay?" Gabrielle managed to ask.

"He will have several more surgeries over the next few months to repair his back and hip," the doctor said. "We aren't seeing any signs of paralysis, but I estimate it will take him at least ten to twelve months before he will be able to walk unassisted."

Silence enveloped them for several seconds before Gabrielle forced out another question. "Will he be able to return to the police force?"

The doctor put his hand on Gabrielle's shoulder. "I'm afraid it's too early to tell."

More tears flooded her eyes, and she nodded. "Thank you, doctor."

"He'll be in ICU for at least a few more days. If all goes well, he'll be moved to a regular room sometime this weekend."

"One step at a time," Kyla said.

"I know," Gabrielle said. "Right now, I'm grateful he's still alive."

"Believe me," Tia said, "so are we."

* * *

Colby arrived in the ICU waiting room to find it full of coworkers and Raul's family. Gabrielle held a little girl on her lap, the child's hair dark and curly like her mother's. No one seemed overly distraught, so Colby wasn't sure why there had been such an increase in visitors since the last time he had stopped by.

He looked past Wesley and Chief Jarvis to where Tia was standing in the corner talking to a woman who appeared to be around her age. The woman glanced at him, and immediately, Colby saw the resemblance. He didn't know how exactly, but he was certain she and Tia were related.

"Hey, Colby," Chief Jarvis said. "I didn't expect to see you here this time of day."

"I thought I would come over on my lunch break and check on Raul." He looked around the room again. "Is everything okay?"

"Good news," he said. "Raul's going to pull through."

"That's a relief."

"He's going to be on disability for the next year or so, but that's a lot better than the alternative." Chief Jarvis pulled him aside. "I know you only expected to work at the high school for a few weeks. Would you be interested in making this your full-time assignment, at least through this school year?"

Colby's eyes swept the room until they landed on Tia. "Yeah. I'd be fine with that."

"Great." The chief wandered back to where Wesley was talking to Raul's wife.

Again, Colby's gaze was drawn to Tia. She looked up and saw him, a flush creeping into her cheeks. She said something to the woman beside her and crossed the room. "Hey, Colby. I'm sorry I left without letting you know. Mr. Butler offered to let me come over here early, so one of my friends picked me up."

"No problem. Do you need a ride back to the school?"

"No, thanks. I'm going to hang out here for a while," Tia said. "Besides, my sister's here, so she'll give me a ride home."

"Well, give me a call if anything changes and you need a ride." Colby paused. "Wait. Do you even have my number?"

"No, I don't think so."

"Give me your phone, and I'll put it in for you."

Tia hesitated slightly before unlocking it and handing it over. Odd. Colby put his information into her phone and texted himself so he would have her number. Finally.

"Can you excuse me for a minute?" she asked as soon as he handed her phone back. "I promised I'd call Mr. Butler with an update."

"No problem."

He watched her go, wondering if she would come back before he had to return to his shift. A glance at the clock revealed he had only a handful of minutes before he would have to start the long trek to the hospital parking lot.

Colby made a point of speaking to Raul's wife for a moment before leaving the waiting area. He looked up and down the hall, but Tia wasn't anywhere in sight.

Frustrated they'd had so little time together, he started down the hall. Tomorrow they would spend time together, he promised himself. Tomorrow.

* * *

Evan checked the time on his phone for the third time in five minutes. Tia hadn't answered his first two attempts to call her. Figuring she might still be at the hospital where she couldn't use her phone, he resigned himself to waiting. Only another five minutes passed before her ringtone sounded.

"How's your friend?" Evan asked as soon as Tia appeared on his screen.

"He's going to be okay."

"What a relief." Evan could see the family photos hanging in the hallway as Tia moved through her house and settled into a seat at her kitchen table.

"He's going in for surgery tomorrow to have a pin put in his leg, and it looks like he's going to have several more surgeries in the future, but he's alive. From what I heard about the accident, he's lucky to be that."

"Sounds like it." He heard a door open in the background. "Is someone there with you?"

"Yeah. My sister is staying here tonight." Tia turned to look behind her. "Hey, Kyla. Come meet Evan."

A pretty brunette plopped her chin on Tia's shoulder. Her face was rounder, her eyes darker, but the expression was one Evan had seen on Tia's face often enough, one of curiosity and humor.

"Hi, Evan. Nice to finally meet you."

"You too," Evan said. "Glad to hear your friend is going to be okay."

"Thanks." Kyla moved slightly. "Okay, what is this with the background? You're in Paris and you're sitting in a tiny room with nothing on the walls?"

"I'm sitting here talking on the phone, looking out my window," Evan corrected. He stood and turned the phone so Kyla could enjoy the view of Paris, the Eiffel Tower visible in the distance.

"Not bad," Kyla said.

Evan shifted so he was leaning against the window and held the phone facing him again. "I agree."

"Well, I'll let you two talk," Kyla said. "Good meeting you."

"Hey, Kyla," Evan said before she could retreat.

"Yeah?"

"Can you try to keep Tia out of trouble while you're there?"

"Evan, if you know my sister at all, you know we can try all we want, but that never seems to matter."

"It was worth a shot."

"Hey!" Tia protested.

Kyla giggled and stepped out of view.

"What?" Evan asked innocently. "I'm only looking out for you."

Tia jerked a thumb to her left. "That's what Kyla is always saying."

"Great minds!" Kyla called from a distance.

"Did you end up going back to work today?" Evan asked, changing the subject.

"No. My principal said I could take an extra day. I think he knew I wasn't going to be able to concentrate," Tia said. "I may try to go in early tomorrow. The building is usually quiet until eight during the summers. If I go in at six, I'll have time to go through the physicals that were turned in while I was gone."

"You know, I miss you already."

"I miss you too." Tia leaned forward. "And I miss having chocolate croissants for breakfast."

"I'll bring you some for your birthday."

"Promise?"

"I promise."

Chapter 21

COLBY HOVERED NEAR THE HALL outside the trainer's room on Wednesday. If Tia followed her normal routine, she should be leaving for lunch any minute. Tia had been home a full week, but even though they were now working in the same building, he hadn't seen her nearly as often as he'd hoped.

He noticed Al Schroeder, the athletic director, heading his way.

Colby continued down the hall to the nearest exit and went about checking the doors to ensure they were properly locked. When he turned back, Al had disappeared from sight.

Colby glanced at his watch. Tia was already late for her usual run up to Jerome. He opted for the direct approach and lifted a hand to knock, hesitating when he heard Tia's voice.

He strained to hear but was unable to make out the words. Realizing she must be on the phone, he rapped on her door and pushed it open.

Tia looked up and immediately glanced back down at her phone. "I've got to go. I'll talk to you later."

Colby heard a man's voice say goodbye before Tia ended the call.

"Who was that?"

"Oh, I was just talking to my boyfriend." Tia stood. "You met him at the volleyball camp."

Lava heated inside the volcano of his emotions. Exercising great control, he kept his voice casual. "Evan, right?"

"Yeah."

"I thought he didn't live around here."

"He doesn't," Tia said. "Right now, he's living in Paris."

"Talk about long distance." When Tia didn't respond, Colby said, "I was thinking about running up to Jerome for lunch. Are you interested in joining me?"

"Thanks, but my sister is picking something up for me from Grapes. She should be by any minute."

"Your sister is still in town?"

"Actually, she's back in town. She and her girls are staying with me for a couple days," Tia explained. "Kyla wanted to be here when Raul has his next surgery."

"That's right. It's his back this time, isn't it?"

"Yeah." Tia's body tensed. "This should be the last major surgery for him."

"I'm sure it will be a relief for everyone when he's home for good."

"It will," Tia agreed. She patted the stack of paperwork on her desk. "I'd better get back to work."

"I'll see you later." Colby stopped when he reached the door. "Do you want this open or closed?"

"Open is fine."

"Okay. Enjoy your visit with your sister."

"I will. Thanks."

Colby continued out of her room, his jaw clenching. Boyfriend? How could she think she could build a future with a man who lived halfway around the world?

He made his way out to his car. With or without Tia, he needed to grab some lunch. He was already behind the wheel when he saw a silver minivan pull up and Tia's sister get out.

Kyla unbuckled a toddler from her car seat and settled the child on her hip. She then juggled the takeout bag she carried so she could also hold her older child's hand.

Then she ushered her children inside, and the truth washed over Colby. Tia might call Evan her boyfriend, but that wasn't who she was having lunch with or who she was spending her free time with.

If Evan chose to live in Paris, away from Tia, he didn't deserve her. It wouldn't be long before Tia realized she was missing what was right in front of her. She belonged with someone, but it wasn't the man she called her boyfriend.

* * *

Evan wondered if he was crazy to think about buying. He circled the two-bedroom apartment, stopping in the modest kitchen. For Paris, it would be considered large. One of the counters opened to the living room and was wide enough to put two stools beside it.

The last two places he had looked at, the kitchens had been little more than narrow closets with the appliances shoved on facing walls. When he cooked, he wanted to be able to move. And breathe.

He wasn't sure he could have afforded something here in Paris if his sister hadn't suggested he rent rather than sell his place in Detroit. She and his parents had been kind enough to go in and pack all his personal belongings. Within two days, he had a tenant who wanted his condo for the next six months. The rent would cover his mortgage for the year and then some.

When he'd looked at rental prices in Paris, he had quickly discovered buying wouldn't be much more, especially with the signing bonus he had received for his latest contract. In truth, if he used Airbnb to rent out his Paris home during his trips back to the States, he would make money on the prospect.

The real estate agent said something in English, her words heavily accented. Evan preferred she speak in French. He could understand her better.

He looked down at the information sheet in his hand and took in the price. Expensive—certainly pushing the upper range of what he could afford—but the neighborhood was good, the views amazing, and he could envision Tia and him making a life here. At least in the summers.

The thought of the obstacles they faced in making their relationship work deflated him, but he had to admit, their frequent phone calls had helped them get to know each other better than if they had been in the same city. They talked. Really talked.

Hopes, dreams, fears, and everything in between.

He glanced at his phone to check the time. He had deliberately set up this showing for Saturday afternoon so Tia would be awake and able to give her opinion. He pressed the video icon on his phone to call her. A moment later, her face filled the screen.

"Did you find something you like?" Tia asked.

"I think so. Do you have time for a quick tour?"

"Yeah. Tell me about it."

"Two bedrooms, great view, decent kitchen." Evan adjusted the view on his phone and slowly turned in a circle so she could see the cabinets, counters, appliances, and the space where a small table could go.

"This one has a lot more space than the last one you showed me."

"That's one of the things I like about it. And the bathroom is off the hall instead of being in the master bedroom." Keeping the camera facing away from him, he entered the living room to show her the entryway, the wooden floors, and the built-in shelves. He proceeded to the back of the apartment to let her view the bathroom and two bedrooms.

When he held the phone up to the window, she said, "What a great view."

Evan flipped the camera around so she could see his face again. "What do you think?"

"This is my favorite, by far, but it doesn't matter what I think. Can you be happy there?"

"I can be happy if you'll be here with me this summer."

"You know I'm not going to room with a boyfriend even if it is only for a few months." Tia hesitated. "I was actually thinking that if my grandparents would go for it, I might do a house swap so I would have my own space in Paris next summer."

"That could work," Evan said, though he couldn't keep other possibilities from crowding his mind on how to make sure he and Tia achieved their goal to be in the same city by June. "Pretend for a minute that you didn't have this traditionalist thing going—would this be somewhere you could be happy living?"

"Evan, any time we're together, I'm happy," she said. "But to answer the question you're really asking: yes, I like the apartment. It suits you."

Evan looked around the master bedroom once more. "Thanks. I think this is the one."

* * *

Tia pulled open her top desk drawer at work and riffled through it. When she didn't find the bottle of lotion she kept there, she closed it and repeated the process with the other two drawers.

"That's odd." The lotion was one she had tried in Paris and liked so much that she had purchased two bottles to last her through her birthday. She had already put in an advance request for Evan to bring her some more in October.

Her phone rang. "Hi, Evan." She clipped her phone to the cell phone stand she had invested in a few days earlier. "How did the testing go on your new security program today?"

"Good. We found a couple of bugs I need to work out, but the company seemed very pleased with the results."

"Awesome." Tia began her search again. "Did you get approval for the time off to meet me in Detroit?"

"Yeah." Evan didn't elaborate, silence filling the room, except for the clatter Tia caused by digging through her office supplies. Finally, Evan asked, "What are you doing?"

Tia looked up. "Sorry." She shut the drawer again. "I was sure I put a bottle of lotion in my desk drawer, but now I can't find it."

"Do I need to bring you an extra bottle when I see you in Michigan?"

Tia mentally retraced her steps, again coming to the same conclusion. She was certain she had left the lotion here in her office. "Maybe."

"I'll pick some up on my way home tonight. I need to go to the market anyway."

"Thanks. I'll pay you back."

"Don't worry about it. It's only a few euros." Before she could argue, he lifted a croissant into her view. "You know, it's really too bad you aren't here right now. I got to the bakery right after these came out of the oven."

"Oh, that's cruel." Tia watched him take a bite, slowly savoring it as he chewed. "Keep that up and I'm going to tell your mom on you."

"You don't even know my mom yet," Evan countered.

"But I will in September."

Evan took another bite. "I'm simply showing you why you need to think about coming to Paris for spring break."

"I thought spending time with you was supposed to be temptation enough."

"It should be," Evan agreed easily. "But fresh croissants are my backup plan."

"That's not a bad backup plan," Tia said. "I like the first plan better though."

Evan grinned and took another bite. "Good."

* * *

Chief Jarvis stood at the front of the briefing room and tapped on the folder he held. "We got the forensics report back from Raul's car accident."

The room fell silent, all the officers anxious for news. Colby drummed his fingers on his leg as he waited for the latest update.

The chief continued. "They blamed faulty brake lines."

"So it was an accident?" Wesley asked.

"I'm not convinced," Chief Jarvis said. "The repair log shows the brakes were replaced only six months ago. That doesn't mesh with the age of the brake lines the forensics team took off the car."

"You think someone switched them?" Colby asked. "What's the motive?"

"That's the million-dollar question," the chief said. "Since officers share squad cars, it's hard to know if someone was randomly targeting a policeman or if they were after Raul specifically."

"I have to think it was specific," Wesley said from the seat beside Colby. "Raul's the only person who doesn't share a car."

"And his car is parked at the high school all day, every day," the chief agreed. "It would be easy to tamper with it, especially during the summer when there aren't many people around."

"What now?" Colby asked. "How do we identify who is behind this?"

"Colby, I want you to pull up the surveillance video feed from the high school for the two weeks leading up to the accident," he said. "Wesley and Lance, check out the traffic cameras at the intersections nearby. I'll have the night shift help with that too."

"What are we looking for?" Wesley asked.

"Cars heading to the high school."

"Chief, the school is right behind our main shopping district. We won't be able to distinguish who is going to the school and who is heading into the Walmart parking lot."

"Do the best you can. Zero in on the day of the accident and expand backward from there."

Wesley nodded his assent.

"Let me know if you find anything," Chief Jarvis said. After he dismissed everyone, he called out, "Colby, I need to talk to you for a minute."

Colby's pulse quickened. "What do you need, Chief?"

"You've been at the high school for almost two weeks now. Have you overheard anything that would make you think someone had a problem with Raul?"

"Not at all. In fact, he seems to be well-liked by everyone."

"Keep your ears open," Chief Jarvis said. "Let me know if you need help going through the video feed. I can send an extra officer in for a few days."

"Thanks, but I can handle it," Colby said.

The chief nodded and headed toward his office. Colby turned for the door and wondered what the video feed would reveal.

Chapter 22

EVAN RUSHED INTO HIS HOTEL room three minutes before nine. His sprint up the stairs had him breathing heavy, and he leaned down to hold his knees as he caught his breath.

His phone rang an instant after he shut his door, the notes of "Proximity" confirming it was Tia on the other end. After more than a month apart, somehow, they still managed to talk twice every day.

"Hey, there," Evan managed to say. "How's your day going?"

"Not so good. Our starting wide receiver came in to see me today. Looks like he's been trying to play through a stress fracture in his foot."

"Oh man. That stinks." Evan took a deep breath.

"I know. First game of the season is tonight, and this kid was not happy when I didn't clear him to play."

"I can imagine." Evan held the phone out so he could see Tia's image as he continued through his hotel room and dropped the keys for his new apartment on his desk.

"Did I catch you at a bad time?"

"No. Why?"

"You're out of breath."

"I was running late after picking up the keys to my new apartment. I sprinted the stairs so I wouldn't miss your call."

"I forgot that you're moving in tomorrow. You have to be thrilled to be getting out of the hotel."

"After almost three months of this, I'm looking forward to having a kitchen again," Evan admitted. "By the way, I found out I'm going to have to run some testing on Tuesday night, so I might miss your call that day."

"It's not a problem," she said before adding, "You know, if talking so often is stressing you out, we can scale it back. Twice a day sounded great when we were sitting together in Paris, but I know your schedule is crazy right now."

"Tia, I love that we can talk so much. It makes me feel like I'm still part of your life even though we're on different continents." He hesitated. "Is talking this often making things hard for you?"

"No. You know I always tell you if I can't talk long." She adjusted the phone in her hand, and he could see the flash of her classroom behind her. A couple of treatment chairs lined the back wall, and desks occupied the center of the room.

"Do you have anything big going on first thing tomorrow morning?" Evan asked.

"Sleep?" Tia said, phrasing the word as a question. "Why?"

"I was hoping you would help me pick out some things for my apartment, but the shops here close at five. If you're up at eight, we'd have a couple hours."

"Eight I can do. I was afraid you were talking about six o'clock," Tia said. "I usually don't get to bed until midnight on game days."

"Call me if you're up," Evan said. "I'd love your input since you'll be living here next summer."

"Evan, you know I'm not that type."

"And I love that about you," Evan said. "We really will have to think about when we want to get married."

Tia's smile lit up her face. "You keep talking like that and I'm going to start expecting a ring."

Evan couldn't stop his own smile from forming. The first time he had mentioned getting married before summer, the words had escaped him as though he'd had no power to hold them in. The more he thought about it, the more he liked the idea. Now he had to convince Tia they should get married even though they would face another year apart after saying "I do."

"The first weekend in June would be good."

"June is a good wedding month," Tia agreed with humor in her voice. "It's a bit hot here, but at least school would be out."

"We could get married in Detroit," Evan offered.

"No. Sorry. I'm putting my foot down on that one."

"Now you sound like Drew and Julie."

"Worse things could happen." Her eyes lifted to look past her phone as her name was called. "Sorry, Evan. I've got to get back to work."

"I'll talk to you in the morning."

"Okay. Love you."

"Love you too."

Evan disconnected the call and let their last words linger. This wasn't the first time Tia's students had cut one of their calls short, but he couldn't remember her ever expressing her love in front of anyone before.

They were getting closer to getting that ring on her finger, and she didn't even know it.

* * *

Tia watched as the ambulance pulled away, its lights flashing. This wasn't the way anyone wanted to see their season start. First the stress fracture. Now a concussion.

A man's voice sounded behind her. "What bad luck."

It was Colby.

"Yeah. Preston was so excited to make varsity. Now this," she said.

Behind them, the crowd streamed out of the stadium, brake lights visible in the darkness where the line of cars waited to leave the parking lot. Tia started toward the field where she had parked the small tractor she used to haul the water jugs and equipment to the sidelines. She wasn't surprised when Colby fell in step beside her.

"Any big plans for the weekend?" he asked.

The question had become a routine one that Colby asked every Thursday or Friday at school. Once, she had made the mistake of saying no and had nearly gotten cornered into going on a date with him. Thank goodness Raul had been coming home from the hospital that day, providing her with a handy excuse.

"Actually, I'm helping a friend move into a new apartment."

"That's nice of you. If you need an extra set of hands, I'd be happy to help out."

"Thanks, but we're mostly going to be shopping for pots and pans and stuff."

"Gotcha," Colby said, apparently unfazed by the latest rejection. "You'll be at our softball game in the morning though, won't you? It's the last one of the season."

Though she had considered skipping it, with Raul still recovering, she didn't have the heart to let the rest of the guys down. "Yeah. I may be a little late, but I'll be there."

Tia reached the tractor, relieved her athletic director, Al, was standing beside it, talking to the football coach.

"What's the deal with Preston?" Al asked.

"He tested positive for a concussion," Tia said.

Colby tapped her on the shoulder and leaned down to speak into her ear. "I'll see you later."

Vince, the football coach, stepped closer as soon as Colby was out of earshot. "Tia, are you dating Colby?"

"No." She shook her head. "Why?"

"He's made a couple of comments around campus that made it sound like you're a couple," Vince said. "And Julie said something about you having a boyfriend."

Tia's phone chimed. "Sorry." She pulled her phone out of her pocket. She considered refusing the call from Evan, knowing she could call him back in a few minutes, but she decided now was as good a time as any to set the record straight.

The moment she answered it, Evan asked, "Are you still at the game?"

"Yeah. It just ended."

"If you aren't too tired, call me back when you get home."

"I will, but before you go, I want you to meet a couple people."

His eyebrows drew together. "Okay. Who?"

Tia shifted so he could see the two men standing behind her. "This is Vince, our head football coach, and Al, our athletic director." Tia glanced behind her and motioned with her free hand to the screen. "Gentlemen, this is my boyfriend, Evan Spence."

"Good to meet you both," Evan said.

The other two men offered basic greetings before Tia hung up.

Still looking confused, Vince pointed at her phone. "I give up. Why is your boyfriend FaceTiming you at ten o'clock at night?"

"Because he lives in Paris, and that's one of the times we usually talk during the day."

"Does Colby know about Evan?" Al asked.

"Yeah. In fact, they met at volleyball camp."

"Then why is he always hanging around you?"

"I don't know. I think he just doesn't have many friends here yet." Tia's shoulders lifted.

"I guess," Vince said. "Now, about Preston—what's the deal?"

"They're taking him to the hospital to get him checked out. I should get a call as soon as the doctor sees him."

"You'll let me know?" Vince asked.

"I will, but I'd think about who you want to take his place as linebacker. He's not going to be in there for at least a couple weeks."

"You're just full of good news today, aren't you?"

"I do my best."

Chapter 23

THE BAND PLAYED THE SCHOOL fight song from the far bleachers in the gym, and Tia wished for earplugs to counteract the echo. The last few students filed in, the stands nearly full as everyone waited for today's pep rally to begin.

They were already a few minutes behind schedule because of a shouting match between two groups of sophomore boys. A couple teachers were currently questioning two of the boys in one corner of the gym while Colby talked to three more boys on the opposite side.

Colby motioned for his group to leave through the main doors leading to the office, all of them angling across the basketball floor.

Tia caught movement from the other corner when one of the teachers decided to follow Colby's example. Instead of going out the opposite door, however, they headed in the same direction.

"That's a disaster waiting to happen," Tia said to Julie, who stood beside her.

"What?"

"Cameron ought to take those two kids out the back door to keep them apart." Tia took a step forward to suggest exactly that when one of the boys nearest her sprinted toward Colby's group.

"Colby!" Tia shouted, but her voice was lost in the roar of the crowd as chaos broke out.

The first punch landed, and instantly, the five boys who had been separated by the length of the gym now engaged in an all-out brawl.

Several teachers rushed forward and managed to get one kid controlled, but the other four kept their fists flying. Then, in a blink, they weren't the only ones striking out. Like the Hulk following his transformation, Colby's leg swept out and knocked the boy nearest him to the ground. An instant later, he used the same ploy on another. His hands struck out to separate the remaining two, his left hand lifting to intercept a punch. Colby held the boy's fist, squeezing until the boy dropped to his knees with a whimper.

The two on the ground scrambled to their feet. A few seconds later, they recognized their error when they found themselves on the ground again.

Tia watched, her own body tensing. She had expected Colby to be able to defend himself, but she had never seen anything like this. She caught a glimpse of his expression, the lack of emotion sending a chill through her.

"Wow," Julie said. "I'd never want to be on his bad side."

"No joke."

Colby flattened another teenager before he hauled him back off the ground. Gripping a second boy by his shirt, Colby held two boys in place and barked out orders to the staff members nearby.

Two minutes later, the subdued culprits were escorted out of the gym, and the band once again began to play.

* * *

Tia followed Gabrielle into the living room, where Raul was sitting in a recliner with his feet up. The evidence of his accident last month was now limited to the scar down the left side of his face and the walker parked beside his chair.

Raul looked up when she entered. "Hi, Tia."

"How are you doing?" Tia asked. She lowered herself onto the couch opposite him. "I see you no longer have the wheelchair."

Gabrielle moved to her husband's side but didn't sit.

"The physical therapist didn't want me to get used to it."

"Your physical therapist is very wise," Tia said. "Are you going to the place by the hospital?"

"Not yet. Right now, home health care is coming in."

"That's great."

Gabrielle put her hand on Raul's shoulder. "Can I get either of you something to drink?"

"A glass of water would be great," Tia said. "Thanks."

"No problem." Gabrielle picked up the cup on the end table by Raul and carried it into the kitchen.

Raul lowered his voice. "She worries."

"With good reason. You've been through a lot this past month."

"I'm actually glad you stopped by." Raul shifted in his seat. "I was wondering if your grandparents would be willing to rent out the bungalow on your property."

"I don't know. I can ask. Why?"

"We're looking to downsize," Raul said. "Our lease is up in early November, so it wouldn't be until then."

Tia read between the lines, and her heart went out to her friend. Undoubtedly, medical bills were taking priority over rent payments. Even if the police department covered the medical, Tia knew Gabrielle had already exhausted her vacation time to take care of Raul and was now on leave without pay. "I was planning on calling them in the next couple days. I'll ask."

"Thanks."

Tia leaned forward and wiggled her eyebrows. "You know I'll be thrilled if you move next door. That means I'll get to play with Olivia more often."

"As long as you don't teach her how to play baseball near any windows, I'm perfectly fine with that."

"Are you still sulking over that broken windshield?" Tia asked. "I was twelve when that happened."

"Yeah, and I'd only had that car for two weeks when you broke it."

"It was a little crack," Tia countered.

Gabrielle walked back in holding two glasses of water. She handed Tia one before setting Raul's next to him.

"Thanks, Gabrielle," Tia said.

"You're welcome." Gabrielle settled onto the couch beside Tia. "How are things at school?"

"Okay. We miss you though." Tia shook her head. "The person they have filling in for you is driving everyone crazy."

"How come?"

"She hordes the school credit cards like they're made of platinum, and the purchase orders for our basketball uniforms have been sitting on her desk for over two weeks."

"Those should have gone out a month ago to make sure we get everything in on time," Gabrielle said.

Raul shifted in his seat again and spoke to his wife. "Maybe if we get my mom to watch Olivia in the morning before her nap, you could go back at least a couple days a week."

"Maybe."

"I think Olivia should come to school with you."

"I wish," Gabrielle said.

"Actually, you might be able to pull it off if you shift your hours," Tia said, contemplating. "If you came in when she goes down for her nap, you could come home and take your lunch break at dinner time and then take Olivia into work with you for a few hours in the evening. Or bring her in for a while in the morning and let her play until lunchtime."

Gabrielle looked over at Raul and back at Tia. "Do you think Mr. Butler would let me?"

"It can't hurt to ask. Everyone has been wanting to help you guys out however they can. Maybe this is a way to make it happen," Tia said.

"I'll give him a call on Monday," Gabrielle said. "Now, tell us what's going on with your life. Julie said something about a new boyfriend?"

Tia could feel her face light up. "His name is Evan."

"Oh, she's hooked," Raul said. "Look at her face."

"Shut up, Raul."

"And she's blushing," Gabrielle added.

Tia acknowledged the burning in her cheeks and held up a hand. "Okay, so I really like him."

Gabrielle gave her hand a squeeze. "We couldn't be happier for you."

"Did I mention that he doesn't live around here?"

"No. Where does he live?" Gabrielle asked.

"Paris."

Raul shook his head. "You sure can pick 'em."

"It's a gift."

Chapter 24

EVAN STOOD OUTSIDE THE SECURITY checkpoint, a single red rose in his hand. He had arrived in Detroit two days ago so he would have time to start sorting through the things his family had packed for him from his old apartment. Already, he had half a suitcase full of clothes he wanted to take with him. He had also chosen several items to leave in his old bedroom so he wouldn't have to pack much when he came home to visit.

Home. That word rolled through his head as he struggled with where that was for him now. He loved this old colonial he had grown up in. His condo in Detroit had served him well and would always remind him of his early success that had allowed him to enter into home ownership.

The new place in Paris was becoming more and more his home, though, especially with how Tia had helped him pick out various furniture and decorations. He hadn't realized she thought he was only renting until she commented on what he would do with his furniture once he moved back stateside.

Evan planned to correct that misconception this weekend when he could explain in person. The last thing he wanted was for her to think his purchase meant he was staying in Paris for good. Not that he would mind, but only if Tia could be there with him.

A stream of passengers exited past him, and he rose on his toes to try to get a better view. He had received Tia's text message telling him she had landed fifteen minutes ago.

His smile was instant when she rounded the corner. Her hair swung loose over her shoulders, and she was dressed in the same casual chic style she had adopted for her trip to Paris—yellow blouse tucked into fitted jeans and a wide belt at her waist.

Her face lit up when she saw him, and her steps quickened. The moment she cleared security, he scooped her into his arms and held on. Another passenger bumped into them, and Evan moved, keeping one arm around her waist.

"Do you have everything?" he asked, glancing at her carry-on.

"Yeah."

Evan reached over and took her suitcase by the handle, pulling it behind him as he led her toward the parking garage. "I should probably warn you that my family is really excited to meet you. I was hoping for a quiet dinner tonight, just the two of us, but I got overruled."

"I'm looking forward to meeting them," Tia said. "Tell me their names again."

"My mom and dad are Paula and Richard. Landon and Robin are my brother and sister." They reached the parking lot where he had parked the small SUV he had purchased six months after graduating from college. "This is us."

Evan loaded her suitcase in the back and circled to open the door for Tia.

Instead of climbing in, she looked at him, a cloud of concern visible on her face. "What if your family doesn't like me?"

"They're going to love you."

"How can you be so sure?"

"Because I love you, and you make me happy." Evan leaned forward for a kiss. His hands rested on her shoulders, and he let the sensation of rightness settle over him. His heart stumbled when he pulled back and saw her golden eyes staring at him.

"You make me happy too."

"Good, because right now, that's what matters the most to me."

* * *

Tia forced her shoulders to relax and followed Evan into his childhood home. She looked at the sturdy banister running the length of the stairs and could imagine Evan sliding down it as a child. The high ceiling in the living room to her left appeared to be made for an oversized Christmas tree, and the two couches were positioned for intimate family conversations.

"Oh, you're here!" Evan's mother hurried into the hallway, immediately offering her hand. "You must be Tia. I'm Paula."

"It's so good to meet you," Tia said. "Thank you for having me this weekend."

"It's our pleasure." She waved toward her son. "Evan has told us so much about you."

Tia looked over her shoulder. "Should I be worried?"

"Of course not," Evan assured her. "I didn't mention anything about painting Drew's car or how you're always late or—"

Tia clamped her hand over his mouth and said to his mom, "Don't listen to him."

Paula chuckled. "Evan, why don't you show Tia her room? Your sister is planning to stop by in a little while."

"Okay." Evan carried her suitcase up the stairs, and Tia followed him up. "Mom put you in my sister's room. I hope that's okay."

Tia followed him into the bedroom. A thick white duvet offset the mahogany of the bed frame, and a scatter of trophies filled half of a bookshelf.

Tia crossed the room for a closer look. "You never told me your sister was into sports."

"She didn't have much choice. Landon and I were always playing basketball and baseball. She didn't want to be left out."

"I can hardly blame her," Tia said. "For me, it was my dad who got us into sports. He didn't have sons, so we got the benefit of his coaching. That's how I ended up in a men's softball league."

"Why don't you play in a women's league now?"

"My granddad is good friends with the police chief in Cottonwood. He talked me into playing during the summers when I was in college. Every year, they ask me to sub for a game, and somehow, I always get signed onto the team."

"You must be pretty good."

"I can hold my own."

"How are you at wrestling?"

"Never tried it. Why?"

"Just curious." His hands came to rest on her waist. Her heartbeat quickened as she anticipated his lean-in for a kiss. Instead, his fingers played over her ribs, tickling her.

She squeaked in surprise and tried to pull free. "Stop!" she gasped.

When he simply moved his hands to her stomach and she stumbled a step closer to the bed, instinct took over. She threw her weight back and swept out her leg. Evan fell to the floor with a thud.

He stared up at her, first stunned, then amused. "I thought you said you didn't wrestle."

"I don't." She held her hands up. "I did mention Granddad being good friends with the police chief though, right?"

"What does that have to do with wrestling?"

"Nothing, but the police department is where I got roped into taking self-defense classes every year during high school and college."

Steps sounded on the stairs, and Evan's mother rushed into the room. "What in the world is going on up here?"

Tia's face flushed. She made a helpless motion toward Evan. "Sorry. He tickled me."

Paula chuckled and spoke to Evan. "You were right. I do like her."

"I knew you would." Evan pushed himself to a stand. "Is lunch ready?"

"As a matter of fact, it is."

* * *

Evan scooped potato salad onto his plate and passed the bowl to Tia. As he had predicted, after only a few hours of his family knowing Tia, they were already enamored of her. Tia had talked football with his dad and brother and had helped his mom and sister in the kitchen. Or more specifically, she had helped set the table after admitting she could do a few basics but was overall a disaster waiting to happen in the kitchen. Evan suspected she wasn't exaggerating by much.

Tia served herself and passed the potato salad along.

"Okay, I have to ask"—Robin motioned to Evan with her fork—"What in the world do you see in my brother?"

"He knows how to cook," Tia said without missing a beat.

Laughter erupted around the table, and Robin waited for it to subside before continuing. "You may want to set your sights a little higher."

Tia reached out and took Evan's chin in her hand. "But look at him. He's so cute."

Evan pushed her hand away. "You guys realize I'm sitting right here."

"Yeah," Robin said. "It's no fun to pick on you behind your back."

"Thanks."

"You know I love you," Robin said.

"She always says that right before delivering the final blow," Landon muttered. "Evan, run and hide. It may be your only chance."

"It's always such a delight to have all the kids back home," Paula said. "Don't you think so, Richard?"

"I think *adventure* might be a better word for it," Richard countered.

Evan glanced over at Tia, wondering how she would view the banter that was so common in his household. She met him with a grin. Relieved that her sense of humor still appeared to be intact, he took a bite and proceeded to ignore his sister.

"How is business, Evan?" Richard asked.

"Busy, but I'm enjoying the work," Evan said.

"The money must be good for you to have bought an apartment there," Robin said.

Evan's jaw clenched, annoyed that Robin had brought up his purchase before he'd had the chance to talk to Tia about it. Keeping his response neutral, he said simply, "It was a good investment."

Tia stiffened beside him. Evan looked over as Tia's confusion melted into something else. Whether it was hurt or anger, he couldn't tell.

Dinner conversation continued around them, though Tia interacted only when someone spoke directly to her. The reserve that came over her unsettled him, and his stomach lurched when she pushed back from the table.

"If you'll excuse me for a minute, I realized I forgot to call to let my folks know I made it here okay."

"No problem." Paula studied her before asking, "Is everything okay?"

"Yeah, fine." She scooted around the edge of the table. "Thank you for lunch. Everything was wonderful."

Evan watched her leave the room and stood.

"Is something wrong?" Robin asked.

"She didn't know about the apartment."

"Evan, I'm sorry. I assumed she knew," Robin said.

"It's okay. I was planning to tell her about it this weekend anyway." Hoping he could repair the damage, he followed after Tia. She was already in her room with the door closed when he reached the top of the stairs.

"Tia." He rapped on the door. "We need to talk."

He expected resistance and was surprised when the door immediately swung open. He recognized the fury on her face. Staying on her side of the door, she spoke in an even tone. "You lied to me. You said you were renting an apartment in Paris, not buying one." She took a breath, and he heard the waver in her next words. "What happened to trying to make this work? I thought you were only going to stay in Paris for two years."

"I never meant to mislead you." He reached for her hand only to have her snatch it out of reach. "I thought you understood I was buying an apartment until we were talking about my furniture. It was then I realized you didn't know. I was afraid you would think the purchase meant I was staying there, so I wanted to talk to you about it in person."

"We're in person now. Explain it to me."

Where to start? Evan blew out a breath and tried to back up onto even ground. "Remember how I told you that I was going to rent out my condo in Detroit?"

"Yeah."

"When the contract came through, I found out the condo would only have to be rented for six months a year to cover my expenses."

"That's great," she said, still angry.

"When I started doing the math, the cost difference was negligible between renting and buying," Evan explained. "I figured I could list the apartment as a furnished rental anytime I'm here in the States visiting you or my family."

"Evan, people don't buy condos if they're only planning on staying there for a short time."

"You're right," Evan said. "I'm hoping at the end of this contract that I can renegotiate to renew it but only work there for part of the summer." He reached for her hand, and this time, she didn't pull away. "You have summers off, and you seemed to enjoy Paris."

"That doesn't mean I can afford to live there every summer," Tia said.

"I was serious about wanting us to get married someday," Evan told her. "I'm thinking of ring shopping at Christmas."

"Now you're trying to distract me."

"No, I'm being honest," Evan said. "If it turns out that you don't want to spend your summers in Paris, I'll look into hiring a business manager to help me solicit shorter contracts or something long-term in Arizona."

"Arizona is a big state."

"I know, but Phoenix isn't that far from Cottonwood. I could commute if I had to."

"It's a hundred miles each way. That would be a miserable commute."

"You're missing the point," Evan said. "I'm telling you you're worth whatever sacrifice I have to make."

"Evan, *you're* missing the point. This isn't going to work if either of us is making huge sacrifices like that." Tia held her arms out and let them fall to her side. "I love living in Cottonwood, but if you found a job in Phoenix, or somewhere else in the States, for that matter, I would be willing to look for a new school to transfer to."

"You would?"

"Yes, I would."

"I thought . . ."

"You assumed," Tia corrected.

Gauging that the turmoil had passed, he said, "I'm sorry I wasn't clearer about the apartment."

"Just promise me you'll make sure I understand next time," she said. "If there is a next time."

"I will." He tugged her closer and pulled her into an embrace. He held on for a minute, savoring the moment. He eased back and looked down at her. "Now that you know what's really going on with my place in Paris, can we talk about more important things?"

Her eyebrows rose. "Like what?"

"I don't know. Like how many kids do you want?"

"Eleven."

His jaw dropped. "What?"

Tia gave him a sweet smile and patted his cheek. "Just making sure you were paying attention."

Chapter 25

TIA PULLED INTO THE GAS station on her way into Cottonwood. Back to reality.

Her weekend with Evan had been much too short and made her yearn for what she couldn't have. She wanted to see him every day. And not just his image on a screen, but him, live and in person.

His family had given her insight into the person he had been before becoming the man he was now. Their humor was very much like her own family's, and they had all been so warm and accepting of her. Given the opportunity, she would enjoy spending more time with them. If only Evan didn't have to be so many miles away for so much of the year.

The shock of finding out about his apartment in Paris had dissolved into another kind of astonishment when she'd found out the price he had paid. She knew he made a decent living, but apparently, his contract in Paris was even more lucrative than she had thought.

She turned off the engine and climbed out of her car. Another car pulled into the spot opposite her as she unscrewed her gas cap and put the nozzle in place.

"Hey, Tia."

She peeked around the gas pump at Colby standing on the other side. "Hi, Colby. How are you doing?"

"Doing well. It's been a quiet week so far."

"In your line of work, quiet is good."

"Absolutely." He waited until gas was pumping into his car before he said, "Are you going to the volleyball game tonight?"

"Yeah. It's a home game, so I have to be there." She rolled her shoulders to loosen the tension that had settled there during her drive from the airport in Phoenix. "It should be a good match. Coconino hasn't lost so far this year."

"I look forward to watching it."

"Are you getting used to this whole high school scene?" she asked.

"I think so. The kids here are pretty good, and busting a few of them last week on drug possession seemed to go a long way in putting some fear into those who were trying not to be good."

"Setting an example is usually the best way to get things done," Tia said.

"True."

Tia's gas pump shut off, and she replaced the nozzle. "I guess I'll see you later."

"That you will."

* * *

Tia met Evan at the Phoenix airport. Their trip to Michigan had been perfectly timed, breaking their separation into two six-week stints instead of a full three months apart. Evan had told Tia he could rent a car, but she insisted on driving down to Phoenix to get him. He didn't mind forgoing the extra expense, but he knew how tight her schedule was this time of year. For Tia, October was filled with trying to keep football and volleyball players healthy as they headed toward postseason.

At least his flight had landed a few minutes early.

He exited the south-side doors and looked around until he saw her truck. He could hardly miss it. The 1946 bright-red Chevy couldn't hide if it tried.

He angled toward her and lifted his suitcase into the back, choosing to keep his computer bag and his other precious cargo up front with him. He pulled open the door, and she grinned at him.

"Welcome back," she said.

"Thanks." He slid the bag onto the floor and scooted into his seat.

Tia eyed the bakery box he held, guessing at what was inside. "Are those . . . ?"

"Chocolate croissants?" Evan handed it over. "Yes. Along with a couple chocolate tarts for you and some fruit tarts for me."

"Oh, I really love you."

"Good, because I would hate to think I carried these all the way from Paris for someone who didn't."

Tia opened the box and grinned over the top at him. "Best birthday present ever."

"I thought me coming was the best birthday present ever."

She leaned in for a kiss. "That too."

"Am I still going to meet your sister this trip?"

"If you aren't too tired, I was hoping we could stop by tonight." Tia pulled out into the airport traffic.

"We can stop if you want to." Evan looked at his phone. "It's only six thirty."

"Great. She's actually on our way out of town." She grinned at him again. "And Kyla said something about making banana bread today."

"Then we have to stop."

"My thoughts exactly."

* * *

Tia couldn't stop smiling. Having Evan here, meeting her friends in person, really was the best birthday present ever. Their intended short visit with her sister and her family last night had stretched into two hours. She and Evan had been exhausted by the time they'd arrived in Cottonwood, but seeing him interact with her family had been worth it.

The box of bakery items had been a bit lighter when they'd left, but Kyla had made up for it by sending a whole loaf of banana bread home with her. She guessed her sister approved of Evan.

Now, standing along the sidelines with Evan, waiting for the football game to start, she suspected her friends approved too. Otherwise, they never would have let Evan down on the field with her.

She brushed a strand of hair back behind her ear, the silver bracelet Evan had given her sliding higher on her arm. Another birthday present. Between the bakery items and the jewelry, she had to admit the man had good taste.

"How is the other team?" Evan asked.

"They've only lost one," Al said. "We have all of our starters healthy again, though, so this should be a good match up."

"Let's hope they stay healthy," Tia said.

The band marched onto the field for the pregame show, and Vince approached Tia.

"Hey, Park. Nathan's hamstring is tightening up again. Can you help him work it out?"

"Yeah. Send him over to the cart, and I'll get the roller."

Evan put a hand on her shoulder. "Hon, I'll get out of your way while you work. I'm going to sit with Drew and Julie in the stands."

"Okay. I'll meet you down here after the game."

"Sounds good." She watched him make his way to where Drew and Julie were sitting halfway up the left side of the bleachers. When she saw Drew introducing him to the people around them, Tia suspected Evan would end up knowing half the residents of Cottonwood before he left town this time.

* * *

She was making a fool out of him. Colby watched the pretty boy Tia had brought to the game as he made his rounds, shaking hands with her friends, worming his way into her social circles. Who did he think he was?

What happened to him living in Paris?

Colby clenched and unclenched his fists.

"Hey, Colby. What are you still doing here?" Wesley asked, stepping beside him.

"Thought I would stay and watch the game."

"Dude, you have got to get a life outside of work and hanging around this high school."

"I have a life," Colby countered, his gaze falling on Tia.

"Then we need to get you a girlfriend."

"I'm working on that too."

"Really?" Wesley's eyebrows rose. "Anyone I know?"

"You know everyone in town." Colby forced his voice to remain light, even though envy hummed through the words.

"True. So who is she?"

"Oh, no." Colby shook his head. "I know how small towns work. I'm not giving anything away until I know how things are going to turn out."

"Fair enough," Wesley said agreeably. He motioned to the field. "What do you think? Can our defense stop these guys tonight?"

Colby's shoulders lifted casually. "I've always heard that the best defense is a good offense."

"That's what they say."

* * *

Evan answered the knock at the door to find a Hispanic woman a little older than Tia standing on the other side of the threshold, a little girl propped on her hip. Beside her, a man stood awkwardly holding a cane. Tia had mentioned they were going to rent the bungalow and wanted to drop a few things off before they moved in next weekend.

"You must be Gabrielle and Raul. Come on in." Evan motioned them inside and introduced himself. "I'm Evan Spence."

Raul hobbled through the door, planting his cane and shifting his weight before shaking Evan's hand. "Good to meet you."

"Tia said you wanted to take another look around and drop some stuff off. Feel free to take your time. I was heading out to throw some burgers on the grill. We were hoping you would join us."

"Thanks." Gabrielle looked at Raul, and a silent communication passed between them before she said, "We'd love to."

Evan looked down at the little girl. "What's your name?"

"Olivia."

"That's a pretty name." Evan watched her squirm to get down. "Did you know that there's a swing set in the backyard?"

Her eyes lit up, and Evan's smile was instant. This little one was going to be a heartbreaker when she grew up.

"Tia said she'd love for you to come play with her on it," Evan said, quickly looking up at Gabrielle. "That is, if it's okay with your mom."

Gabrielle glanced out the window to where Tia was picking something in the garden. "That would be great. Thanks."

"No problem."

Gabrielle lowered her daughter to the ground. Instantly, Olivia took Evan by the hand. Charmed, he headed for the sliding glass door that led to Tia's house. "We'll see you in a bit."

Evan escorted his young charge through the bungalow's fenced side yard and into the main yard at Tia's house.

As soon as they cleared the gate, Olivia saw Tia and shouted, "Run!" Olivia tugged him along with her, making a beeline for Tia. Evan paced himself at a jog to keep even with her.

"There she is!" Tia squatted down and held out her arms, waiting for Olivia to race into them. Then she stood and swung her around, sending the girl's feet flying through the air.

"I want to swing."

"We can do that," Tia said. She turned to Evan and held out a fat zucchini. "Not sure if you want to grill this, but it needed to be picked regardless."

"Do you have any olive oil and seasoned salt inside?"

"Yeah. They're both in the cabinet to the left of the stove."

"In that case, you two play, and I'll get dinner started."

"Thanks." Tia put Olivia down and immediately challenged her to a race to the swings.

Their laughter rang out, and Evan let himself watch for a bit longer. This could be them in a few years. A little one of their own, planning their meals together, Tia gardening and him cooking. Summers in France, Christmas with whichever parents demanded a turn.

Warmed by the possibilities, he moved into the kitchen and set the zucchini on the counter. After retrieving the oil and spices he needed, he set his supplies and a cutting board in front of the kitchen window. With a view like this, who could blame him if he wanted to appreciate it every chance he got?

* * *

Tia leaned back on her chair, enjoying the cool breeze. After playing hard while waiting for dinner, Olivia had snuggled onto her mother's lap after dinner and fallen fast asleep. "I'm so glad you guys were able to come over tonight. I've missed seeing you."

"Dinner was great," Raul said. "This has been so nice to get out of the house and feel like a normal person again."

Tia motioned to Evan. "Thank him. He did all the cooking."

"And you did a great job of it too," Gabrielle said. "Tia said you live in Paris. How soon do you have to go back?"

"I'm here for a few more days. I'll leave Monday afternoon so I can be back at work on Tuesday morning."

"What do you do?" Raul asked.

"Computer programming, mostly. At the moment, I'm working with the transit authority in Paris, enhancing their surveillance and security on their subway system," Evan said. "With the constant threat of terrorism in Europe, we have to upgrade the programming at least every year."

"What kind of surveillance are you using?"

Gabrielle put her hand on Raul's arm before the men could start talking technology. "Raul used to work in computer forensics before he joined the police force up here."

"What made you change careers?"

"The company I was working for lost its contract, and I wanted to move up here anyway. Gabrielle and I both wanted to be closer to family."

Evan looked at Tia. "I can understand that."

"Any idea when you'll be back next?" Gabrielle asked.

"Probably not until Christmas, but I'm hoping to convince Tia to visit me in Paris for Thanksgiving."

"Wow. I'd love to visit Paris," Gabrielle said.

"The bakeries there are amazing," Tia told her.

"I think if she could get a job as an athletic trainer over there, she would come just for the food," Evan said.

"Probably." Tia leaned forward and spoke to Gabrielle again. "But seriously, the bakeries have these tarts that are to die for."

"Don't forget the croissants."

"And the croissants . . ." Tia agreed with a hum of approval.

Gabrielle turned to Raul. "Maybe for our next wedding anniversary, we should go to Paris."

"You let me know when you're coming. I have a spare bedroom. You're welcome to it."

"Seriously?" Gabrielle asked.

"Yeah." Evan said, surprising everyone with his offer. "Give me at least a few weeks' notice so I can make sure I don't have renters, but I'd be happy to let you stay there. And if you come during the summer, Tia will be there."

"Summer in Paris." Gabrielle shifted the child in her arms. "Tia, I think you found yourself a keeper."

"I agree," Tia said, "but I'd think so even if we could live the rest of our lives right here."

Raul cast an adoring gaze on his wife. "I know what you mean."

* * *

Evan held Tia close, not ready to leave. "I really hate goodbyes."

"Me too." A tear spilled over onto Tia's cheek.

"Thanksgiving?" Evan asked. He had brought up the idea of her coming for another visit a couple times throughout the weekend, but she had yet to commit one way or another.

"I just worry my parents will be upset if I don't spend it with them."

"How about this: Why don't you come to Paris for Thanksgiving, and I'll come with you to visit your parents at Christmas."

"You would do that?"

"I think it's only right for me to meet your father before I ask for permission to marry you." He saw the mixture of emotions on her face. "And no, I don't think we're rushing things."

"We've only known each other five months," Tia said. "And we've been apart for most of it."

"Yeah, but we've talked more often than most couples who have been together for a year."

"True."

"The only thing I really care about is if I ask the question, will you say yes?"

"There's only one way to find out." Tia leaned in for a kiss. "But I think the odds are in your favor."

Chapter 26

He watched her sleep.

Tia's hand curled under her cheek, her hair fanning across her pillow. Shadows played over the room as a cloud slipped in front of the moon. Tia didn't stir.

The sounds of the night floated through the open window—toads croaking, crickets chirping, and the occasional dog barking at whatever local wildlife was invading its territory. The scent of late summer roses and pomegranate hung in the air as though setting a scene at a romantic restaurant.

He had missed seeing her.

She had disappeared after school last Friday, an instant after the bus had left to take the football team to their game. He thought she was on her way to watch them play, but she hadn't been there. He would have noticed. Four days she had been gone, but she was back now.

A coyote howled.

Tia rolled onto her stomach, and her long hair fell forward, curtaining her face. Colby reached out to brush it back and stopped himself. She looked so peaceful; he didn't want to risk waking her.

He let his hand drop, surprised when her eyes flew open. The scream that escaped her pierced the air.

In a blink, she scrambled out of her bed on the far side. He barely had time to appreciate her trim figure clad in boxer shorts and a tank top before a baseball bat lifted above her head, poised to swing.

"Tia, it's okay." Colby held both hands up, palms out. "It's just me."

The screaming stopped, but the bat didn't lower. She gasped in a breath, followed by a second one before she managed to find her voice. "What are you doing here?"

What was he doing here? He supposed that was a valid question. "I was driving by and saw someone in the shadows of your house. It looked like a break-in."

Tia continued to gulp in air, and a new wave of fear was visible on her face. "Someone was in my house?"

"You're safe now. I must have scared off whoever it was."

Her arms relaxed enough to rest the bat on her shoulder. Rapid footsteps sounded outside, and Colby instinctively reached for the weapon holstered in the back of his waistband.

"Tia!" a man's voice called from outside. "Tia!" he shouted again.

"I'm okay!" Tia shouted back. She lifted wary eyes and stared at Colby before skirting along the far wall to the bathroom. She reached her arm inside and grabbed a robe off the back of the door. After slipping her arms through the sleeves, she headed out of the room, belting her robe as she went. Pity.

Rushing to her front door, she retrieved an old-fashioned key out of a decorative bowl on the entry table and slipped it into the lock, jiggling the key to unlock it, then opened the door.

Colby lifted his weapon, just in case the newcomer wasn't friendly. As soon as he saw the middle-aged man holding a hunting rifle on the porch, he shouted, "Put down the weapon!"

Tia instinctively held her hands out. "It's okay, Mr. Peterson. He's with the police."

The rifle lowered.

Tia drew a shuddering breath. "Colby Farren, Bob Peterson. Mr. Peterson lives next door."

"What in the world is going on over here? I heard a scream."

"Possible break-in," Colby said. "If I can, I'd like to ask you to return to your house, sir."

Mr. Peterson took a long look at Tia, apparently reading the fear still lingering there. "If it's all the same to you, I'll stay."

"I'm afraid I must insist," Colby said in his most commanding tone. "This is a possible crime scene. I need to preserve it."

"In that case, Tia, why don't you come over to my house? You can stay with us tonight."

Immediately, she nodded. "Let me grab my phone."

Before Colby could protest, she raced into her bedroom, returning an instant later, her baseball bat replaced with her cell phone.

"Tia, it would be easier if you stay here. I need to ask you some questions."

"You can ask her all the questions you want at my house," Bob said. He turned his attention to Tia. "Don't forget your purse and your keys."

Tia opened a narrow door to the side of the front door and retrieved her purse from the top shelf of the coat closet. Then, without a word, she stepped outside and let her neighbor take her away.

* * *

Tia couldn't get her heart to stop racing. She'd nearly brought her baseball bat with her but had decided Bob Peterson's rifle and Colby's sidearm would protect her well enough for her to make the short journey next door.

Bob ushered her into his living room, where his wife, Lucy, was. Lucy stood at their entrance. "Is everything okay?"

"The cops think someone broke into Tia's house," Bob told her. "They think he took off, but the cop wants to check it out before he comes over to talk to Tia."

"How terrifying." Lucy took Tia by the arm and guided her to the rocking chair. "Did you get a good look at him?"

"I never saw him." Tia settled into the chair and looked at Lucy, who appeared confused. "But I heard you scream."

"I woke up, and Colby was in my room," Tia said.

"Colby?"

"He's the cop," Bob said.

"Why was a policeman in your bedroom?"

"I don't know. He said he saw someone come into my house. I guess he was searching all the rooms, and I woke up when he came into mine."

"Well, you're safe now." She patted Tia's arm. "Did you want to call your folks and let them know what's going on?"

"No. I don't want to wake them." Tia's hand fisted around her cell phone. "If you don't mind, there is someone else I'd like to call."

"Of course. I'm going to go fix some hot chocolate for you," Lucy said.

"And I'm going to call Chief Jarvis. I don't like the attitude of that guy over at your place," Bob said. "He wasn't even in uniform."

"He works the day shift."

"Then what in the Sam Hill was he doing driving down our street at two thirty in the morning?"

Tia's heartbeat picked up speed again. "I have no idea."

"You make your phone call. I'm going to get to the bottom of this. Tell me to lower my weapon," he muttered as he left the room. "I've been shooting this Winchester since before he was born."

Bob's rant eased the sharpest edge of fear away. Tia hit the button to FaceTime Evan, relieved when he picked up.

"Hey, Tia. What are you doing up in the middle of the night?"

The simple question was all it took. Tears spilled over, and she fought for control.

Concern immediately illuminated Evan's face. "Hey, what's going on? What happened?"

"I woke up, and Colby was standing in my bedroom."

"What?" Evan bobbled the phone as he shot up to a stand. "Colby was in your bedroom?"

"He said he saw someone trying to break into my house." Tia used her free hand to wipe at a tear that spilled over. "I'm sorry to bother you. I know you're working, but I wanted to talk to someone."

"Don't apologize. You can call me anytime," Evan said. "But I do want to know why Colby was in your room. He should have identified himself before he ever entered your house."

"I don't know," Tia said wearily. "Everything is kind of a blur."

"You must have been terrified." Evan's voice shifted from annoyed to comforting. "I'm sorry I'm not there."

"Me too."

Lucy came back into the room. "Here you go, dear."

"Thanks, Mrs. Peterson." Tia accepted the thick mug with her free hand. She looked down at her screen and said, "Evan, this is Mrs. Peterson. Her husband came over when he heard me scream. I'm staying with them tonight."

Evan waited for Tia to angle the screen toward the older woman. "Thanks so much for looking after her for me."

"Oh, you're welcome. I'm only sorry Tia had such a fright."

"Me too."

Tia turned the phone to face her again. "I guess I'd better go. Thanks for letting me cry on your shoulder, so to speak."

"Anytime." Evan blew her a kiss. "I'll talk to you in a few hours."

"Okay." Tia ended the call, and Bob walked back into the room.

"The chief is going to look into this." Bob held up his cell phone. "In the meantime, Tia, you can stay in Lizzy's old room."

"Thanks." Tia stood, grateful when her knees wobbled only a little.

"And another thing," Bob said. "When you get up in the morning, I'll go with you and check out your place. I don't want you there alone until the chief has a chance to check things out himself."

"Thanks. I would appreciate that."

* * *

The chief escorted Colby into his office and slammed the door hard enough to make the glass rattle. "What in the world is this about Tia Parker waking up to find you standing in her bedroom?" Chief Jarvis demanded.

Colby stared at his chief's flushed face and irritated scowl. "Like I told you on the phone, I was searching the house. I saw someone climb in through one of her windows."

"That doesn't excuse this. I don't know what you were thinking," he boomed. "You go in, off duty, and don't even call it in? That's sloppy police work. And then to send Bob Peterson away instead of letting him stay with Tia—that was downright stupid."

"I was trying to preserve the crime scene."

"What crime scene?" Chief Jarvis asked. "A couple of muddy footprints in the garden and a missing window screen? Bob wouldn't have interfered with those."

"I'm sorry. I was trying to do what I thought was best."

"Why didn't you call it in?" Chief Jarvis demanded again.

"I wasn't sure what I saw at first. It wasn't until I was out of my car and within earshot of the perpetrator that I realized what was going on."

"What were you doing out on Airport Road at that time of night anyway?"

"I couldn't sleep. I went for a drive and thought I might hit the Circle K to pick up something to snack on."

"Airport Drive isn't on your way to the store."

"I know. I used to circle through that neighborhood on my patrol, especially knowing Tia lives alone," Colby said. "I made the detour out of habit and didn't think anything of it until I saw someone lurking in the garden."

The chief tapped his pen on his desk. "Write it up and file your report." He put both hands on his desk and leaned forward. "But if you ever go into a home without knocking or announcing yourself first, I'll personally charge you with trespassing."

"Yes, sir."

Chapter 27

EVAN HATED THIS. ABSOLUTELY HATED it. He had barely gotten home before Tia had called in hysterics. The thought of some man standing in her room while she slept sent a shiver of apprehension through him. He didn't care if that man was a police officer. Evan didn't like it. He especially didn't like being on another continent when Tia was feeling threatened.

He had talked to Bob Peterson at length this morning when Bob had walked Tia home and waited while she got ready for work. Bob's call to the police chief had given him some comfort that this situation would be dealt with, but it didn't take away the helpless feeling Evan had been fighting since that first call.

A glance at the paperwork on his desk sent another bolt of irritation through him. Nothing here needed his presence. He easily could have stayed in the States for a few weeks and worked remotely. In fact, he might propose to do just that when he went back to the States for Christmas. Europeans often took an extended holiday. He hoped they would let him enjoy the same benefit.

He glanced at his watch, wondering if it was too early to call Tia. It was only six in the morning in Arizona, but Tia had gone home from work early yesterday.

Eager to check on her himself, Evan made the call. He had expected it to go unanswered or to have Tia answer with a groggy hello. Instead, she answered on the first ring, already dressed in workout clothes.

"I was worried I was going to wake you," Evan said.

"Not much chance of that lately." Tia yawned. "Sorry."

"Have you gotten any sleep?"

"I took a nap during my planning period yesterday."

"Maybe you should have someone stay with you for a few days. Or you could move over into the bungalow for a while."

"I thought about it, but the lights would let anyone coming onto the property know I was over there anyway." Tia dragged her fingers through her hair. "I hate being paranoid like this."

"Didn't you say your football team is away tonight?"

"Yeah. Why?"

"If you don't want to have someone stay with you, you could go somewhere for the weekend."

"I don't want to blow money on a hotel room because I'm afraid to sleep in my own bed."

"What about Julie's cabin in Pinewood?" Evan suggested.

"Julie and Drew are heading to Phoenix this weekend for some family thing."

"They don't have to go with you," Evan said. "Unless it would freak you out to be there alone."

"That's not a bad idea." Tia seemed to ponder the possibility. "I'll talk to Julie at work today."

"Let me know what you decide," Evan said.

"I will." She moved to her front door. "I'm heading out for a run. Want to come with me?"

Evan smiled at the casual invitation. "As much as I'd love that, I should get some work done."

"Okay. Thanks for checking on me."

"Anytime. Love you."

"Love you too."

* * *

Tia waited in the hall outside Julie's classroom. The moment the bell rang, she slipped inside to avoid the stampede of kids crowding through the doorway.

Julie set aside the book she had been teaching from. "Hey, what's up?"

"I have a favor to ask." Tia waited for the last students to depart. "Any chance I'd be able to stay at your family's cabin this weekend? I kind of want to get away."

"No problem. In fact, you'd be doing me a favor if you don't mind shutting it down for the winter," Julie said. "Since my entire family is going skiing in Colorado for Christmas, I doubt anyone will be up there before spring."

The worst edge of her uneasiness lifted. "Do you have a key, or do you want me to use the hidden one?"

"I'll give you mine. It'll be easier for when you lock yourself out." Julie retrieved her purse from the bottom drawer of her desk.

"I only did that twice."

"Yeah, but since one of them was only last year, it's better safe than sorry." Julie handed Tia the key.

"Thanks, Julie. You're a lifesaver."

* * *

The drive to Munds Park dragged out compared to the last time Tia had made the trip. She had chatted with her sister on the phone for the first few minutes of her drive, but she'd had to make do with the radio for company since reaching the freeway.

The scare of waking up with Colby in her bedroom had made it nearly impossible for her to sleep well at night. Chief Jarvis had come out himself and checked out her house and yard, but as far as anyone could tell, nothing was missing and only a single window screen had been removed. The presence of some workmen at her house the previous day fixing the heater made it difficult to determine which footprints might have belonged to the culprit behind her scare.

For once, Tia looked forward to some time to herself. In a way, it would be just her and Evan. She made the turn off the freeway and headed to the general store to pick up some groceries. The thought that she should have gone shopping in Cottonwood before she left didn't strike until she was already on the road, and something about announcing her plans for a weekend away didn't bode well with her at the moment.

She parked in the lot and ran her hand over her right wrist in a habitual gesture and looked down to see she had forgotten to put on the bracelet Evan had given her. She knew she had forgotten something this morning.

With an annoyed sigh, she climbed out of the truck. She made it only halfway to the door before it swung open and Kendra Blake stepped outside.

"I was hoping that was you," Kendra said.

"What?"

Kendra closed the distance between them and gave her a friendly hug. "Your boyfriend called Charlie earlier to let him know what's been going on. He wanted us to check on you."

"He didn't." Tia couldn't believe Evan would call someone to babysit her, much less a man who was married to one of the most famous women of their generation. "I am so sorry. I know you and Charlie have better things to do than to check up on me."

"Don't be embarrassed. I know what it's like to be involved with someone who is overprotective," Kendra said. "Regardless, my family has two cabins across the street from each other. Charlie thought with everything going on, you'd feel safer if you stayed close by."

"Wait. What?" Tia shook her head, not sure she was hearing Kendra correctly. "You're inviting me to stay in one of your family's cabins?"

"Yeah." Kendra ushered her into the store. "It's literally across the street from where we're staying, and it will help you get a good night's sleep knowing an FBI agent is close by."

"That's probably true, but I promised I'd close down my friend's cabin for her for the winter."

"We can send Charlie over tonight to take care of it."

"I wouldn't want to impose."

"No imposition at all." Kendra motioned to the older lady sitting at the counter. "Mrs. Burgess, you met Tia, didn't you?"

"Yes. Good to see you again."

"You too."

Kendra motioned to the grocery carts. "I know you'll probably want to pick up a few things for yourself, but Charlie and I hope you will join us for dinner tonight."

A refusal formed, but Mrs. Burgess intercepted it. "Don't try to say no to her," she warned. "Kendra doesn't like that word."

"It's true," Kendra said.

Tia weighed the options and couldn't deny that having friends nearby would give her a needed sense of peace. "Then I guess I'll say thank you instead."

"Good idea," Mrs. Burgess said.

Kendra took the cart from her and started for the nearest aisle. Logic caught up with her, and she turned to face Kendra again. "Wait. How did you know I would stop here on my way to my friend's cabin?"

"I didn't know for sure, but Evan gave us a pretty good idea of when you'd get here. I needed to go shopping anyway, so I told Charlie I would try to catch you here," she said. "If I missed you, Charlie was going to call you on his way home."

Tia's cell phone rang. Charlie's name illuminated the screen. She held it up so Kendra could see. "Guess who."

"Oh, can I answer it?" Kendra asked.

"Sure." Tia handed over her phone.

"Hi, honey." Kendra giggled. "Yes, I found her. We're at the store now."

"I'm going to shop," Tia said and started down the aisle. She selected the few things she would need to make herself meals through the weekend. Or more specifically, she gathered the items she would need that would let her limit her cooking through the weekend. Milk and cereal could go a long way.

She went to pay, and Kendra handed her phone back to her. "Charlie said he's almost home. He's going to swing by here before we leave."

"Why?"

"Remember what I said about overprotective men?"

"Yeah."

"You're about to get a firsthand view of what I meant."

* * *

This had to stop. She was gone again.

Every time Colby wanted to stop by and spend time with Tia, she disappeared. He thought for sure after Evan left town, she would be around for good, at least until Christmas break. After all, her job needed her.

He needed her.

He checked his computer for any mention on her social media accounts. He hadn't worked up the nerve to send her friend requests yet, but he was able to access her feed easily enough through his connections with the other guys at the station.

His teeth clenched. Nothing. Did the woman never post anything except about the high school sports teams?

Closing down his computer, he opened an app on his phone, keying in multiple passwords, followed by an encryption key that would protect him from anyone tracking his location. When he found the information he was looking for, he grabbed his keys and headed for the door. Maybe a long drive would help him clear his head.

* * *

Tia followed Kendra out of the store to where Charlie was walking alongside Kendra's car holding what looked like a walkie talkie. "What is he doing?"

"Checking for tracking devices."

"Seriously?" Tia looked at Kendra, certain she must be joking. When she saw the expression on Kendra's face, she said, "You're really serious."

"Yep." Kendra shifted the single grocery bag she carried. "I went into Flagstaff today to do some shopping. He doesn't like for me to go home until he's checked my car out to make sure I don't have anyone trying to find out where we live."

"Okay, I knew that famous people had to worry about security, but I had no idea it was this extreme."

"Like I said, overprotective men." Kendra started toward her car a space away from Tia's truck. "I'm surrounded by them. My dad's even worse than Charlie."

"That's hard to believe."

"I know." She crossed to Charlie and greeted him with a kiss. "All done?"

"Yeah. You're good."

Charlie rounded Kendra's car and approached Tia. He shifted the device he held into his left hand. "Good to see you again, Tia."

"You too." She juggled her groceries in an attempt to open the back of her truck.

"Here. Let me get that for you."

"Thanks."

Charlie skirted past her and lowered the tailgate. A beeping noise started, and Tia wondered if maybe the battery in her phone was dying. She set her groceries in the bed of her truck and turned to look at Charlie staring down at his device. He swept it beside her truck, squatting to look beneath the vehicle.

Kendra crossed to them. "Is that . . . ?"

"Yeah."

Tia looked from Kendra to Charlie, now seeing the way he was sweeping his tool back and forth along the bottom of her truck. "Wait. Does that beeping mean—?" She couldn't finish the rest of the sentence. Her chest tightened, and dread shot through her.

Charlie looked under her truck, then reached beneath it to retrieve something in front of the rear wheel. "Got it." He stood and looked down at a device that wasn't even as big as the palm of her hand. "I think you may have bigger problems than someone breaking into your house. You have someone following you."

"You're talking to me?" Tia asked in disbelief.

"Yeah."

Tia pressed her hand to her chest. "Everyday, ordinary, small-town girl me?"

"I'm afraid so." Charlie fell silent for a moment. "Here's what we're going to do. I want the two of you to drive over to the country club and park Tia's truck there. Then drive in Kendra's car to our cabin."

"What are you going to do?" Kendra asked.

"I'm going to see if Jed would be willing to send this tracking device on a little ride."

"Who's Jed?" Tia asked.

"Mrs. Burgess's son," Kendra said. "Come on. Let's put your groceries in my car and get you to the cabin. You'll feel better once we get you settled."

Tia let out a shaky breath. "You sound like you're speaking from experience."

"I am."

* * *

"What do we do now?" Evan asked. He had felt ridiculous calling Charlie to ask for a favor. Now he couldn't believe his concerns had been so well founded. He paced across his living room and tried not to think about the fact that it was three in the morning.

Tia had FaceTimed him only to hand the phone over to Charlie a moment later. He could now see pine trees in the background and suspected Charlie had walked outside so they could have a private conversation.

Evan heard a door close before Charlie answered him. "I'm going to call the police chief in Cottonwood and make him aware of the situation."

"What can they do?" Evan asked. "She's already friends with half of the department there, but that didn't prevent someone from tracking her or from someone breaking into her place last week."

"Yeah, but they probably didn't connect that the break-in might not be random."

"So you think whoever broke into her house is the same person who put the tracking device on her car."

"It's worth checking out." Charlie glanced behind him before he continued. "I'm having the tracking device delivered to the FBI office in Phoenix. One of my friends there will plant it on a car parked in plain sight of a security camera. That will give us a chance to see if we can identify and catch this guy. I'm also going to winterize her friend's cabin and make sure no one is looking for her there."

"Charlie, I can't thank you enough for your help," Evan said. "Not being there for Tia right now is killing me."

"I've been in your shoes," Charlie said. "But if there is any way you can get on a plane and be here while we sort this out, it would be a good thing."

"I started looking into tickets last night," Evan said. "We've had increased chatter about a possible terrorist attack on the Paris subway system, so I have to do a security check this weekend, but I'm going to talk to my boss on Monday. Once I finish my current testing, I'm hoping to work out of the office for the next few weeks. I'd like to be on a plane by Monday night."

Charlie nodded his approval. "I know we talked about having Tia stay at the cabin across the street, but if it's okay with you, I think I'm going to see if Kendra and I can convince her to stay here with us."

"I'd feel a lot better about that, but I'm sorry to impose on you like this."

"It's not a problem," Charlie insisted. "Honestly, I'll sleep better knowing she's upstairs than if I'm worried someone might find her at the other cabin."

"Are you sure your wife will be okay with that?"

"She'll love having the company." Charlie moved back inside and asked, "Did you want to talk to Tia again?"

"Yeah. Thanks." Evan crossed to his window and looked out at the city lights. A moment later, Tia's voice came over the line.

"I'm really sorry I woke you."

"It's okay. I told you to call me anytime," Evan said. "Charlie wants you to stay with them tonight."

"Kendra already offered. I feel bad about invading their weekend together, but I don't want to be alone tonight."

"I know. I'm sorry I'm not there."

"That wasn't what I meant," Tia said quickly.

"I'm sorry I'm not there all the same," Evan repeated. "Try to enjoy your time in the mountains."

"I will. And you try to get some sleep." Tia blew him a kiss. "Love you."

"I love you too."

Chapter 28

TIA WALKED INTO THE KITCHEN to find Kendra standing at the sink and Charlie sitting at the table. She fought back the awkwardness of staying with people she barely knew.

She had always liked Kendra as an artist, but she had no idea that as a person, she was even more impressive. Her husband was no slouch either.

"Good morning." Kendra moved to the cabinet by the refrigerator. "Can I get you something to drink?"

"Kendra, I can get it."

"It's fine." She pulled out a glass. "Orange juice, milk?"

"Orange juice sounds great." She looked at the wall clock; it was nearly nine o'clock. "I can't believe I slept so late."

"You needed it," Kendra said, retrieving the juice from the refrigerator.

"You're right. I forgot what it was like to sleep for more than a few minutes at a time." Tia picked up one of the muffins she had bought at the store yesterday and carried it with her to the table. "You guys are welcome to eat anything I picked up from the store. I always buy way too much for one person."

"I was hoping you would say that." Kendra put a glass down in front of her and set another beside Charlie.

"Careful," Charlie warned. "She's going to be cursing your name when she meets with her personal trainer next week."

Kendra selected a muffin of her own. "But I'm singing your praises this morning."

"I don't know what you have planned today, but if you're up for it, we could go hiking this morning and burn off some of these calories," Tia suggested.

"That's a great idea," Kendra said. "It's supposed to be gorgeous out today."

"Do you hike often?" Charlie asked. "I know there are some great trails near Sedona."

"And in Sycamore Canyon too," Tia said. "I don't go as often as I would like. It's hard to find people to go with, and I don't hike alone."

"Smart." Charlie bit into his banana. "I can't tell you how many missing persons cases we have that turn out to be either someone getting lost hiking by themselves or, worse, having a fall."

"I can only imagine. A friend of mine from college lost her sister that way. She fell into a canyon and died from her injuries before they found her."

"That's heartbreaking," Kendra said.

"I know. I haven't hiked alone since."

"If you two don't mind waiting about an hour, I'll come with you," Charlie said. "After the week I've had, some time in the fresh air is exactly what I need."

"Works for me." Tia bit into her muffin and rolled her eyes in pure appreciation. "These are so good."

"I know. Aren't they?" Kendra said, taking a bite of her own. She broke off a second piece. "We'd better make it a long hike."

* * *

Tia saw Colby's car parked at the gas station coming into town. How was it that he was always everywhere she was? Had she been able to avoid driving by him, she would have, but he had chosen to buy his morning coffee by the one intersection she had to pass through to get into town.

Charlie and Kendra had convinced her to stay Sunday night with them, extending her weekend away. Rising early had been a small price to pay for the comfort of knowing Charlie and his gun were close at hand. She hadn't slept as well as she had at the cabin since Evan left the last time. The light turned green, and Colby walked out of the convenience store and stopped to look around.

Tia scrunched down in the seat of her truck, hoping he wouldn't notice her. After dealing with the possibility of someone stalking her, the last thing she wanted was to have him hovering around. He was the only member of the police force she didn't know well, yet she saw him more than all her friends combined. The thought that Colby was starting to feel like a stalker entered her mind, but she pushed it aside. The man was a police officer.

Colby waved, and she forced herself to wave back.

He was a police officer, but he was giving her the creeps.

Though she had planned to gas up this morning, she passed her intended stop and headed for the high school. She would be earlier than usual, but after taking so much time away, she needed to catch up on her paperwork. With any luck, she would be shut inside her office long before Colby got to school.

* * *

Colby looked up as the delivery man walked into the main office, a huge bouquet of red roses in his hands.

"Wow," Sharla said. "Who are those for?"

"Tia Parker."

"Looks like things are getting serious with her new boyfriend," she said. "Either that or he's in deep water for something."

"It's usually one or the other." The delivery man set the bouquet on the reception counter and handed Sharla a tablet. "Can you sign here, please?"

"Sure." She took the electronic pen and scribbled her name.

Something primitive bubbled up inside Colby, and he struggled to keep his calm facade in place. "Hey, Sharla, I'm heading down that way. I can take these to Tia."

"Are you sure? I don't know if she's in yet."

"Yeah. Not a problem. I need to head out on patrol for a while, but I'll leave them on her desk if she isn't here." Colby picked up the bouquet and carried them out of the office. Had it not been for the two teachers talking in the hallway, he would have smashed the roses, vase and all, to the ground. Instead, he nodded a greeting and continued toward Tia's room.

The little white card stuck up through the sea of red. He turned the corner and glanced around. Finding himself alone, he plucked the card out of the bouquet and ripped it open.

Just a little something to take the edge off your worries. See you soon. And I was serious about what I said last time we were together. Ring shopping at Christmas. Love, Evan

Colby stuffed the card in his pocket. Who did Evan think he was? Tia would never marry him. She already belonged to someone else. She belonged to him.

* * *

Memories of Colby ate at Tia throughout the early morning. She had arrived at the school a bit before seven, but the pile of paperwork hadn't diminished in the slightest over the past hour and a half.

How many times had she run into Colby at the gas station? Or outside her classroom? Had she ever had a sporting event this year when he hadn't been the last to leave? He always remained in uniform, but she knew from Raul that his hours at the school ended at five, leaving sporting events the responsibility of one of the other officers.

Going back to summertime, she could add seeing him in Jerome as well as the odd mix-up after the softball game where they'd ended up at The Chaparral but the rest of the team had gone to the 10–12 Lounge. Could Colby have told her the wrong restaurant on purpose, or had it really been an honest mistake?

The possibility that he could have been responsible for her flat tires entered her mind. Had that not happened, he wouldn't have given her a ride home and he wouldn't have known where she lived. She glanced at the clock. Another twenty-five minutes until she could call Evan. He wouldn't be able to do anything about her concerns, but at least he might be able to talk her down from the ledge she was tiptoeing on right now.

Surely Colby would have had to undergo psychiatric evaluations to get hired by the police department. And this was his second job in law enforcement.

She thought of his old position and the woman he had intended to marry in Alaska. Maybe his ex could shed some light on how to handle the man who always seemed to be lurking nearby.

Tia crossed her room and cracked her door open wide enough to peek out and make sure no one was hanging out nearby. When she was satisfied her call wouldn't be overheard, she moved back to her computer and opened a search bar on the internet. Unable to remember Lexi's last name, Tia opted for a more direct approach.

"Valdez Police Department. How may I direct your call?"

Tia read the name of the police chief off the Valdez Police Department's website. "May I speak with Chief Webster, please?"

"May I ask who is calling?"

"My name is Tia Parker." Tia opened her mouth to explain the reason for her call and couldn't come up with the words. Thankfully, it wasn't necessary.

"One moment, please."

A gruff voice came over the line. "Chief Webster."

"Chief Webster, this is Tia Parker from Cottonwood, Arizona. I'm sorry to bother you, but I'm hoping you can help me with some information."

"What are you looking for?"

"I'm trying to get in touch with Colby Farren's ex-fiancée."

Silence stretched over the line for several seconds. "I don't know where you're getting your information, but as far as I know, Colby didn't have a girlfriend before he left Valdez, much less a fiancée."

"What? He said they broke up when he moved to Arizona. I know her name is Lexi, but I don't have a last name." More silence. "Chief, are you still there?"

"Could you be talking about Lexi Dyer?"

"I don't know. He only mentioned her first name."

"What did you say your name was again?"

"Tia. Tia Parker."

"Miss Parker, can I ask what this is all about?"

"I'm sure it's nothing. I just hoped to talk to her."

"Lexi Dyer's body was found three weeks ago. The last time she was seen alive was May 30."

"What?"

"I think you'd better tell me everything."

A sickness rose within her, along with an overwhelming sense of dread. "I woke up last week, and Colby was standing in my bedroom. He said he saw someone breaking in and came in after him."

"Was there any evidence of a break-in?"

"A window screen was pulled off. The window was unlocked, so there's no way of knowing if someone came in or not."

"Anything else?"

"A tracking device was found on my car last Friday. An FBI agent friend of mine found it and sent it down to the Phoenix office to see if they could catch whoever might be following me," Tia told him. "When I got back into town this morning, I noticed Colby parked by the gas station at the edge of town, and it got me thinking. Since he's been here, I run into him all the time. Maybe more than is normal."

"Look, I don't want to scare you, but we had a similar break-in at Lexi's apartment six weeks before she disappeared. The report was very much like what you described."

"Would Colby have made up the story about the intruder?"

"All I'm saying is I'm concerned for your safety. From what you're describing, I'm concerned Colby was responsible for Lexi's death and may now be fixated on you. If that's the case, you aren't safe."

"If you thought Colby was involved with Lexi's disappearance, why wasn't he questioned? Surely you knew where he moved to."

"Everyone around here thought Lexi had gone to visit her folks in Anchorage. Apparently, her parents thought she had traveled overseas for the summer," Chief Webster explained.

"Her parents didn't think it was odd they hadn't heard from her?"

"They did, but my department wasn't notified that she was missing until about a month ago. When we started piecing together her movements, the last person we knew to have seen her alive was her boss, but that put her disappearance around May 27. An old college friend confirmed a couple days ago that she talked to her on the phone May 30." He paused, then added, "I hadn't put together that her disappearance date and Colby's move were so close to the same time until just now."

Tia wavered and grabbed the edge of her desk to steady herself. "What do I do? He works here at the school."

"I want you to go straight out to your car. If anyone asks where you're going, say you're going to the hospital to check on a friend."

"Then what?"

"Drive to the police department, but not the one where Colby works," he said. "Is there another one close by?"

"Clarkdale is down the street, and Sedona is about twenty-five minutes away."

"Go to Sedona, then. If Clarkdale is that close, they may share their dispatcher," Chief Webster explained. "Leave now. I'll call the Sedona police chief and let him know you're coming."

"Okay."

"Tia, it's going to be okay," Chief Webster promised. "I'll have the Sedona police chief wait to contact his counterpart in Cottonwood until after you get to Sedona. That will ensure your safety when they take him into custody."

"Thanks." She hung up the phone and grabbed her purse. She caught the scent of flowers as she headed for the door.

Then she saw the enormous bouquet and the face behind the roses.

Chapter 29

FOR THE FIRST TIME IN her memory, Tia wished Evan hadn't called. The notes of "Proximity" jingled from her pocket, announcing the location of her cell phone.

Colby slipped into her room, forcing her to back up so he could kick the door closed. His hand reached for his sidearm, and he pointed it at her through the roses. "Hand it over," he said, his voice eerily calm. "You won't need that anymore."

Tia stared at the gun, unable to look past it.

"Hand over your phone," Colby repeated.

Tia forced her gaze to lift to his. Pure evil stared back at her. "I don't understand."

"I'm tired of waiting."

"Waiting for what?"

"Why is Evan sending you flowers?" Colby demanded. "He should know you belong with me."

Tia swallowed hard. Chief Webster had been right. Colby was a threat, and now he was less than two feet away. *Think!* she ordered herself. Digging into every creative fiber of her being, she said, "He's trying to win me back. We broke up before he left town last week."

"I'm not stupid," he growled in a low voice. He set the roses on the counter running the length of her treatment area and dug a crumpled piece of paper from his pocket. Tossing it beside the flowers, he scowled. "Ring shopping?"

"It's not what you think," Tia insisted. She didn't know what the card said, but if it had been enough to set Colby off, Evan must have been behind the surprise delivery.

"Give me your phone," Colby demanded a third time, raising his gun again.

Her hand shaking, she pulled it from her pocket and set it on the counter. Instantly, it started to ring again.

Colby looked down and read the screen. "You broke up, huh? Then why is he calling you?"

"I broke up with him," Tia lied. "He isn't happy about it."

"Why should I believe you?"

"Have I ever lied to you?" Tia asked, fighting the childish urge to cross her fingers now to ward off evil karma.

"I don't know."

Struggling for calm, Tia pressed on. "I thought we were friends. There's no need for that gun."

"I've heard this before. Lexi treated me differently too once she had a gun pointed at her."

"Colby, I'm not Lexi," Tia insisted. Terror bubbled up into her throat, and she had to swallow before adding, "I'm nothing like her."

"We'll see soon enough."

* * *

Evan shut his suitcase and zipped it closed. His conversation with his boss this morning had gone even better than he could have anticipated. Not only had he approved Evan's request to telecommute from the States for the next few weeks, but he had also indicated that he would be open to allowing it in the future. If Evan could accomplish the same level of productivity from across the Atlantic, his time in Paris could be limited to a week or two each month.

He couldn't wait to tell Tia.

If he had his way, he would reduce his time in Paris even further, concentrating his testing and in-office presence to the summer months when Tia could be there with him. A few trips back during the school year and he could make it work to live in Arizona. Too bad Tia had rented the bungalow next door to Raul and Gabrielle.

He checked the time. Only ten more minutes until their scheduled call. He had tried calling her early, but apparently Tia had been away from her phone.

He pulled his suitcase into the entryway and set it by the door, along with the computer bag he had already packed. Circling back into the master bedroom, he removed another suitcase from his closet to pack the clothes he didn't plan to take with him. He had listed his apartment on Airbnb for the days he would be gone, and he wanted to ensure he left the closets and dressers clear. Thankfully, he had stored most of his personal items in a locking cabinet in the corner of his closet when he'd first moved in, knowing short-term rentals were a likelihood.

His phone chimed, and he looked down to see it was a confirmation for a booking on Airbnb. After storing his large suitcase in his storage closet, he locked it and made one last sweep of his apartment to make sure everything was ready.

He planned to talk to Tia over breakfast, and then he would have enough time afterward to cross the street to the subway for the first leg of his journey toward home. He checked the time and smiled as he pressed the video button beside her name. It went unanswered.

Evan shook his head. Of all the days for her to not be on time. He paced through his apartment and fixed his breakfast before trying again. He checked the time once more. Where was she? The only time she had been late for their scheduled calls was the day she had visited her friend in the hospital after that awful car accident, and even then she had been only ten minutes late.

Fifteen minutes had already passed since their normal time. He finished his breakfast and cleaned his dishes before gathering his things. With limited time to spare, he tried calling a third time. When once again, the call went unanswered, he texted Julie.

Can you check on Tia? She isn't answering my call.

He gathered his suitcase and computer bag and headed out the door. He was nearly to the subway station when Julie texted him back.

She doesn't come to work this early, but I'll check on her at lunch.

When is that?

10:40.

An hour and ten minutes. Might as well be an eternity.

Thanks.

Realizing he would be going through security about the time Julie would be able to catch up with Tia, he sent another text, only this time to Charlie.

Did Tia get off okay this morning?

Charlie's reply was instant. *Yes. Is there a problem?*

Not sure. She missed our scheduled call. That's never happened before.

Evan dug out his transit pass and entered the subway. He was all the way to his platform when Charlie texted him back. *No reported accidents along her route. I have a call in to the principal at the school to see if she's already there.*

Thanks, Charlie. Sorry to make a big deal out of this, but I'm worried.

Not a problem. I'll be in touch.

The train pulled into the station. Evan juggled his computer bag so he could carry it on top of his suitcase. He needed his other hand to hold his phone.

* * *

Everything in Tia's office had been reduced to three things: her cell phone on the counter, the gun pointing at her, and the man who was standing between her and the exit. The notes of "Proximity" rang out again.

Colby's hand tightened on the gun. With his other hand, he picked up Tia's phone and handed it to her. "Unlock the screen."

Having little choice, Tia did as he asked. Her fingers itched to send a message to somebody, anybody, but he snatched the phone from her the moment the screen opened. He scrolled through her text messages briefly and, an instant later, started typing something.

"What are you doing?"

"Letting Principal Butler know you're taking another day off." He glanced at the roses again, and his lips drew into a thin line. "Those really are beautiful. It would be a shame to leave them here."

He lifted the bouquet again, adjusting them in one hand so he could continue holding his firearm without it being seen. "Let's go."

Not seeing any other option at the moment, Tia led the way out of her office into the empty hallway. "Out the back door," he whispered.

She made the turn, passing the currently empty weight room as she made her way to the door. The thought surfaced of using the door as a weapon, or at least a possible means to knock Colby's gun loose, but he crowded her, so they went through the door together with almost no space between them.

"We'll take your truck," Colby said, nudging her toward her reserved parking spot. They were fifteen feet from her vehicle when an engine sounded and a car made the turn toward their side of the parking lot.

The possibility of someone coming to her aid lifted her. Then she recognized the car and feared for her friend's life. Gabrielle parked two spaces away, little Olivia strapped inside with her.

"It's up to you if they live or die." The flat, almost emotionless tone scared her more than when she had heard the intense jealousy in his voice.

Gabrielle climbed out and proceeded to open the back door to collect her daughter.

"Hi!" Olivia called out brightly.

"Hi, Olivia. Are you coming to work with your mama?" Tia managed to ask.

She nodded. "I get to play with crayons."

"You have fun."

"Where are you off to?" Gabrielle asked. "You're usually coming this time of day instead of going."

"I know. I was just checking on some paperwork. I decided to take another day off. It's a beautiful day for a hike."

"True. It's not often you get a day in November that isn't too cold." Gabrielle's eyes narrowed, and she spoke to Colby. "Are you going too?"

"No. Just carrying these out to the car for Tia."

"Well, have fun, Tia." Gabrielle took her daughter by the hand. "See you guys later."

"A hike?" Colby asked as soon as they disappeared into the school.

"It's the only thing I could think of that I knew she'd believe. If I wanted to go for a run, I would go before or after work."

"Smart." He nudged her closer to the car. "I always knew you were smart." He motioned to her purse. "Unlock the door and then hand me your keys."

She followed his instructions, her heart sinking even lower when he had her climb behind the wheel. Keeping the roses and gun pointed at her, he skirted around the front of the car and climbed in. He balanced the flowers between his knees, his weapon now laying across his lap, hidden from plain sight but still pointing right at her.

"So far so good."

"Where are we going?"

"Somewhere where we can be alone. Somewhere where everyone else will cease to exist." He waved the gun upward an inch. "Start the engine."

Helpless and nearly paralyzed by fear, Tia slid the key into the ignition, praying someone would realize something was wrong and save her from the lunatic sitting next to her.

Chapter 30

HAVEN'T SEEN TIA AT WORK today.

Evan read the text from Julie, and his anxiety rose another notch. He had yet to hear back from Charlie, and it had been nearly an hour since they had spoken. Evan got in line for customs, grateful it appeared to be moving quickly.

Once he passed through that obstacle, he moved to the security station, using his wait time to send another text message to Tia. When again he received no reply, he sent two more, this time to Tia's sister, Kyla, and another to Drew in the hope that one of them would be able to reach her.

Kyla responded first. *What's wrong? She isn't answering me either.*

Evan texted her back. *I don't know. Julie said she wasn't at work.*

I'll try Mr. Peterson next door. He should know if she's home or not.

Thanks.

As though getting to his gate faster would speed up his travel time, Evan picked up his pace. He wasn't sure if he would be able to sit still, so he opted to stand in the corner of the waiting area instead.

His phone rang, and his heartbeat quickened when he saw Charlie's name on his screen. "Did you find her?" Evan asked the moment he answered the FaceTime request.

"I need you to do me a favor. Call or text Tia's phone."

"I texted her a couple minutes ago. She's still not responding."

"Try again," Charlie said.

"Okay. I'll call you back." Evan hung up and tried calling Tia again. When it connected on the first ring, relief poured through him. Then he saw Charlie's face on his screen, and his relief plummeted into fear and despair.

"Charlie, what's going on?"

"I'm in Tia's classroom right now. Her phone was sitting on the counter."

"She must be in the school somewhere," Evan said. "She wouldn't leave her phone if she was going somewhere."

"She left a jacket on her chair, but her car isn't here."

"Sometimes she runs to school," Evan said, grasping at any logic that would make her safe.

Evan heard a man's voice in the background. "What's this all about?"

Though he couldn't see the other man clearly, he recognized the police uniform.

"I'm Charlie Whitmore, FBI," Charlie said and shook the policeman's hand.

"Chief Jarvis. What's going on here that would bring in the FBI?"

"I'm trying to locate Tia Parker. She missed a scheduled phone call earlier, and no one has seen her since she left Munds Park this morning."

"She probably got sidetracked on her way back to town," Chief Jarvis said. "That girl isn't ever on time."

"Her principal said he received a text saying she was taking another day off, but that doesn't explain why her phone is here," Charlie countered. "Principal Butler also mentioned that she hasn't ever asked for time off by texting before. She's always called him."

"Charlie," Evan said to get his attention. "Tia may be late for a lot of things, but she's never late for our calls."

"Evan, I'm going to call you back on my phone. I want to have her phone dusted for fingerprints."

Evan couldn't respond. The line went dead, and he fought the wave of nausea rolling inside him.

A text came through, this time from Kyla. *She's not at her house. Ask Bob if her truck is there.*

Evan's phone rang again, this time from Charlie's phone. Evan opened the new video chat.

"Okay, we're going to dust her phone for prints in case someone else might have been handling it," Charlie said. "Is there anything else you can think of that might help us narrow down where she might have gone?"

"No. Nothing."

"What's this?" Chief Jarvis's voice carried over the line. In the background, Evan could see him pick something up off the floor.

"Looks like a card from a florist," Charlie said. He adjusted the phone so Evan could see the crumpled note. "Evan, when did you send Tia flowers?"

"Saturday. They were supposed to be delivered today."

Another text buzzed, and Evan saw the message flash across the top of his screen. He read it to Charlie. "Tia's car isn't at her house."

"What?"

"Her sister had a neighbor check for me. Wherever Tia is, her car should be with her."

The announcement for Evan's first flight sounded. "They're calling my flight."

"Give me a call when you land."

"Charlie, we have to find her."

"I know, Evan." Charlie said. "For now, just concentrate on getting here."

Helpless, he watched the screen go black.

* * *

Colby gave Tia driving instructions, having her take a route through Verde Village that would avoid traffic lights. He wasn't thrilled that they were in Tia's truck. Everyone in town knew what she drove, but then again, she had told Gabrielle she was going hiking. That would buy him time.

"Where are you taking me?" Tia asked, her voice quivering.

"You said you wanted to go hiking."

Tia's lips pressed together, and a tear trickled down her cheek.

"Don't cry."

"Then let me go," Tia said. "I thought we were friends."

"We are." Colby reached out and brushed the tear away. Her skin was so soft, just as soft as he'd imagined. He saw the way her shoulders tensed at his touch, and anger flowed inside him. "Why do you do that?" Colby demanded.

"What?"

"Flinch when I touch you."

Her eyes darted from the road to meet his, a well of terror illuminating the deep gold. "You startled me."

Colby's jaw clenched at the lie.

She quickly turned her eyes back to the road, and he stared at her profile. So beautiful.

A flash of memory pricked his brain, a similar drive in Alaska. But he wasn't driving this time, and Tia wasn't screaming. Or rather, he hadn't been forced to tie her up and stuff a bandana in her mouth to keep her screams from being heard.

Hadn't Lexi understood they'd belonged together? Maybe the reason things hadn't worked out with her was because he was destined to come here, destined to meet Tia.

Things were different this time. Tia was his friend, and now she knew they should be more. He could give her the opportunity to change. They just needed time alone, time without distractions.

They reached a stop sign.

"Turn right," he instructed, sending them toward Cornville.

She turned right.

No, she was nothing like Lexi.

Colby looked down at the roses he held in his lap. Rolling down the window, he lifted the bouquet, glass vase and all, out the window. He dropped them to the pavement with a satisfying crash.

Immensely pleased that he had removed the lingering reminder of other friends from her mind, his hand tightened on the grip of his pistol. Maybe this day would turn out even better than he'd planned.

Chapter 31

Tia waited until they were a mile from Casey's Corner before she mentioned her nearly empty gas tank. "If we're going much farther, we need to stop for gas."

Colby leaned closer to look at the gauge. Tia suppressed a shudder.

He didn't respond to her comment. They approached the top of the rise, and she added, "There's a gas station up on the left."

"No, we'll wait until we get to the freeway." When Tia glanced in his direction, her eyes met his. "You know too many people around here. We don't want anyone to talk you out of taking that hike today."

Tia's throat constricted. Once they passed Cornville, the likelihood of anyone recognizing her diminished greatly. Stopping at Casey's Corner would have been perfect. It was right next door to the firehouse, right next door to people who might be able to help her escape.

She glanced at the small gas station and convenience store that many of the locals used for their basic grocery shopping. Her hope that someone would be outside, anyone who might notice her, was dashed in the twenty seconds it took for them to drive by. At this point, her only hope of getting away appeared to be if someone saw her car and remembered the direction she was heading. She hoped it didn't take long for the police to realize she was missing.

She looked at Colby again, his uniform perfectly pressed. Would her friends in the department make the connection that Colby was the person to fear?

They drove in silence for several more miles until they approached the highway entrance.

Colby nodded to the gas station on his right. "Pull in there."

She did so, instinctively scanning for some means of escape. If he let her out of the car, would she dare try to run away? All her self-defense classes had taught her to run, but those hadn't assumed a trained police officer was the person who would be shooting at her.

"Pull in there." Colby motioned for her to take the slot farthest from the gas station building.

Tia noticed the way the gun twitched in his hand. He was nervous, she suddenly realized. This trip, taking her hostage—none of it had been planned. But how could she use that knowledge to her advantage?

People driving by on the freeway primarily accessed this gas station, and the town of McGuireville wasn't much more than a dot on the map. In fact, she wasn't sure it even ranked its own dot.

No one was going to notice her here, at least not anyone who would sense something wasn't right. She would have to run. She didn't have a choice.

"Turn off the engine and give me your keys." As soon as she did, he tugged his hat down and grabbed her purse off the floor board. He dug through it until he found her wallet.

Tia fought the sense of invasion, staring as he selected one of her credit cards and handed it to her.

"Don't even think about running. If you do, I'm not going to waste a bullet on you. I'll shoot the gas pump and blow up the whole station." An SUV pulled up at the next row of pumps, two kids visible in the back seat, and a look of victory stole over Colby's expression. "Don't say anything to anyone. Don't do anything but put gas in the car. Understand?"

Tia swallowed hard and nodded.

"Roll down your window before you get out."

Tia cranked it halfway down, jiggling it when it got stuck.

"That's good enough." Colby motioned with the gun, keeping it low enough so the other customers couldn't see it. "Now top off the tank and keep your body facing me. Trying to flag someone down will get everyone at this station killed."

Tia moved slowly, climbing out of the car and shutting the door gently. She moved to the pump and slid her credit card into the slot to pay. At least someone would know she had been here. If they thought to look. Not wanting to open the car door and face Colby any sooner than necessary, she slid the credit card into the back pocket of her jeans and uncapped her gas tank.

Her eyes darted around again. Colby had her trapped, and he knew it.

She put the nozzle into the tank and began fueling at medium speed. Her vision caught on the box of window paints in the back of her truck. She had meant to return them to school after decorating for Homecoming but had never gotten around to it.

Shifting so her arm would be in Colby's blind spot, she reached in and grabbed a bottle of paint. One handed, she flipped open the top and aimed the tip at the pavement. Keeping her body as motionless as possible, she squirted paint onto the ground.

The gas pump shut off, indicating the tank was full. Rather than try to put the paint back in the truck, she dropped it to the ground when she replaced the nozzle.

Fighting every instinct within her, she forced herself to open the truck door and climb back inside. Colby handed her the keys, and she started the engine.

Slowly, she pulled away, leaving the bottle of paint on the ground and a message scrawled on the pavement.

* * *

Tia couldn't believe it when Colby instructed her to turn off at the Munds Park exit. What were they doing here? Did Colby know this was where she had been last weekend? Questions burned on her tongue, but she kept them to herself.

The fact that Charlie was living here entered her mind, but she knew he would have already left for work by now. She glanced at the general store without moving her head. Only one car sat in the lot, and Mrs. Burgess stood on the front porch, a broom in her hand.

Tia continued past, driving along the main road, the country club parking lot relatively empty this time of year. With temperatures cooling and summer over, they were the only car on the road.

"Turn left," Colby ordered.

Tia turned left. She followed his directions, confusion settling in. Every turn was familiar to her. Every street was one where she had been before.

When he instructed her to turn into the driveway of Julie's family cabin, she wasn't able to hold her silence any longer. "I don't understand. What are we doing here?"

"Julie said something last week about you staying here. That was nice of you to offer to close it down for the winter."

"How did you know . . . ?" Tia trailed off, realizing she had already said too much.

"I was standing outside her room when she gave you the instructions of what she needed you to do," Colby said. "I tried to come visit you here over the weekend, but you were never home."

Tia didn't respond. She parked at an angle, her side of the truck only a few feet from the steps leading to the front door.

Colby reached out and turned off the engine for her, pulling the keys from the ignition and pocketing them.

Tia kept her eyes trained forward. In her mind, she mapped out the woods by the cabin. The thick pine tree ten feet to her left, a cluster of three smaller pines a few yards beyond that. The cabin next door wasn't far. If she could make it past it, maybe she could hide. Maybe she could live.

Colby lifted his gun. He reached with his left hand and opened his door. He pushed it open, climbing out while keeping the gun trained on her. "Let's get settled in."

Tia reached for her purse, but Colby snatched it away as though he was afraid her ticket to freedom might be contained within. "I'll carry that for you."

Without a word, she reached for the door handle and pushed it open. Colby was already rounding the hood when she got out.

The moment Tia's feet hit the ground, it was like a starting whistle went off. She darted behind the closest tree and kept going.

She heard Colby's oath and something fall to the ground. Then all she could hear were footfalls coming much too fast, much too close.

A cry escaped her, her own feet pounding the ground, her heart racing in her chest, her pulse echoing in her head. Her sleeve caught on a low branch, but that didn't slow her.

Heavy breathing drew closer, and Tia let out another cry, again changing direction to put a tree between them.

Then she felt the hand on her back, the pressure of the contact knocking her off her feet. She flew forward onto the forest floor with a grunt, the weight of Colby falling with her and pinning her to the ground.

"That," he panted out, "was very stupid."

She tried to buck free, but he pinned her arms behind her back. Her shoulder twisted at an unnatural angle, and she yelped in pain.

Colby rolled off her and pulled her up by her wrists. "Come on." He hauled her toward the cabin, apparently unconcerned when her feet continued to stumble. He was practically dragging her by the time they returned to the truck.

Her purse lay at the bottom of the stairs, but he didn't concern himself with it or any of the contents that had spilled free.

Forcing her up the steps, he retrieved his handcuffs from his belt and slapped them on one of her wrists. He locked the other side around the porch railing, leaving her trapped beside the door.

"Where's the key?"

"I don't know," Tia lied.

Anger erupted on his face, and his hand struck out, connecting with her face. Pain exploded behind her eyes, a bruise instantly swelling along her cheekbone. She stumbled back two steps, her back crashing against the railing as specks of light flashed in front of her eyes.

"Where is the key?" Colby asked again, his words slow and deliberate.

She saw his hand raise again, and she instantly pointed to the flower-bed below. Keeping his eyes on her, he jogged down the steps and kicked at the rocks until he found the false one that contained the key.

He returned and opened the door before retrieving his handcuff keys. Grabbing her by her free arm, he unlocked the cuff from the railing and yanked her inside.

Before he bothered to close the door, he snapped the handcuff on the stair railing inside to hold her in place, then yanked off both of her shoes.

Tia could only stare helplessly when he closed the sliding glass door and slid the curtains into place.

Chapter 32

EVAN CHECKED THE AIRPORT DISPLAY for his connecting flight information. He had enjoyed Amsterdam when he had visited before, but today, all he wanted was to leave and get to his final destination. And he wanted to find Tia safe and sound when he got there.

After identifying the correct gate, he read the signs and started forward. He did a quick calculation of what time it was in Arizona and pulled out his phone. He tried Tia first, praying she would answer and prove this whole thing was a big misunderstanding. Maybe she really had gone out somewhere and had forgotten to take her phone. He wished he could believe that.

When his call went unanswered yet again, he dialed Charlie's number, hitting the button to FaceTime. A moment later, Charlie's face filled his screen.

"Where are you?" Charlie asked.

"Amsterdam. I go from here to Detroit before I catch my flight to Phoenix," Evan said. "Any word?"

"Nothing yet." The frustration and concern were evident in Charlie's voice. "Is there anyone she might have gone hiking with? Any other friend I should contact?"

"I haven't met many of her friends, but between Julie, her sister, and the Petersons, I think they would know of everyone she might go with."

"I followed up with all of them, and they have been calling friends and family to see if anyone has heard from her. Nothing yet."

"I should have called the police myself after the break-in," Evan said, kicking himself. "Tia was so freaked out from finding that cop standing in her bedroom that I didn't trust the police to protect her."

Charlie's eyes narrowed. "Wait. What happened?"

"Tia woke up, and this guy—Colby Farren—was standing in her bedroom. He said he saw someone breaking into her place, but something sounded fishy to me." Evan dragged a hand over his face. "I thought cops had to identify themselves before entering someone's home."

"They're supposed to unless they perceive doing so would put someone in imminent danger," Charlie said. "It's odd enough, though, that I'm going to check him out. You said he's a cop in Cottonwood?"

"Yeah. He moved there several months ago."

"From where?"

"Somewhere in Alaska."

"Wait. Could it be Valdez, Alaska?" Charlie asked.

"I'm not sure. Why?"

"I need to make a phone call," Charlie said. "How long until your next flight?"

"An hour and a half."

"Okay. I'll call you back." Charlie disconnected the call, and Evan stared at his phone for a full ten seconds before he slid it into his pocket. An instant later, it rang. He snatched it out, but it was his mom calling rather than Charlie. Seeing his mother's face on the video chat should have given him some comfort, but instead, he felt like a little boy hiding under his bed during a thunderstorm: helpless and afraid.

"Any word yet?" she asked.

Evan swallowed hard and fought back the tears burning in the back of his eyes. Not trusting himself to speak, he shook his head.

"You look exhausted. Have you gotten any sleep?"

Taking another second to regain his composure, he took a steadying breath. "Not really."

"I know you don't want to hear this right now, but you need to take care of yourself. You won't do Tia or anyone else any good if you don't."

"I know, Mom."

"Please make sure you eat something while you have the chance. I don't want you passing out from hunger when you get to Phoenix, and you don't want me to show up at the Detroit airport to force you to eat."

The image of his mother trying to make her way through security amused him. She would do it too, even if it meant buying a ticket to get past TSA. "Okay, I promise I'll go get something to eat right now."

"Do I need to stay on the phone to make sure you're telling me the truth?"

"Probably, but I'm actually waiting on another call. How about you trust me this time?" Evan noticed a deli on his right. "I found a sandwich shop right here. See?"

He switched the camera to the outside view to show her the menu.

"That will work." She nodded her approval. "And get one of those yummy cookies they have there in Amsterdam."

"Why? Did you want me to bring you one?"

"No, but you'll want one," she said. "Comfort food."

"I love you, Mom."

"Love you too. Let me know if there is anything we can do to help."

"I will." Evan hung up and got in line. He wasn't sure his stomach could handle food right now, but his mom was right. If he didn't eat something, he might pass out before he ever reached Phoenix.

He managed to eat the better part of his sandwich before Charlie called him back.

"Evan, I need to ask you something," Charlie said. "Does the name Lexi Dyer mean anything to you?"

"No, why?"

"The last call Tia made before she disappeared was to the police chief in Valdez," Charlie said. "She was trying to get in touch with Lexi."

"Is there any way we can talk to Lexi and find out why Tia was trying to talk to her?"

"I'm afraid not," Charlie said, his voice grave.

"Why?"

"Lexi Dyer is dead. She disappeared from Valdez, Alaska, around the same time Colby Farren left town. They found her body a few weeks ago."

Evan absorbed the news like a punch to the gut. His breath whooshed out before he managed to ask, "What are you saying?"

"I'm saying, I think I know who Tia is with. The police chief from Valdez called the police chief in Sedona. Apparently, the Valdez chief was concerned for her safety."

"What?"

"Tia never showed up." Sympathy and concern reflected in Charlie's face when he continued. "Not only that, Colby had told a jeweler in Valdez that he was engaged and that his fiancée was moving with him to Arizona. The police chief uncovered the story a couple hours ago after Tia called and said Colby mentioned being engaged to someone named Lexi. The police have been trying to piece together what happened to her ever since."

Evan grasped at whatever straws he could find. "How sure are you that Colby was involved in his ex-fiancée's death?"

"Evan, they were never engaged." Charlie's voice grew even more serious. "In fact, according to the girl's friends and family, they never dated."

"I don't understand. He invented their relationship?"

"We suspect he did more than that." Charlie let the implications sink in. "The time line is still vague, but there's one thing the police chief is certain of: the last time Lexi was seen alive was three days before Colby left town."

Chapter 33

THIS MIGHT WORK BETTER THAN Colby had planned. He read the instructions in the laundry room on how to open the cabin back up. With Tia secured to the stair railing, he set about turning on the water and electricity, opening the water line to the water heater, and bringing in firewood. His search of the cabin revealed there wasn't a landline phone.

When he discovered an oversized tarp on a shelf, he carried it outside to where Tia had parked. He took note of the suitcase and box of paints in the back of the truck. Deciding the suitcase might have some essentials Tia would need, he set it aside before draping the tarp over the vehicle.

He set the suitcase in the utility room where the washer and dryer were located and then assessed the rest of the cabin. The backyard sloped away from the house and was clear, except for a single mature pine tree spearing up through the center. The branches had been carefully trimmed to protect the house, the nearest one more than fifteen feet from the upstairs window.

He dug through the tool box in the utility room, selecting a screwdriver, a handful of two-inch screws, and an electric drill.

Tia was still tugging at her cuffed hand when he passed back into the living room, the motion causing the metal to gouge the wood.

"You're only going to make your wrist bleed," Colby said, moving past her and onto the stairs.

She stopped and looked up at him, determination on her face. She was going to fight back. What was she thinking? Didn't she understand her destiny?

He shook his head and continued upward. She would come around soon enough. They would both be so happy when she did.

Passing into the upstairs bedroom, he inspected the window from the inside. Because the cabin had a three-foot crawl space beneath it, as well as ten-foot ceilings inside, the distance from the window to the ground was at least fifteen feet. If Tia tried to jump out, she wouldn't get far. She'd be too crippled from a broken leg. Or worse.

Best not to take any chances. Colby put one of the screws above the portion of the window that would normally slide up. Using the drill, he screwed it into place, leaving it sticking out a half inch. He repeated the process on the other side.

Testing it, he tried to open the window. As expected, it went up only a half inch before running into the screws. Always cautious, he screwed in two more, these an inch above the first ones.

Satisfied, he repeated the process with the bathroom window. He riffled through the contents under the sink, removing the cleaning caddy and all its contents. Checking the drawers, he discovered a couple of new tooth-brushes, toothpaste, some disposable razors, a package of miniature paper cups, soap, shampoo, and conditioner. Maybe he wouldn't have to go out for supplies as soon as he'd thought he would.

He searched the rest of the room, finding nothing of interest except for extra linens and a pair of sweats in the closet.

Recognizing the bedding as a possible escape tool, Colby stripped the beds and piled all the sheets and blankets on the loft outside the bedroom door. Leaving only the pillows and the pair of sweats in the room, Colby proceeded to switch the doorknob around so it would lock from the outside. Pleased with his progress, he straightened and looked at the pile of linens in the corner. If the temperatures dropped tonight as much as they were supposed to, he suspected Tia was going to be much more cooperative by morning.

* * *

Evan passed through security, and Kyla was waiting for him. Immediately, his steps faltered. For the past fourteen hours, he had fought back the demons that had continued to plague him. News stories of car accidents, abductions, people lost in the wilderness. Every possible negative outcome to Tia's disappearance had needled into his mind, and he had used every ounce of energy to replace them with happy endings.

He continued to grasp for any explanation of where Tia could be, why she would have gone somewhere without her phone.

Kyla must have read his expression. She closed the distance between them. "No news so far."

"What are you doing here, then?"

"Picking you up." Kyla held up a set of car keys.

"You didn't have to do that. I have a car reserved," Evan said.

"It's silly for you to rent one when we have a spare," Kyla said. "I assume you can drive a stick shift."

"Yeah." He fell in step beside Kyla, worry gnawing endlessly. "How are you holding up?"

"Probably about the same as you." Kyla pressed her lips together, and her eyes watered. "She has to be okay."

"She will be," Evan said with confidence, praying his words were true. "Tia's smart, and she's strong. We'll find her."

Kyla fell silent for a moment. "I forgot to tell you my parents got here a few hours ago. They're staying with me too."

"I thought they would have gone up to Cottonwood."

"The police said they don't know where she is. At least if my folks stay with me, my kids can distract them a bit," Kyla said. "I'm sorry Tia isn't here to introduce you to them."

"Me too."

They reached the parking lot where an ancient Toyota Land Cruiser was parked. The gray paint was probably similar to the original color, and it had a winch attached to the front.

"How is it that you and your sister both drive classic cars?" Evan asked, grasping for some piece of conversation to distract him.

"Tia got Granddad's old truck. I got my dad's old hunting vehicle." She used the key to open the driver's side and reached across to unlock the passenger door. Evan lifted his suitcase over the front seat and set it in the back. After sliding into his seat, he set his computer bag on the floor by his feet. "You're welcome to stay at my house tonight, but either way, you can use the Toyota while you're here."

"Thanks."

"There's also a key on here for Tia's house. The guest room is the door on the left."

"You think of everything, don't you?"

"Not really." Kyla shrugged. "I didn't make banana bread today."

"You probably had a lot on your mind."

"Yeah, speaking of which, the FBI agent you've been talking to called and asked you to call him when you got here."

That was all the invitation Evan needed. As Kyla started the engine, he whipped his phone out and dialed Charlie's number even though it was nearly midnight.

"Evan, where are you?"

"Phoenix. Any news?"

"Some." Charlie hesitated long enough to make Evan brace for the bad variety. "There was a hit on her credit card at a gas station in McGuireville."

"Where's that?"

"It's a little town right off of I-17, not too far from Cottonwood."

"Did anyone see her there?"

"The security cameras at the gas pump caught a glimpse of her, but it was what she left behind that has us worried."

"What did she leave behind?"

"Right next to where she gassed up her truck, there was a message painted on the ground. It said 'SOS,' and she signed her first name. The bottle of paint was lying on the ground right next to it."

The nightmares bloomed in his mind full force. "Colby has her."

"That's our assumption," Charlie confirmed gravely. "The good news is that we know she's still alive."

"How do we find her?"

"We've put out an APB, and we've alerted the media. If they're still in her truck, there's a good chance someone will have seen them. The '46 Chevys aren't common, especially painted that bright red," Charlie said. "Do you know if Tia normally carries much cash with her?"

Evan thought for a moment. She had gotten some Euros out of an ATM machine when she'd visited him in Paris, but typically when she bought something, she used a card. "I don't think so. In fact, when I first met her, some of her students commented about the oddity of her having cash with her."

"From what I can tell from Colby's bank records, it doesn't look like he's carrying much cash with him either."

"What does that mean?" Evan asked.

"It means they won't be able to get far without leaving an electronic trace."

"What can I do to help?"

"At this point, there's not much you can do besides wait and pray."

"I'm not good at either of those, especially when I have to do them together," Evan said. "Look, I work with security systems for a living. I'm sure I can help somehow."

"What kind of security systems?"

"Mass transit surveillance, mostly."

"Where are you staying tonight?" Charlie asked.

"I haven't decided yet. Tia's sister offered to let me stay at her place, or I can go up to Cottonwood to stay at Tia's house."

"Stay in Phoenix tonight," Charlie suggested. "I want you to go into the FBI's Phoenix field office in the morning. I'd like you to brainstorm with one of our agents there on where to focus our search."

"I don't know how much help I'll be on that."

"You and Tia talk all the time. I bet you know more than you think you do."

"I hope so," Evan said.

"I'll talk to you tomorrow."

"Yeah. Tomorrow." Evan hung up and moved his computer bag. He would go talk to the FBI, all right, but he wanted to go well beyond brainstorming. It was time to put his computer skills to work.

Chapter 34

EVAN'S TIME WITH THE FBI left him with a knot in his stomach and a new dose of despair. No sighting of Tia or Colby. No electronic signatures to trace. Nothing.

Colby had apparently left his cell phone in his office at school, and the attempts by the Cottonwood Police Department to raise him on the radio had gone unanswered.

Though Kyla had offered to let Evan stay with her, he found himself driven to head north. For all he knew, Colby could have taken Tia out of the state by now, but he wanted to be where she should be, where their memories had been made.

His mind kept playing over the questions the FBI agent had asked him this morning. He drove up Interstate 17, the thought that Tia could have passed by here yesterday invading his thoughts, his eyes constantly scanning for her classic pickup.

He should have been here. None of this would have happened . . . He blinked hard and fought against that thought.

He reached Camp Verde and took the exit toward Cottonwood. It wasn't until he passed through the stoplight leading into town that inspiration struck.

He dialed Charlie's number.

Charlie didn't bother to greet him. "Sorry, Evan. Nothing new."

"I had an idea," Evan said. "I assume you have someone running through traffic camera images."

"Yeah, but those are only helpful if someone does something wrong."

"Not necessarily," Evan said. "There's a forty-eight-hour backup on the image feed."

"That's great, but we don't have the manpower to search through every camera in the entire state looking for them. At least not before the data recycles."

"I can create an image search and run it through the feed results," Evan said, a flutter of hope blooming in him. "If someone can get me a photo of Tia's truck, I can use that to see where they've been."

"Assuming they've been somewhere where there are traffic cameras. We don't have cameras this far north on the interstate."

"Yeah, but that pickup only gets about ten miles to the gallon. They'll have to fill up every hundred and fifty miles or so."

"Could you do the same search program for the security cameras at gas stations?"

"You get me access, and I'll make it happen."

"How soon can you meet me at the police station in Cottonwood?"

"I'll be there in twenty minutes."

"Ask for Chief Jarvis when you arrive. I'll let him know you're coming."

"Thanks, Charlie."

Evan hung up and increased his speed. It was time to find Tia and end this nightmare.

* * *

Tia huddled on the bed, four pillows layered on top of her. She had changed into the sweats Colby had left in the bedroom, but the warmer clothes hadn't been enough to battle the cold.

She had used the first several hours after Colby had locked her in the upstairs bedroom searching for anything she could use to escape. Colby had been annoyingly thorough when he'd cleaned out the room.

Her cheek throbbed, a reminder of her runaway attempt. What she wouldn't give for a Tylenol right now.

He had given her a sleeve of crackers as a means of nourishment. She had rationed them, not sure if and when he would feed her next. Fears and possibilities had invaded her thoughts through the night as she had paced her room. At least her movement had helped her keep warm during those first few hours after the sun had gone down. When exhaustion had taken over, she had tried the huddle method to battle the cold. The layer of pillows had combined with her body heat to warm her somewhat, but not enough for her to truly sleep.

Her door creaked open, and she forced her eyes closed. Maybe if he thought she was sleeping, he would go away.

Footsteps padded across the carpeted floor. A finger brushed across her cheek. She fought against a shudder.

"You are so beautiful."

Tia didn't open her eyes.

"I love you so much." The finger traced along her jaw before Colby tucked a lock of hair behind her ear. "I know you're awake. I have a fire downstairs. Come and warm up."

Tia debated briefly before opening her eyes. Anything to get out of the bedroom was worth it.

"That's better." He backed up slightly, giving her room to swing her legs over the bed. A pillow tumbled onto the floor.

She forced herself to stand, her legs trembling from lack of circulation. Colby took her by the arm, but this time, she didn't resist. She needed the warmth of the fire.

He escorted her downstairs, the two of them walking side by side so that Tia's shoulder brushed against the wall. A photo above the sixth step swung on contact, tilting to the left.

When they reached the first floor, she noticed a pile of her clothes on a chair in the corner. Her cheeks heated. She could have happily lived her entire life without Colby knowing that she owned bright-pink underwear.

Colby retrieved his handcuffs and locked her to the wooden arm of the couch. She reached with her free hand, retrieved the afghan from the back of the couch, and pulled it onto her legs and up over her shoulders.

"I did some laundry last night. You can put some of your clothes away when you go back upstairs."

"What about the rest of the stuff in my suitcase?"

"I'll make sure you have everything you need. There isn't a lot to eat here besides canned food," Colby said as though she had deliberately come here with him on holiday.

"I could make some pancakes," Tia suggested. "There should be some mix in one of the canisters in the pantry." If she could get him to release the handcuffs . . .

"Maybe tomorrow," Colby said noncommittally. "I heated up a can of soup." He moved to the kitchen and began dishing up their meal. She watched him put a spoon in each bowl and carry both toward her. "It's nothing fancy, but it'll have to do until I can go after some supplies."

Trapped for the moment, Tia accepted the bowl and let the heat warm her hands before eating the meal.

The thought that he might try to slip something into her food popped into her mind, but when she saw him eating his portion, she followed suit. Their food had come out of the same pot, and the truth was she was starving.

She wiggled her toes, the feeling seeping back into her limbs. Lifting the spoon to her lips, she glanced up at the clock: 9:00 a.m. Under normal circumstances, this is when she would be talking to Evan.

She swallowed her first bite. Somehow, someway, she was going to find a way to get back to him. Somehow, she would fight her way free.

Chapter 35

"WHAT DO YOU KNOW SO far?" Evan asked Chief Jarvis.

"Still no sign of Tia." Chief Jarvis ushered him through a squad bay and into his office.

"Have you found Colby?"

"Not yet." Evan heard the frustration in the older man's voice. "His car is in the lot here at the station, and his squad car is parked at the high school."

"No one at school knows where he is?"

"No. We went through the security footage yesterday. We saw someone leaving with Tia at 8:45, but we couldn't see his face. It was hidden by a big bouquet of roses. It looked like he was carrying them out to her car for her."

Evan's heart plummeted. "I sent her roses yesterday."

"I know," Chief Jarvis said. "The parking lot camera caught a glimpse of Tia on the edge of a frame a minute later. She appeared to be talking to another staff member."

"Who?"

"Gabrielle Sanchez. We questioned her, and she said Tia told her she was going hiking."

"That's why Charlie was asking me if I could think of anyone Tia might have gone hiking with."

"Yeah. Charlie insists that there's no way Tia would have gone hiking alone. I agree with him."

"So do I. For someone so independent, she's very security conscious."

Chief Jarvis paused before adding the next blow. "When Gabrielle saw Tia, the man with her was Colby Farren."

Evan struggled not to envision Tia alone with Colby, alone against her will. "I assume someone checked out his apartment."

"One of my men went by yesterday to make sure he wasn't there," Chief Jarvis said. "The search warrant came through an hour ago, and I have a couple of men there checking it out. I'd like for you to drive over with me to take a look as well."

"I thought you would want me to start working on the image search program."

"Colby only lives a few minutes away," Chief Jarvis said. "There were a couple of items in his place that seemed out of character for him. I want you to help us identify if any of them could have belonged to Tia."

His stomach curled, but he forced the words out. "Lead the way."

* * *

Tia's body trembled, a result of exhaustion rather than temperature. She stretched so her toes were peeking out from underneath the afghan. A hole had worn through her left sock from the constant pacing last night, the ball of her foot now exposed to the heat of the fire.

Feast or famine, she thought to herself. Last night, she had shivered for hours. Now, beads of sweat formed on her forehead from being too close to the fire. Under normal circumstances, she would have pushed the afghan aside, but she clung to it like a shield. Logically, she knew it wouldn't protect her from Colby, but at least it kept him from leering at her. She hated it when he stared.

Before she had seen the glimpse behind his mask, she had mistaken his attention toward her as a harmless attraction. How could she have been so wrong?

She poked her foot out a little farther and looked out the front window. At least Colby hadn't kept the curtains drawn today. Not that someone passing by would see anything out of place. The trees in the front yard secluded the cabin, shielding it from view, and she could see now that a tarp protected her pickup from the elements and from being seen.

Trying to appreciate her only contact with nature at the moment, she watched a squirrel collect an acorn from the ground and stuff it into its mouth. A blue jay called from high in the tree beside it.

Colby had gone into the kitchen to clean up their midday meal. Soup again. The odor lingered, competing with the scent of pine.

She reminded herself that she should be grateful for any food at this point. Things could be worse. Her gaze met Colby's, and she shuddered again. A lot worse.

The clang of metal sounded outside. The blue jay took flight. A burst of hope rose within her only to twine with fear when Colby rushed through the living room with his gun drawn. He held position inside the door for a moment before sliding the door open.

"Get out of here!" he yelled out. A moment later, Tia saw a raccoon scamper into view before disappearing into the trees. Her hope disappeared with it.

"Darn raccoon," Colby muttered when he came back inside. He holstered his gun and secured the door. A moment later, she heard the water running in the kitchen again.

With the fire dying and her feet exposed to the cooling air, exhaustion threatened to overtake her. Colby came back into the living room and sat in the recliner beside her. Feeling his gaze on her again, she closed her eyes. Despite the feeling of complete vulnerability, she forced her body to relax and willed herself to sleep.

* * *

Evan followed the chief into the one-bedroom apartment. The living room looked normal enough. A simple couch and chair facing a television screen hanging on the wall. A connector cable for a computer hung from the side.

"Evan, do you know Wesley?"

"Yeah. We met the last time I was in town," Evan said.

"Show me what you've got," Chief Jarvis said, snapping a pair of forensics gloves on his hands.

"We haven't found his computer yet, but look in here." Wesley started for the bedroom.

Evan braced himself before he followed, afraid he might find some huge collage of photos of Tia or a ridiculously large gun collection. When he entered the bedroom, he found little more than a neatly made bed and an alarm on the nightstand.

"It hardly even looks like anyone lives here."

"I thought the same thing, but check this out." Wesley opened the nightstand drawer to reveal a bottle of lotion. "This label is in French. I didn't take Colby for the type to use lotion, much less import it."

The sickening feeling in Evan's stomach increased. "Can I see that?"

Wesley lifted it from the drawer. "Don't touch it. We may need to lift fingerprints off it."

Evan swallowed hard. "My fingerprints are already on it. So are Tia's." He lifted his gaze to Wesley's. "I bought that for Tia in Paris."

"What's this?" The chief put his hand on Wesley's shoulder and nudged him to the side so he could get to the nightstand. He reached into the drawer and pulled something out. Evan absorbed another punch to his gut. Dangling from the chief's finger hung Tia's bracelet.

Evan struggled to find his voice. "That's Tia's too."

* * *

Tia walked up the stairs, Colby's grip firm on her arm as they made their way toward the cold, unheated upstairs room. When she had woken from her nap, the sun had already lowered in the sky. She had asked to use the restroom, hoping he would let her use the one downstairs, but instead, he was escorting her back upstairs.

Though she had several changes of clothes from her suitcase, he had let her take only one set with her to her room. She had a second pair of socks now, but that wasn't going to do much against the freezing temperatures that would plague her tonight.

She glanced at the pile of linens in the corner of the loft. "Can I at least have a blanket? It gets so cold up here."

He escorted her inside as though she hadn't spoken.

"Please, Colby."

He pushed her through the doorway and drew his gun. "Go into the bathroom."

Immediately, her heart started hammering. Faced with his weapon for the first time since yesterday, Tia did as he asked. She left the door open and watched him cross to the single bedroom window. After inspecting the screws locking the window closed, he backed out of the room. A moment later, she heard something flop onto the floor.

"Sleep well, Tia," Colby said.

Tia peeked through the bathroom door to see a blanket lying on the floor.

She held her ground, not sure what to expect. The door swung closed, and a moment later, she heard the flick of the lock.

Chapter 36

"ARE YOU SURE THIS PROGRAM of yours is working?" Chief Jarvis asked from where he sat beside Evan. "I thought we would have had some hits by now."

Evan wanted to say he was sure, but the lack of success made him waver. He had spent a good four hours adapting some of his existing programming to be compatible with the local camera feeds. "Only one way to find out. Can you give me another vehicle to search, one we're sure has been around the area in the last couple days?"

"Use mine," Charlie offered. He pulled up his phone. "I have a photo I sent my folks after I bought it last month."

"Perfect." Evan took Charlie's phone from him and loaded the image into his search. Two minutes later, search results started filling the screen. "Based on this, you were in Flagstaff two days ago and came to Cottonwood yesterday morning."

Charlie pointed to the screen. "You can use the hits to see exactly where I went while I was in town."

Chief Jarvis stood. "You aren't from around here, so you were on the main roads."

"True," Charlie said.

"Would Colby know the location of the cameras well enough to avoid them?" Evan asked.

"He was on patrol for the first six weeks after he arrived," Chief Jarvis said. "It's not impossible, especially since we have a lot of roundabouts along Highway 89A instead of traffic signals."

"We need to focus on gas station security feeds," Evan said.

"I'm still working on access, but you can run through what we have so far."

"Give me the access code, and we'll fire it up," Evan said, eager to contribute.

"I have to say, this sure shows us where our blind spots are," Chief Jarvis said.

Charlie and the chief looked at each other, a silent message passing between them.

Evan looked at the other two men, trying to read between the lines. "What?"

"Blind spots," Charlie said. "That's where we need to concentrate our search."

"Still a lot of ground to cover," Chief Jarvis said.

"Yes, it is."

* * *

Colby checked Tia's bedroom door one more time before he walked into the crisp night air. He shivered. Tia was right. Tonight was going to be a cold one. He'd never really thought about Arizona having chilly temperatures. Of course, compared to Alaska, this was summertime.

He'd have to keep her fair disposition in mind when he chose their next home. Someplace where they could have their privacy with moderate temperatures. In a country this size, surely they would have plenty of options. He only wished he had his computer with him so he could search the possibilities.

He walked out to the road and looked to his right and then to his left. Darkness everywhere. He'd been right. This was the perfect place to come.

Changing direction, Colby walked toward the back of the house. The light from Tia's room glowed through the window. He stopped at the base of the pine tree in the center of the yard.

A shadow passed in front of the window, and Colby couldn't help but wonder if she was standing there looking at him. Did she sense his presence as she had that night in her room? Was she so in tune with him that she could anticipate his movements? Would she someday be able to expand that connection to sense his dreams of the life they would build together?

A howl sounded in the distance. A wolf or a coyote—he couldn't tell.

Tia moved in front of the window again, remaining there for several long minutes. Colby stood in the shadows, entranced.

When she moved out of view and the light flicked off, a stab of disappointment shot through him. She was so close, and yet he yearned for so much more.

"Someday," he whispered to himself. "Someday soon."

* * *

Evan stared at the blank screen. "I don't know why it's not working."

"Your search returned the hit for the gas station in McGuireville," Chief Jarvis said.

"Maybe the image search isn't picking anything else up because the cameras are seeing the truck from different angles," Charlie suggested. "Kind of like how facial recognition software needs a head-on shot to be effective."

"I put in images from every angle. The ones I didn't have from the photos at Tia's house, I pulled off the internet for other cars of the same make and model and used the computer to change the color to match Tia's."

"Maybe we're going about this all wrong," Charlie said. "We've been assuming that Colby would take Tia and try to stay ahead of the search. Since we're pretty sure he's the one who sent the text message to her principal asking for another day off, he should have had a good head start."

"Right," Evan said. "Had it not been for our regular phone calls, she could have been gone a day or more before anyone knew for sure she was missing."

"What if he's doing the opposite and holding her somewhere nearby?"

"Someone would have seen her truck by now," Chief Jarvis said. "And staying in town would be risky. Tia grew up here, and most residents at least know who she is."

"Then someplace away from Cottonwood but close enough that he could hide out without drawing attention to them."

Evan clued into his thought process. "You're saying that the reason I haven't found another hit on the gas stations is because there isn't one."

"Exactly," Charlie said.

"Which means our search area is limited to the distance they could get on a single tank of gas."

"Chief Jarvis, it's time to coordinate with the other local police departments," Charlie said. "We need to assume she is within a hundred-and-fifty-mile radius."

"We talked about focusing on blind spots," Evan said. "How do we narrow it down further?"

"We know they left the high school and made their way to McGuireville," Charlie said. "With a tankful of gas, they could have made it past Flagstaff or all the way down to Phoenix, but we know he avoided the cities because they weren't on traffic cameras."

"So we need to search for exits that don't have traffic cameras," Evan said.

"Even if we narrow it down to the I-17 corridor where they aren't present, there are still a lot of possibilities."

"Focus on the area to the north," Chief Jarvis said.

"Why north?"

"Because Colby drove here from Alaska," Chief Jarvis said. "I don't think he's even been to Phoenix yet."

"I agree. He came up to Flagstaff when Tia was there for a week during the summer. He might have become familiar with some of those exits if he had to stop for gas."

"I'm going to call in the search helicopters. I think we have a good enough idea of where they should target to help us narrow the search field. Someone has got to be able to spot that pickup."

* * *

Evan didn't know how many hours had passed since his call to Tia had gone unanswered. He crossed the squad room to the water cooler and poured himself a cup. The helicopters had called off their search for the night and would begin again at first light. Evan wondered how long they would keep up their efforts. He also wondered if this nightmare would ever end.

Chief Jarvis moved beside him and put a hand on his shoulder. "Go home, Evan. There's nothing more you can do tonight."

Evan opened his mouth to protest but closed it again. After nearly two days of worrying, almost half of that spent on planes, trains, and in cars, he didn't have the energy to argue. "I'll be back in the morning."

"Do I need to have someone drive you where you're going? You're dead on your feet."

"I'm staying at Tia's house. It's not far."

"I'll let the Petersons know you're coming. Bob has gotten extra protective of Tia since Colby was in her house."

"Thanks." Evan gulped down his water and tossed the cup in the trash. "You'll call me if you hear anything?"

"Yeah. I have your number."

With a nod, Evan left the room and fumbled with the borrowed car keys. He managed to drive the short distance to Tia's. He parked along the road and stared at the charming brick house for a moment before pushing himself into motion.

He grabbed his suitcase and passed through the wrought-iron gate as he walked along the brick front walk. The old-fashioned key for her front door had enchanted him the first time she had explained how to lock the door from the inside. Now it made him yearn for her to be beside him.

He pushed the door open and stepped inside. The sensation of being in Tia's home without her nearly undid him. The scent of her lingered in the air, that essence that was uniquely hers mixed with strawberries and vanilla.

Locking the door behind him, he pulled his suitcase through the living room and into the guest room. His emotions were in turmoil, and he wandered through the house and his memories for the better part of an hour, stopping to stare at where they had snuggled together on the couch for her birthday, lingering in the kitchen as he thought of his first visit. He could almost smell the pancakes and chocolate chips.

A bottle of the lotion she had discovered in Paris stood on the kitchen counter. A pair of old sneakers lay inside the back door.

Knowing he needed sleep, he headed back into the guest room and collapsed on the bed. The thought surfaced that he should change into something more comfortable, but he gave into the urge to close his eyes. Eight hours later, he awoke still fully dressed, his shoes lying on the floor.

For a moment, he struggled to remember where he was. When the events of the past few days came flooding back, he bolted up to sit on the side of the bed. Too wired to feel any lingering exhaustion, he pushed himself to a stand.

After showering and changing, Evan loaded his suitcase back into the borrowed Land Cruiser. He assumed he would return to Tia's house tonight, but he wanted to be prepared for anything, including going to pick her up from this nightmare she had fallen into.

Chapter 37

FOR TWO DAYS, COLBY HAD watched the road for cars coming and going. None came or went. Not once since he and Tia had arrived.

When he had heard Julie talking about this cabin, the thought had bloomed that it might be a nice place for him and Tia to get away. He hadn't appreciated how secluded it would be. They could stay here for weeks, months even, and never be seen. To make that happen, he needed supplies.

He paced by the wide bank of windows along the front of the cabin, considering his options. Tia hadn't complained about the simplicity of their morning meal. That was good. He didn't want to be with a woman who was so picky she made things difficult.

If only he could trust her. That would come in time, he assured himself.

After letting her eat and warm up, she had asked to be uncuffed to go to the bathroom. Not willing to have her look for anything she could use to leave, he had escorted her back to her room and locked her in. With this time apart, he decided it was a good opportunity to reassess their situation.

He still wore his police uniform and was irritated that he didn't have something else to change into. While there had been a few items of clothing in the closets, all of them had been women's clothes. The canned goods also weren't as extensive as he would have liked.

His research into this area had revealed that most of these cabins were vacation homes, primarily used during the summer months. With that in mind, he straightened his uniform and headed for the door. Time to do some shopping.

* * *

Tia had mentioned playing on the police department's softball team, but until today, Evan hadn't understood how close she was to the men she called her teammates. Their concern was palpable, their frustration every bit as visible as his own.

Wesley had made a spot for him at the desk beside him in the police squad room. On the other side of him, Raul sat at another desk, his fingers tapping on his computer. Apparently, his injuries weren't going to keep him from helping in the search.

An old-fashioned bulletin board stood on an easel a short distance away, photos tacked to it. A rolling white board contained the time line, beginning with Tia's exit from the school. The only other dot on it was her stop at the gas station forty minutes later.

The flow of officers coming and going continued, but the only added clues today had been the discovery of Colby's cell phone in his office at school and the lack of hits appearing on Evan's image search. If only he could get his hands on Colby's computer, maybe he would be able to find a more concrete clue.

"Come on, guys. Give me something." Chief Jarvis threw down the folder he'd held on Wesley's desk. "Colby's new to the area. We've got to be able to have something. GPS data from his phone or car. Spending patterns. Something that will give us a clue as to where he might be hiding out."

"His car is in the impound lot, but it wasn't GPS enabled," Wesley said. "We're still piecing together his routes for the various police cars he used before he took over for Raul."

"Any patterns?" Chief Jarvis asked.

"Yeah. He went by Tia's house at least twice a day. By the looks of it, I'd guess he was trying to see her when she was going to and from work."

"I can't believe none of us saw this."

From his spot by the bulletin board, Charlie said, "You saw what you were supposed to see." He lifted the file he held in his hand. "His psych evals were clean both here and in Alaska."

"I don't understand how that's possible," Evan said.

"Sociopaths can make themselves believe whatever truth they invent," Charlie said. "Some go through their whole lives and are able to adjust, mimicking feelings and succeeding in all aspects of society."

"And some break," Wesley said.

Chief Jarvis looked at Charlie. "Any word from our search helicopters?"

"Nothing yet," Charlie said.

As Charlie and Chief Jarvis discussed possible areas to focus on next, Raul shifted his chair so he was facing Evan. "I've been thinking. Maybe we should try your image search using Tia's and Colby's image. It's possible they could have walked into a gas station and bought gas using a gas can."

"That would make sense. Colby would know you guys would put out an alert looking for Tia's truck as soon as everyone realized she was missing."

"I can pull up Colby's picture from his file. Do you have any of Tia?"

"Yeah. I'll load them into the search." Evan scanned through some of his photos of Tia in Paris, selecting several so as to include her profile as well as a direct view of her face.

He loaded them in, his fingers slowing. Turning to Raul, he said, "Someone said Colby's cell phone was at the school."

"That's right."

"Do you know if he had any photos of Tia on it?"

"Let me check with our forensics guy." Raul picked up the phone and made a call. A moment later, he hung up and shook his head. "The phone didn't have anything in it. In fact, he didn't have any pictures at all."

"Doesn't that strike you as odd?" Evan asked. "I know my understanding of stalkers is limited to what I've seen on TV, but I expected to walk into his apartment and see her image everywhere. Instead, he only had two items he must have taken from her."

"I'll admit, that is odd." Raul looked past him, his eyes focusing on the bulletin board. He reached for his cane and pushed himself to a stand. Hobbling forward, he moved closer, fixating on one picture. "He doesn't have his laptop with him."

"What?" Evan asked.

"Someone mentioned that a computer wasn't found, but there was evidence that he owned one."

"Yeah. He had an HDMI cord hanging from the flat screen on his wall."

"Then where is the computer?" Raul asked.

Wesley perked up and inserted himself into the conversation. "We searched his apartment and his cruiser and didn't find it."

"What about his office?" Evan asked.

"Nothing there either." Wesley stood. "I'm going over to his apartment to look again."

"Do you mind if I come with you?" Evan asked.

"No problem."

Evan turned to Raul. "Can you keep an eye on the image search?"

"Yeah. I'll load Colby's picture in and let you know if anything pops up."

"Thanks." Evan pushed to a stand.

Wesley started for the door. "Let's go."

* * *

Tia stepped out of the shower, hesitant to leave the warmth the steam created. She didn't think it was possible to be even colder last night than she had been the night before, especially with the extra clothing Colby had given her, but she had barely slept. And she had shivered incessantly.

The clean clothes she had brought with her upstairs last night hung over the towel bar, along with a hand towel. She grabbed the miniature towel and dried off as quickly as she could. As soon as she was dressed, she used the towel to work the excess moisture from her hair.

When she walked out of the bathroom, she heard something outside and saw Colby cross the yard toward the next-door neighbor's cabin. What was he doing? Deciding his actions didn't matter, she moved closer to the window and used her fingers to try to turn the screws Colby had put in the frame. They didn't budge.

She moved to the door and jiggled the knob. Had she really expected it to be unlocked?

Certain there had to be something she could use to break through the barrier of the door, she checked the closet, as she had the day before. Still empty. Under the beds. Nothing. Why had she and Julie done such a good job of cleaning the last time they had stayed here? Normally, there would at least be a stray bobby pin somewhere.

Moving into the bathroom, she pulled the drawers out of the vanity in the hopes that something might be hidden within. Again, no luck.

She opened the cabinet and peered under the sink. A flimsy piece of metal was clamped around the pipe. Thinking it might slide between the door jamb and the door, she tugged at it to find it firmly caught. Determined, she angled her body so she could get a better look. Identifying the screws holding it in place, she worked at the first one, rubbing her fingers raw.

Afraid Colby would notice if her fingertips started bleeding, she went to the closet, where she had stored the clothes she had been wearing when she'd arrived two days ago. Two days. She could hardly believe that was possible. Part of her barely remembered what it was like to come and go as she pleased. Had the past forty-eight hours multiplied somehow?

Grabbing the T-shirt hanging in the closet, she sat in front of the bathroom cabinet again and used the fabric to pad her fingers. She managed to get the first screw loose and set to work on the second one. Taking breaks and switching between both hands, fifteen minutes later, she finally worked it loose and managed to pull the thin metal strip free.

Quickly, she checked the window. The raccoon was back, scuttling along the back of the cabin toward the garbage cans, but Colby wasn't anywhere in sight.

Eager to take advantage of her time alone, she hurried to the door. She tried to slide the metal between the door and doorjamb, and her heart sank. The strip was a fraction of an inch too thick. She tried again, this time pressing the rounded edge right below the section where the doorknob was. Again, the metal caught, refusing to budge.

Wondering if she could gouge the wood along the door jamb to inch her way toward freedom, she pressed the edge against the doorjamb again. The aluminum immediately bent beneath the pressure, leaving the door and doorjamb undamaged.

"Great," she muttered under her breath.

She heard movement outside and crossed to peer out the window.

Colby was back, two large garbage bags in one hand and some smaller grocery bags in his other. Had he gone shopping? She estimated he had been gone for at least an hour. Maybe two. She supposed it was possible he had walked to the general store. It would make sense, actually, so her truck wouldn't be seen by anyone. Too bad. Mrs. Burgess might have noticed her truck and helped the police narrow their search area. Assuming they were actually searching for her.

Doubts crowded her mind, and her sense of dread returned when she heard footsteps on the stairs. Quietly, she moved back into the bathroom and closed the cabinet under the sink. She returned to the bedroom and slipped the piece of aluminum under the bunk bed closest to her an instant before the door swung open.

* * *

Evan tugged at the edge of the latex gloves on his hands. Wesley had insisted he wear them so he could help in the search without compromising evidence.

With the idea that the computer might be deliberately concealed, Wesley had gone to extremes in his search, pulling out all the drawers in the dresser, searching through every box, piece of clothing, and even feeling along floorboards, looking for hidden compartments.

Evan had been tasked with looking behind the few pieces of artwork on the wall in case a safe had been hidden. Nothing. The single bookshelf contained only a handful of hunting magazines and a softball mitt.

Evan searched through the end table drawer to find the television remote. This guy certainly was a minimalist.

Wesley came into the living room. "Anything?"

"No."

"Let's try the kitchen," Wesley suggested.

"That would be a random place to keep a computer."

"If he went to the effort to hide it, he would go for unexpected." Wesley opened the pantry door and pulled down two cereal boxes.

Evan opened the cabinets above the refrigerator but found them completely empty. Continuing to the other cabinets, he found pots and pans that appeared to be well used. Cups, plates, bowls, four of each, that looked brand new. A kettle, blackened on the bottom, rested on the stove.

He straightened and looked around the room. If he wanted to hide a laptop, where would he put it? His eyes lowered, and he opened the oven. Nothing. Squatting down, he pulled open the drawer beneath the oven.

Two cookie sheets sat on top of the pile. A burst of hope bubbled, and he pulled the cookie sheets out only to find a broiler pan underneath.

"I've got nothing over here," Wesley said, shoving a pasta box back into place.

"Me neither." Evan dropped the cookie sheets back into the drawer with a clatter. He straightened and started to close the drawer.

A smooth black surface caught his eye, and he opened the drawer wide again. He lifted the cookie sheets again and set them on the floor. Then he pushed aside the top of the broiler pan. Tucked in the hollow portion was a slim laptop.

Anticipation shot through him. Evan lifted it from the pan. "Found it."

* * *

Colby's visit to three more houses on the block had given him more supplies than he had hoped for, enough that they would be able to live here for months without leaving the cabin. Apparently, he and Tia were staying.

The cabin two doors down had an ample supply of firewood, but Colby didn't see any point of hauling it over here prematurely. He could go get it as he needed it throughout the fall and winter months.

When it came time to move on in the spring, the search for Tia would be long over, and they would be free to find somewhere to begin their new life together.

He changed out of his uniform, hanging it neatly in the closet. His search yesterday hadn't uncovered any clothes that would fit him, but today, he had hit the jackpot. The house six doors down contained clothes in nearly every bedroom. Based on the decor, Colby suspected the family included a couple of teenage boys. Luckily, between the master bedroom and the boys' room, he had found clothing to last him the better part of the week before he would have to do laundry.

He would need to tamper with the electric and water meters at his cabin to make sure the owners didn't notice a spike during the winter months. That would be easy enough. He'd done the same thing at his home in Alaska when money had gotten tight.

After he changed and finished hanging up his new wardrobe, he moved into the kitchen and set about putting away groceries. He didn't know who lived next door, but he commended them for being prepared. Five-gallon buckets of powdered milk, flour, sugar, and dehydrated eggs. Cases of canned chicken and roast beef. Soups, canned milk, vegetables, and fruits. The spices had been limited to a few essentials, but they'd had everything Colby would need to fix meals for months.

He wondered how long it would take for Tia to accept their new relationship. He'd much prefer to let her do the cooking. After all, women were much more suited to work in the kitchen than men.

He could wait, he told himself. Tia was worth the wait.

* * *

"We found it," Evan announced when they entered the squad room.

Wesley followed behind him, holding the sealed evidence bag containing the laptop.

"Dust it for prints and then have Raul run forensics on it," Chief Jarvis ordered.

Wesley continued through the room.

Evan crossed to Raul. "Any hits on the facial images?"

"Nothing except the one in McGuireville, and that was only Tia," Raul said. "It looks like Colby never got out of the car."

"I'm surprised she didn't try to run," Evan said.

"He was on duty when he took off, so I have to think he was armed. She must not have felt like she could make a clean break."

"I really hate this."

"Don't we all." Raul pointed at a table on the far side of the room. "Someone sent in some food for us. You should eat something."

"I'm not hungry."

"Eat anyway," Raul said. "It will be a few minutes before Wesley brings the laptop back. I thought we could work on it together."

"Okay. You win." Evan glanced at Raul's desk; it was void of any food wrappers. "Can I bring you something too?"

"Sure. Thanks."

Evan was throwing away their trash when Wesley returned a few minutes later. He put the laptop on Raul's desk. Immediately, Raul powered it on.

The screen came on, indicating a password was required.

"Can you bypass the security screen?" Evan asked.

Raul tried but was redirected to a second security screen. He looked up at Evan. "I never would have taken Colby for a computer geek."

"I never thought he was a stalker either," Wesley countered. "He's full of surprises."

"Any idea what he might have used for a password?" Raul asked.

"I'll check his desk," Wesley said. "Maybe he has it written down."

Evan waited until Wesley was out of earshot before he muttered, "I doubt it."

"Me too."

Sure enough, Wesley returned a moment later, unsuccessful.

Evan's phone vibrated, indicating a new email. He pulled it out of his pocket, not sure he could deal with anything in the real world right now. The thought that he should put an autoreply on his work email prompted him to type in his passcode to avoid the distraction of work for the next few days. His fingers froze.

Evan shifted closer to Raul. "Let me try something."

Raul rolled a few inches to his left to give Evan access to the computer. Evan typed in a string of numbers. Wrong password. He tried again, this time increasing the numbers by two. Immediately, the screen opened, and hundreds of images of Tia stared back at them.

"Oh wow," Wesley said.

Raul looked at Evan. "How did you do that? How did you know his password?"

"It's almost the same as mine," Evan said, his eyes somber. "Tia's birthday."

* * *

Dressed in Levi's and a crew-neck sweater, Colby looked approachable. Normal even. He had let Tia come downstairs again, her hand cuffed to the couch as it had been the last time. She had opted to sit on the far side of the couch this time to allow her to comfortably tuck herself under the afghan without getting overheated.

She grasped at how things had been with Colby before, the months she had considered him a friend. Trying for some semblance of normal, she asked, "Did you always live in Valdez before you moved here?"

He looked up, surprise illuminated on his face. He studied her for a moment as though searching for a hidden trap in the question.

"I lived in Anchorage for a while before I moved to Valdez."

"I didn't know that. What did you do there? Did you go to school?"

"No. I worked for a hospital."

Tia hadn't expected that answer. Trust. Tia reminded herself that his trust might be the only thing that would let her regain her freedom. Stepping on those thin threads of their previous friendship, she asked, "What did you do at the hospital?"

"Maintenance mostly."

"What about your family? What do they do?"

Colby stood and headed for the kitchen. "I'd better start on dinner."

Tia watched him open the pantry, her jaw dropping when she saw the contents. Cans lined every shelf, with more stacked on the floor. Even the shelving unit that hung over the inside of the door was completely full.

"Where did you get all that food?"

"Some of the neighbors were nice enough to share," Colby said. His tone made it sound like the neighbors had invited him over and simply handed him their excess. From what she could see, he had cleaned out the entire street.

A heaviness pressed down on her chest. Their limited supplies had made her hopeful that Colby would have to go out shopping. With only one store in town, the police would certainly talk to Mrs. Burgess if they continued their search in this area.

Realizing she would have to come up with a new plan, she said, "It's been hard being inside all day without the chance to work out. Can we go for a walk before dinner?"

"Not tonight."

Tia opened her mouth to press and instantly shut it again. He hadn't said no completely. *Not tonight* could mean maybe tomorrow. And maybe tomorrow could mean she would have several hours to come up with a plan. She tugged her hand toward her, the chain of the handcuffs drawing tight. It was time to find something that would let her pick his lock.

* * *

Evan and Wesley scanned through Colby's photos in search of any clues that might reveal where Colby had taken Tia. Raul had copied all the images onto flash drives for them before starting his own analysis on recent internet searches.

"Unbelievable." Raul tapped a few keys before turning to face them. "You aren't going to believe this."

Chief Jarvis approached from where he had been standing a few desks away. "Did you find something?"

"Unfortunately, nothing that tells me where Colby is now, but I think I found out why there's a discrepancy between the maintenance logs on my squad car and the forensics report."

"What?" Chief Jarvis asked.

"Take a look." Raul motioned to the screen of Colby's laptop. "Colby was researching causes of car accidents."

Evan rolled his chair closer to see the image of how to properly change brake lines. "I don't understand."

"I think I do," Chief Jarvis said. "After Raul's car accident, I put Colby in charge of securing his vehicle. The maintenance guys insisted the brakes were replaced six months earlier, but the forensics report came back that the accident was a case of worn brakes. Not only that, Colby looked through all the high school surveillance video. I think he didn't find anything because he was the guilty party."

"You think Colby cut the lines?" Wesley asked. "Why would he do that?"

"To be closer to Tia," Evan said, his stomach curling. "Raul worked at the high school and saw Tia every day."

"Exactly," Chief Jarvis agreed. "He volunteered to take over for Raul. I never suspected a thing."

"How could you?" Raul asked. "He fooled all of us."

"I don't know about the rest of you, but I'm tired of feeling like a fool," Chief Jarvis said. "Let me know if you find anything else."

Raul answered for all of them. "We will."

* * *

Colby heard the rumble of a distant helicopter. He looked over at Tia where she was cuffed to the couch. It was fortunate she was where he could see her. She still had enough fire in her to try to draw the pilot's attention, but here with him watching her, there was no chance of that. Not that anyone would be able to see through the thick trees surrounding the cabin. With the truck covered with a tarp, nothing was going to draw anyone's attention.

The sound grew closer, and Tia looked upward, apparently now recognizing the source. She glanced at him briefly before training her gaze on the window. Colby stared at her. Why couldn't she understand that they belonged together? Only minutes earlier, she had been acting like the person he had fallen in love with, the woman who was beautiful outside as well as inside. Finally, she had been talking to him again, looking at him with interest again.

The helicopter had squashed their progress in an instant.

Irritated on principle, he moved to the window and watched the evening sunlight dappling through the pines. Though he couldn't see the aircraft overhead, he heard it circle and move on.

Satisfied that the authorities had cleared the area off their search grid, he rolled his shoulders and felt the tension fall away. He hadn't realized how much he had worried about what would happen when someone learned Tia was missing. Now that they had overcome this hurdle, their future was his.

He cast his gaze on Tia and saw the light of hope in her eyes dim to be replaced by tears. She fought against them, immediately casting her gaze to the floor.

Colby sat beside her and reached out to take her chin in his hand. She pulled back, and he instinctively tightened his grip to hold her in place. The despair in her eyes spurred him on. Finally, she understood there was nowhere for her to be but here.

He lifted his free hand and trailed a finger along her jaw, over her lips. She swallowed hard. He saw the awareness come over her, along with the fear. It was the fear that fed him, empowered him.

Trailing his finger down the side of her neck, he let his hand caress her shoulder. Soon, very soon, the fear and despair inside her would turn to surrender.

Chapter 38

Tɪᴀ ʟɪꜱᴛᴇɴᴇᴅ ꜰᴏʀ ꜰᴏᴏᴛꜱᴛᴇᴘꜱ, ᴅʀᴇᴀᴅɪɴɢ the moment Colby would come upstairs to get her. She had seen the change come over him last night, and it frightened her.

She closed her eyes and thought of Evan. She couldn't give up.

A cramp knotted in the arch of her foot, and she reached down to work it out. Her legs trembled. She didn't think she could survive another night like the last one.

Apparently, the presence of the helicopter yesterday had spooked Colby enough that he had cut the power, probably to make sure there weren't any lights visible after dark. She suspected he had also forgone the fire, because she was absolutely freezing.

Dressed in a pair of yoga pants, a T-shirt, and a pair of sweats over the top of both had barely taken the edge off. She had spent the night alternating between jogging in place to keep her blood flowing and diving beneath the layers of pillows. Trying to create an insulation effect, she had topped the pillows with the few pieces of extra clothing she had in her room and the single blanket Colby had allowed her.

The clatter of a metal garbage can lid hitting the ground sounded at the side of the house. The raccoon was back. She heard Colby go outside to chase it off yet again. With the vacation rentals sparse this time of year, the raccoon had chosen to visit them daily. Yesterday, they had been graced with two visits by the furry critter.

While Colby was outside, Tia climbed out of bed and retrieved the aluminum metal strip from beneath her mattress and studied her door again. If she couldn't get it unlocked, maybe she needed to go at this problem backward. She dropped to her knees and tried to loosen the metal pin in the bottom door hinge. The aluminum strip bent beneath the pressure.

She blew out a frustrated breath, a sense of urgency flooding through her. She had to get away. She couldn't wait any longer.

As she had the day before, she tried again to wedge the metal into the narrow space between the doorknob and the doorjamb. Impossible. How come people on television and in the movies could pick a lock in ten seconds flat, yet she had been here for three days and the only escape she had managed had given her a bruised cheek and a chafed wrist?

The sound of the door sliding into place sounded, and a few minutes later, the scent of chili wafted up the stairs. Her stomach curled. The thought of being in the same room with Colby after the way he'd acted last night made her skin crawl. It had taken every ounce of willpower to keep from screaming when he'd touched her. She shuddered at the memory.

Expecting he would come upstairs soon, she replaced the metal strip beneath her mattress and began gathering her clothes that had scattered onto the floor. The T-shirt and jeans she had been wearing at school when this whole nightmare had begun were in desperate need of laundering, but she was afraid to bring that subject up for fear that Colby wouldn't let her replace them.

She scooped them up, grabbing the jeans by the leg. Something fell free of the pocket, and she stared. Her credit card.

Her memory flashed—that moment when she had gassed up in McGuireville. She had automatically stuck her credit card in her back pocket, and Colby hadn't asked for it back. In her moment of terror, she had completely forgotten it was there.

Tossing the dirty clothes in the closet, she snatched the credit card off the floor and approached the door. Lifting her eyes heavenward, she let out a silent prayer. Then in a move that would make MacGyver proud, she slid the credit card between the doorknob and the doorjamb. Hope soared when after only a few seconds of jiggling it, the latch released and the door opened.

She let out a shuddering breath. Now what?

The sound of Colby working in the kitchen sent panic through her. If she tried to run again, he would catch her. She had to get away when she could get a good enough head start.

She pulled the door open far enough to lock the door again, and then quietly closed it, locking herself inside once more. The credit card still in hand, she crossed the room to hide it under her mattress but thought better of it. What if Colby decided to search her room?

His feet sounded on the stairs. Tia reached behind her and slipped the credit card into the hidden pocket in the back of her yoga pants. With the pair of sweats on over them, Colby wouldn't be able to see the presence of the key she had been searching for.

She dropped onto the mattress a moment before the door pushed open.

Colby stared at her for a long moment, his expression unreadable. His lips pressed together for a brief second before he said, "It's time for breakfast."

Tia stood and walked toward him, her legs trembling once again.

* * *

Evan couldn't take this anymore. Three days and no sign of Tia.

Worry had gnawed at his stomach until he was sure there wasn't a lining left. He ate what others put in front of him, slept when the police chief sent him home each night, and searched every other moment in his day. Every night before he went to bed, he checked in with Tia's family to find they, too, were clinging to hope while battling against their worst fears.

The helicopters had yet to find any sign of Tia or her truck, and Evan suspected they didn't have much time before the authorities decided to call off the air search. He also worried that the police were going to realize very soon that he wasn't one of them and decide to send him home for good. He couldn't let that happen.

He parked beside the police station, arriving a moment ahead of Charlie Whitmore. Charlie climbed out of his SUV and crossed to him.

"How are you holding up?" Charlie asked.

"I'll answer that after this is all over."

Charlie put a hand on his shoulder. "Believe it or not, I understand completely."

"I assume we don't have anything new from the searches."

"Yes and no." Charlie started toward the station. "Come on. Today we're going to put together a puzzle."

Evan followed him inside, and within minutes, Charlie had posted a huge terrain map of the region on the wall in the briefing room. The chief waited for everyone to take their seats before moving to the front of the room with Charlie. "Okay, Charlie. Explain to everyone what you have in mind."

"We have identified all the exits off of Interstate 17 where a car could get off without passing through a traffic camera." Charlie pointed at the areas highlighted in blue. "With the helicopters coming up empty, I believe we need to focus our search in wooded areas."

"That narrows it down a lot," Chief Jarvis said.

"What if they never got on the highway?" Wesley asked. "Those roads around Lake Montezuma have a lot of territory to hide without any stoplights."

"Which is why that's one of our primary target search areas," Charlie said. "What I'm hoping you can help us with is identifying which areas Colby would be familiar enough with to know how to stay out of sight."

"Then you can scratch everyplace around Phoenix," Wesley said. "Colby hates the heat, and I don't think he's ever made it past Camp Verde, much less that far south."

"Most of that area south of Cordes Junction is flat anyway. Not a lot of places to hide, and the plant life is mostly sagebrush," Charlie said. "Not to mention we have cameras on the interstate starting at the Anthem exit."

"Logically, he would have either stuck to the backroads around Lake Montezuma and Beaver Creek or gone north and worked his way into one of the wooded areas off the freeway."

"His computer searches didn't show much," Raul said. "He was good about erasing them, and those we recovered were only about places Tia has been recently. It looks like he was following her around without her realizing it."

"I know he showed up in Flagstaff when Tia was at NAU in July," Evan said.

"And we have to assume the tracking device I found on Tia's truck was planted by Colby," Charlie added.

"It looks like these are the four main areas for our search." Chief Jarvis pointed to several areas near the freeway.

Charlie shifted closer, as though seeing the map for the first time. "Were any of Colby's internet searches on Munds Park?"

"Yeah." Raul flipped through his notes. "He did a search on November 2."

"That was last Friday," Wesley said, stating the obvious.

"And it was the day I found the tracking device on her car," Charlie said. "That whole area is made up of summer cabins. Colby could hide out there for weeks without anyone knowing he was there."

"I'll contact the Coconino Police Department and get a search team out there," Chief Jarvis said. "We can have some of our guys work the search by Lake Montezuma and coordinate with the other areas."

"I'm going to head out to Munds Park," Charlie said. "That's an area I know well."

Evan stood. "I'm coming with you."

"Evan, you're a civilian," Charlie countered. "I know you want to help, but the last thing we need is for Colby to see you coming. Your presence alone could set him off."

"Then I can set up at the country club or the general store with a computer and help coordinate the search." Evan waited for Charlie's gaze to meet his before he added, "You know I can't just sit here."

"I know." Charlie let out a sigh. "Follow me up in your car. I'll have you stay at my place with Kendra. I'd rather her not be alone anyway."

Feeling like he had achieved a monumental victory, Evan nodded. He would agree to anything right now if it would put him closer to finding Tia.

Before they reached the door, Chief Jarvis's phone rang.

Charlie and Evan paused, waiting to see if he was receiving news about Tia's case. When he hung up a moment later, he said, "Thunderstorms are rolling through the area. The helicopters are grounded until further notice."

The mood in the room deflated.

Charlie touched Evan's arm. "Come on. Let's go."

* * *

Colby rubbed his hand over the three-day beard on his face, irritated that in his search of the nearby cabins, he hadn't found an electric razor. He was going to have to break down and use the disposable version. At least the boys a few doors down had left some shaving cream under their bathroom sink.

Tia sat at her normal spot on the couch, a blanket tucked around her. He had turned the electricity on before starting breakfast, and a fire once again burned in the fireplace. Whatever smoke rose in the chimney would blend into the looming clouds.

He hadn't heard any aircraft since yesterday. Hopefully, that would be their one and only pass of the area, but he would have to cut the electricity again tonight to make sure they didn't have any light visible.

His gaze landed on Tia. She had grown quiet today, barely speaking to him as they ate their breakfast. He thought of their evening together last night, of the softness of her skin beneath his touch. She hadn't pulled away like Lexi had when they had finally managed to have time alone. No, Tia was different. She was beginning to understand.

Though Tia's eyes remained on the fire, he saw her cheeks flush as though she could feel him staring. Today was the day, he decided. Today things were going to change.

He rubbed his hand over his chin again. Yes, today was the day.

* * *

Evan parked beside Charlie in the general store parking lot and climbed out. "Why are we stopping here?"

"Because if Colby came in for supplies, Mrs. Burgess will know it," Charlie said. "It didn't look like he had planned ahead before abducting Tia, so he would have to come up with food and basic supplies somewhere."

"True." Evan followed him inside.

Mrs. Burgess stood as soon as she saw them. "Charlie, do you know what's going on around here? I've seen three police cars drive by in the past hour."

"We're looking for Tia Parker," Charlie said.

"I saw her story on the news. That poor girl."

"I'm hoping you can help us find her," Charlie said. He pulled his cell phone from his pocket and retrieved an image of Colby. "Have you seen this man in here before?"

Mrs. Burgess took a long look, then shook her head. "Never seen him."

"Any chance you've been missing any inventory over the past few days?"

"Nothing except for the chocolate muffins Jed got into yesterday."

"Could he have been disguised?" Evan asked Charlie.

"Maybe." Charlie pulled up another image on his phone, this time of Tia's pickup truck. He held it out again. "He would have been in this truck."

Her eyes went round. "I saw that truck."

"When?" Evan asked.

"Where?" Charlie said at the same time.

"It was right out on the main road. I saw it driving by when I was outside sweeping the porch." Mrs. Burgess paused for a moment. "Must have been Monday."

"Do you remember what time?"

"After breakfast, before lunch." She gave Charlie an apologetic look. "Sorry. I didn't pay any attention to the clock."

"That's okay. You did great," Charlie said. "Do you remember which direction they were going?"

"Past the country club. I didn't see beyond that."

"If you see this guy or the truck, I want you to call or text me," Charlie said. "He's a police officer, so don't let him fool you into telling him we're looking for him."

"I can do that." Mrs. Burgess picked up a package of muffins and handed them to Charlie. "Here. You take these. And grab yourselves some sandwiches too. Once you get out there searching, you aren't going to want to stop for food."

"Thanks." Charlie grabbed three sandwiches. "Put these on my tab."

"Darling, these are on the house. It's the least I can do." She put several water bottles in a bag and passed it to Evan. "You go find that girl. I want to see her back here safe and sound."

"Yes, ma'am."

* * *

Tia heard the water turn on in the downstairs shower. This was her chance. If Colby held true to the schedule he had established over the past few days, she should have the better part of an hour before he came back upstairs to get her for lunch.

Her hand shook when she fished the credit card out of her pocket. She slid it into the crack by the doorknob, jiggling it to get the latch to disengage. It didn't work.

Panic bubbled inside her. All morning, Colby had stared at her, a kind of cold, glassy stare. Something had changed in him, and it wasn't for the better.

She pulled the credit card free, shook out her hand, and tried again. This time, her efforts were rewarded. The door popped open.

Listening for any sound, she paused for a brief moment, then closed the door and locked it behind her. Taking care to move quietly, she hurried down the stairs. She unlocked the sliding glass door, realizing after she opened it that she had no way to lock it behind her.

The water in the shower shut off, and Tia's heart leapt into her throat. She closed the door completely and climbed through the porch railing, her feet landing on the pine needles covering the narrow flowerbed running the length of the porch.

The clang of metal startled her, and she yelped in surprise. The resident raccoon scampered out of the garbage can and hurried into the trees. She started to follow after it, but the heavy fall of footsteps caused her to freeze.

Would Colby see the unlocked door and know she had escaped? Or would he think he had forgotten to lock it?

She squatted down to make sure she wasn't visible through the glass, her heart beating hard and high in her throat. She leaned against the base of the cabin, a metal handle digging into her hip.

The memory of playing hide-and-seek with Julie as a child flashed into her mind. Tia shifted and pulled on the handle behind her, lifting the panel of wood that allowed workmen to access the crawl space beneath the cabin.

She crawled through a heartbeat before the door above her slid open.

"What the . . . ?" Colby started the sentence only to mutter an oath. "Tia!"

He retreated inside, and Tia could feel the vibration of him racing up the steps. She eased the access panel back into place, closing herself beneath the cabin. A spiderweb caught on her arm. She brushed at it, willing her eyes to adjust to the darkness.

Afraid Colby would find her hiding spot, she used her hand to smooth out the dirt behind her so as to not leave obvious tracks as she crawled deeper beneath the cabin, farther into the darkness.

Her head bumped against something, the sound exaggerating in her mind. Had he heard her?

More footsteps pounded over her head. Colby screamed her name. He was outside now, circling the cabin.

Her breath came in rapid bursts, and she struggled for air in the damp, cold, dark space. She envisioned the cabin above and crawled more than half the width of it. When she reached the spot where the water pipes entered the house beneath the kitchen, she stopped, groping them with her hands to confirm her position. Using the trick that had helped her win at hide-and-seek throughout her childhood, she put one of her feet on a crossbeam. She then used the pressure of her hands against parallel beams to suspend herself above the ground. She placed her other foot against the pipes.

Colby circled the cabin a second time, her name erupting from his lips. She kept hoping he would leave to search for her, but she could hear him drawing closer again. A creak of a hinge was followed by light spilling into the crawl space. But rather than coming from where she had entered, it was on the other side of the cabin, beneath the utility room.

The narrow beam of a flashlight swept from one side to the other. Tia held her breath, hoping the fabric of her sweatshirt wasn't hanging low enough to be seen.

The light swept beneath her a second time and then a third.

Her arms trembled from the exertion of holding her position. Unable to hold her breath any longer, she let the air out slowly, forcing herself to breathe quietly. Any movement, any sound, and her life was over.

The flashlight swept one more time, and he followed it with a curse. Then the access panel slammed back into place, and she was left in darkness.

* * *

Evan paced across Kendra Whitmore's living room, his sandwich remaining untouched. Kendra sat at the kitchen counter and nibbled at hers. He paused long enough to look out the window at the rain pulsing down through the pines.

He turned to make another lap around the room and caught the understanding look on Kendra's face. Since his arrival, she had been uncommonly quiet for a host, as though she knew making conversation was beyond his current capabilities.

Aware that Kendra had experienced a similar horror a few years ago, he asked, "How did you survive being in someone else's control like this?"

"I was fortunate that my ordeal ended the same day it started," Kendra said. "I'll tell you this though. Tia is doing everything she can right now to escape."

Evan turned toward the window and stared into the rain and dropping temperatures. Even if she did get away, where would she go? She'd freeze to death if she tried to hide in the woods overnight. The mountains she had so enjoyed when they'd come for a visit last summer could very well cost her her life.

That visit with Drew and Julie flashed into her mind. "What if she did get away?"

"What do you mean?"

"She doesn't have a cell phone, and there's hardly anyone living in the area this time of year."

Kendra scrambled to her feet and crossed to stand by the window beside him. "She knows where we live. She could be trying to come here."

Evan pulled his phone from his pocket and dialed Charlie's number. "Whitmore."

"Charlie, it's Evan," he began, his heart pounding with eagerness and hope. "What if Tia managed to get away from Colby? Maybe we should be searching first where she would hide."

"Hold on." Charlie's voice sounded in the background, and Evan was able to make out enough words to hear him direct a local police car to check out his street.

"I'm sending a cruiser to stay in the area of my cabin," Charlie said. "Where else would she go?"

"The only other places I can think of are the country club, the general store, or the cabin we stayed at last time we were here."

"If she made it to the club or the store, someone would have called us. What's the address to the cabin you stayed at?"

"I don't know, but I can show you where it is."

"I don't know . . ."

"Please, Charlie. If she got away and is hiding there, it means Colby is somewhere else."

Charlie hesitated briefly. "Okay, meet me at the country club and we'll check it out."

"I'll head there now."

"Hey, do me a favor and tell Kendra to make sure the alarm is on in the cabin."

"I will." Evan hung up and turned to face Kendra. "Charlie is having the police stick around here in case Tia comes this way. He said to engage the alarm."

"I will." Kendra stood. "Evan, good luck."

"Thanks."

* * *

The monster exploded inside him. Colby's entire body shook with fury as he continued his search around the cabin. She had to be here. She had to be close.

His path around the perimeter of the cabin hadn't revealed any footprints. How was that possible? With last night's rain, the soft ground should have made her easy to track.

Raindrops sprinkled onto his face, and he looked skyward. Lightning flashed, followed by a clap of thunder.

"Tia!" He screamed her name only to be met by silence. His hand struck out, impacting the side of the deck railing with enough force to knock it loose.

His hand throbbed, the pain cutting through his fury. He drew a deep breath and forced himself to think. Evidence. He needed evidence. Tia couldn't possibly have disappeared without leaving a trace.

He examined the gravel driveway, unable to distinguish between his footsteps and Tia's. For the second time, he walked the edge of the rectangular patch of rock, only the remnants of their footprints visible from the day they'd first arrived. Could she have traced those original footsteps as a way to disguise her path?

He squatted and traced the indentation her sneaker had made. He had taken her shoes, so her print wouldn't be the same in her stocking feet.

A fresh shower of pine needles lay across the track, no indication visible that anyone had come this way again.

He straightened and moved back to the truck. His fingers gripped the edge of the tarp, and he yanked it hard, sending the plastic flying onto the ground beside him. He checked the truck bed and looked beneath it.

Where was she? Fighting back the worst of his rage, he fisted his hands and stared at the front of the cabin, the home he had made with Tia.

The garbage can lid was once again on the ground, lying haphazardly against the railroad tie that lined the narrow flowerbed on the side of the deck. He crossed to the can, setting the lid back in place, his eyes sweeping the area with a new purpose.

Then he saw it. The faint indentation in front of the access panel. From a knee maybe?

He had already looked beneath the cabin, but now he understood where she had started this game of hide-and-seek. He was right. She was still here. Now he just needed to give her some motivation to come out into the open.

* * *

The muscles in Tia's arms and legs trembled from holding herself in place, and she eased herself back out of the rafters onto the ground. The sound of Colby circling the cabin continued outside, and it was all she could do to keep her breathing steady each time he drew close. The thought that he might look under the cabin a second time loomed, causing her to huddle behind the piping in the hope that his flashlight wouldn't land on her.

Footsteps sounded overhead again. A moment later, Colby bounded across the front deck. When she heard the engine of her truck roar to life, a flood of relief poured through her. A few more minutes and she could abandon her hiding place.

* * *

The decision to take one car took less than a minute. The weather combined with Charlie's lack of four-wheel drive made the antique Land Cruiser the vehicle of choice.

With the skies dark with rain clouds, Evan nearly missed the first turn.

"Are you sure you know where you're going?"

"I stayed here almost a week. I know where I'm going," Evan insisted. He took the next turn with confidence. He was three cabins from the final turn when he saw the flash of red to his right. "Charlie, that's her truck!"

"Keep driving."

"But . . ."

"If Colby has her inside, we don't want him to feel cornered," Charlie explained.

Evan kept driving. "Where do you want me to stop?"

"How far is her friend's cabin?"

"It's around the corner," Evan said. "As a crow flies, it's probably only a few hundred yards."

"Do you think Tia knows her way around here well enough to know that?"

"From what she and Julie said, Tia came here all the time growing up. There's a good chance."

"Go up to the corner and pull over." Charlie retrieved his phone and called for backup.

Evan parked on the side of the road, the rain now beating steadily against the windshield.

"Wait here." Charlie retrieved his weapon from his shoulder holster, checked his ammunition, and put it back in place. "I'm going to take a quick look around."

"What can I do?"

"Stay here so I can concentrate on finding Tia," Charlie said. "I don't want to worry about a civilian getting in the way while we search."

Recognizing that arguing would only delay the search, Evan nodded. "Be careful."

"You too," Charlie said. "I'll call you as soon as I find her."

Evan watched him step out of the car into the rain. Charlie closed his door quietly, the click of the latch barely audible over the wind and rain.

Through his rearview mirror, Evan watched Charlie slip back the way they had come until he disappeared into the trees. Evan's hands tightened on the steering wheel, the culmination of his hopes and fears battling within him.

Realizing that his original hope of Tia hiding out at Julie's cabin wasn't being explored, he started his engine again. Surely, he wouldn't be in the way if he checked it out. Besides, if he found Tia, the police would be able to concentrate on finding her kidnapper without the concern of keeping Tia safe.

He put the vehicle into gear and pushed on the gas. The Land Cruiser rocked forward a few inches and rolled right back where it started. He must have parked in a soft spot of mud. He threw the car into reverse and tried backing up to find more solid ground.

He could hear the tires spin, but the passenger side of the car sank deeper into the mud.

"Great," Evan muttered. Stuck, literally. He stepped into the storm, closing the door quietly as Charlie had done moments before. Frigid rain sluiced over him, soaking his hair and running down his back. He leaned down to inspect the tires, hoping he could figure out how to manually change the vehicle from two-wheel to four-wheel drive.

When he moved to the front of the car, he noticed the winch attached. Seeing a new means of getting free, he eyed the tree on the opposite corner. He figured out how to unlock the winch cable and took hold of the hook on the end. If his estimate was right, he would be able to loop the thick wire around the tree and use the hook to hold it in place. A touch of the button, and the winch should pull the car free. Or pull the tree down. He hoped for the first possibility.

A bolt of lightning flashed overhead. He climbed back into the Land Cruiser in unison with the thunderclap. What a time for a storm.

* * *

Tia waited for the sound of the engine to fade before she crawled toward the nearest access panel. With Colby gone, she opted for the one by the back of the house. Cobwebs caught in her hair, and she tried to brush them away as an eight-legged occupant creeped across her arm.

She swiped at it, hoping it wasn't the black widow variety. Keeping one hand out in front of her so she wouldn't run into anything in the dark, she continued forward.

Her fingers finally brushed against a wooden panel, but this one wasn't movable. She used her hand to press along the boards that protected the crawl space from unwanted guests.

A shiver worked through her. She should have reached the opening by now. Could Colby have secured it from the outside? She was just about to turn and crawl back to where she had entered when her hand pressed against the spot where two panels met. The one on the left moved.

She shifted to the left. The wind howled outside, branches rattling against its force. Determined to get clear of Colby once and for all, she drew a deep breath and pushed the panel open.

After taking a quick look around, she crawled the rest of the way outside and straightened.

Water soaked through her socks, and rain assaulted every other previously dry spot on her body. With a shudder, she headed for the trees. A little over two miles and she would reach the country club, a phone, and a dry, safe place to hide.

* * *

Colby stood at the edge of the cabin next door, waiting, watching. Tia was bound to leave her hiding place soon.

The idea to pretend to leave had been brilliant. He was brilliant. Tia would be his. It was her destiny.

He saw the tarp flap in the wind, irritated for a moment that he hadn't thought to take it with him. Keeping the truck out of sight ensured their privacy. Then again, who would see it anyway? With this weather, the search would be called off, assuming they hadn't given up already.

His eyes scanned the cabin, constantly looking for any movement, always coming back to the access panel beside the front porch. That had to be where she was hiding, some dark corner his flashlight hadn't reached.

Water dripped through the tree he was currently using for shelter, an icy droplet hitting his neck and sliding beneath his collar. He was going to enjoy sitting beside the fire after he had Tia back under control.

He knew now that he had been too patient. He had wanted her to come to him, to realize they belonged together. No more. It was time for him to show her how things were going to be from now on.

He stared at the access panel, fixating on it. Could he have been wrong about her? Had she somehow managed to make it past him?

Impatient, he stepped clear of his hiding spot and began walking around the cabin, keeping a good twenty yards between himself and the structure.

Lightning flashed as he came around the back corner. There, at the edge of the yard, Tia slipped into the trees.

* * *

Tia sensed his presence even before she heard the footsteps. Her head whipped around, and for a fraction of a second, she froze. Then she ran.

Darting between trees, she sprinted forward. She had a bigger head start this time, but not by much. She didn't bother to take cover. If Colby pulled his gun on her today, there was nothing she could do about it. She pressed forward, every ounce of her energy focused on making her escape.

Her toe caught on a tree root, and she stumbled but didn't fall. A cry escaped her and was carried away by the wind.

The pounding of the rain matched her heartbeat, water pelting her with each movement. She kept going.

Using the internal map she had imprinted in her mind from youth, she cut across a neighbor's yard, angling toward the road. Colby's breathing grew close enough that she could hear it over the wind. Another cry of fear bubbled out.

He was getting closer, and she had too far to go. Logic told her she wasn't going to make it, but she couldn't stop. Only two miles to the main road, only two miles to where she could find help.

But Colby was too fast. She wasn't fast enough.

The relatively even surface of the dirt road gave her feet a reprieve from the abuse of the forest floor, and she increased her pace. She could hear Colby's footsteps clearly now. He was closing in on her.

The sound of an engine turning over carried toward her, and she wondered if her mind was playing tricks on her. Then she rounded the corner and saw it.

Kyla? Tia couldn't believe her eyes. She would have recognized her dad's old Land Cruiser anywhere. But what was Kyla doing here?

Tia pushed harder, her legs burning.

Another two hundred yards. Surely she could make it that far. But when she reached the old Land Cruiser, would she find safety or would she and her sister both be doomed to face Colby's wrath?

* * *

With the motor running, Evan reached for the button to engage the winch. A cry in the storm caused him to look up, his jaw dropping when he saw Tia sprinting toward him.

Her path would take her across the winch cable, so he climbed out of the vehicle and yelled, "Tia!"

Surprise flashed on her face before she turned her head to look behind her.

Time stalled in that moment.

Colby. Sprinting at full speed. A gun in his hand.

Unarmed, with the Land Cruiser stuck in the mud, Evan stared at the woman he loved, the woman he cherished, racing toward him. Yet when she reached him, she would still be every bit as much Colby's captive as she had been before.

Not if Evan could help it.

"Tia!" he shouted again. He climbed back into the car and reached across to open the passenger door. If nothing else, her path to that side of the car would give her some shelter from any bullets Colby decided to send their way.

"Watch out!" Evan shouted as she approached the cable lying across the road.

Whether she realized the meaning of his warning or not, Tia crossed the barrier without incident, but Colby had closed to within twenty feet of her.

"Now or never." Evan turned on the winch, the cable slowly pulling tight. It lifted several inches off the ground an instant before Colby reached it.

The cable now ankle high, Colby's front foot caught against it. The speed of his impact sent him sprawling and crashing face first to the ground.

The winch continued to turn, the Land Cruiser slowly edging forward out of the mud and onto the firm surface of the road.

Tia scrambled into the seat on the passenger side.

"Wait here. I have to unhook us."

With a sense of urgency, Evan passed behind where Colby lay motionless and hurried across the street. His fingers were wet and fumbling, but he unhooked the winch from the tree he had used as an anchor and dropped the grappling hook to the ground. Colby was slowly rising to his feet, his gun in hand.

* * *

"No!" Tia screamed. She left the safety of the vehicle, fear for Evan now her dominant emotion.

Following instinct, she reacted, running again, but this time, she raced toward Colby instead of away. His back was to her, her tormentor's fury now directed at Evan.

"Colby, no." Evan spread his hands out to his side. "The police are on their way. Don't make it worse."

Colby steadied his gun, and Tia launched herself at him, tackling him around his waist in a way that would have made her football team proud.

Already off balance, he fell to the ground, but somehow, he maintained his grip on his weapon.

"Tia! No!" Evan shouted. Out of the corner of her eye, she saw him holding the thick metal cable with both hands.

Colby rolled over onto his back, crushing her beneath his weight. "Don't push it, Tia, or I'll kill you too."

He grabbed her by the arm and yanked her up beside him. In a swift move, Tia found herself in front of him, Colby's arm hooked around her neck, his gun hand still free to take aim.

"Colby, don't." Tia tried to wriggle free, but Colby tightened his hold.

"We'll have to start over, Tia," Colby said, his voice unexpectedly calm, distant even. "They won't understand."

"Colby, let him go. Let me go."

"I can't let you go. We belong together. You belong with me." He lifted his gun and took aim. "Sorry, Evan. You should have stayed in Paris."

Her life, Evan's life, and their possible future flashed before her eyes. Tia threw her hips back and jabbed an elbow into Colby's ribs.

The gun went off, the bullet impacting the bark of the tree only inches above Evan's head. Evan ducked. Then his arms went into motion, and he swung the winch cable, sending the slack of it bouncing into Colby's legs.

The impact of metal against his legs didn't appear to faze him. Colby stepped on the cable, neutralizing it as a possible weapon.

Tia swung her leg back, trying to knock him off balance. That only angered him more.

"That's enough!" Colby shifted his grip to her arm, holding her so she was facing him, her back to Evan. "Don't make me hurt you, Tia. I don't want to hurt you."

"Then let me go."

"You don't understand, do you?" He shook his head as though scolding a small child. "You aren't ever going to understand."

"Colby, if you really love me, you'll let me go."

"I do really love you. That's why I can't let you go." He pushed her toward Evan.

Tia felt Evan's hands reach for her, pulling her behind him even as Colby took aim once more. Horror erupted inside her, a scream bubbling within her but unable to find a voice.

Lightning flashed. A single gunshot sounded.

* * *

Evan's heart stopped. He turned Tia toward him, his eyes searching for any sign of injury.

Tia clearly had the same thought about him. Her hands patted his chest, searching for a bullet wound. "Are you okay?"

"I'm fine. You?"

She nodded. Then her gaze strayed to where Colby now lay on the ground.

Charlie emerged from behind the Land Cruiser, gun in hand, and rushed forward, kicking Colby's fallen weapon clear before checking for a pulse.

Instantly, Evan pulled Tia close and buried his face into the curve of her neck. "It's okay," he murmured. "It's okay now."

Over Tia's shoulder, Evan saw Charlie shake his head. Colby was dead. The nightmare was over.

Charlie moved to the shelter of the car to make a phone call, but Evan couldn't move. He couldn't let go.

Tia trembled in his arms. He pulled back so he could see her face. Her cheeks were wet with rain and tears. "I'm so sorry I wasn't here."

She blinked several times as though to bring him into focus. "What are you doing here?"

"I was on my way to see you when you disappeared."

"What?"

Evan didn't answer, except to lower his lips to hers. All the pent-up frustration and fears poured into the kiss, both of them trembling with overflowing emotions.

She shivered, and another flash of lighting skittered across the sky. "Let's get you someplace warm."

Evan leaned down to pick up the winch cable and led Tia back to the car. A police cruiser arrived as he helped her into the passenger seat. Charlie headed over to talk to the two policemen who climbed out while Evan went about retracting the winch cable.

He turned the heat on high and dug a sweatshirt out of his suitcase and handed it to Tia. "Here. You need to get into some dry clothes."

Her teeth chattered. "My clothes are at Julie's cabin. That's where he . . ." She trailed off and tried again. "That's where I've been."

Charlie approached in time to overhear the last part of their conversation. "Evan, take Tia back to my cabin. She can borrow some dry clothes from Kendra. We'll have to process the cabin where Tia was held. I found her car keys on Colby. I'll drive her truck back to my place when I'm done here."

"Thanks."

Charlie nodded. "Tia, I'm glad you're okay."

She let out a shuddering breath. "So am I."

Chapter 39

EVAN HELD TIA'S HAND AS they waited in the hospital examination room. Though he knew Tia wanted nothing more than to go home, he and Charlie had both insisted she get checked out first.

"I'm fine," Tia announced for the third time since their arrival. "Colby didn't hurt me."

"That nasty bruise on your cheek didn't get there by itself."

She lifted a finger to her cheekbone where a yellow shadow marked her otherwise tanned skin. "I almost forgot about that."

"Will you tell me what happened?" Evan leaned forward until her gaze met his.

"I saw Colby on my way back from Pinewood, and I started thinking about how often I ran into him," Tia said. "He was giving me the creeps, so I thought maybe I could call his old girlfriend and see if she could offer any advice on how to handle him."

"But you couldn't talk to her."

"No." Her voice dropped to a whisper, and tears welled in her eyes. "The police chief in Valdez said they found her body a few weeks ago. He thinks Colby killed her."

"If you hadn't gotten away . . ." Evan began but was unable to finish the thought.

"If you hadn't found me when you did, I . . ."

Evan gathered her into his arms. "It's okay. You're okay now."

The doctor entered, his eyes sweeping over them. His brisk, businesslike demeanor melted as he continued forward. "I'm sorry to keep you waiting. I understand the police want both a physical and emotional evaluation on Miss Parker."

Tia swallowed hard. "My emotional state will be just fine if you let me go home."

"Then let's see what we can do to make that happen."

* * *

Tia couldn't sleep. She had arrived home to find her parents and sister waiting for her. After lots of hugs and tears of relief, she had been forced to relive the experience one more time when Charlie had come by to take her statement as well as return her truck. The moment the interview had ended, she had disappeared into her room and slept for hours.

Finally warm and dry, she had woken in time for a late dinner before heading back to bed again. Evan had been entrenched in a conversation with her dad, and her mother had hovered in the best possible way, staying close to take care of the basics. She had no doubt that her clothes were already washed and folded in the laundry room, her kitchen clean, and her refrigerator fully stocked.

Because she was awake, she headed for her refrigerator now, jumping when she heard movement in the living room.

"Sorry," Evan said, straightening from where he lay on the couch. "It's just me."

There was a sheet neatly tucked into the cushions, and a pillow and blanket lay on top of it.

"Why are you sleeping on the couch?" she asked.

"Your sister was too tired to drive home, so she's in the guest room."

"Sorry everything is so tight here. We aren't used to having Raul and Gabrielle living in the bungalow."

"It's fine." Evan crossed to her and took her hand. "Couldn't sleep?"

"I got used to being up all night. I guess it'll take some time to adjust."

"I'm almost afraid to ask, but why were you up all night?"

"It was too cold to sleep." She shook her head to push aside the memories. "I'm going to raid the refrigerator. Want to come?"

"Sure." Evan released her hand and followed her into the kitchen. "Do you want me to make something for you?"

"No, thanks." She opened the refrigerator but closed it again when she saw the container of peanut butter cookies on the counter. She really loved her mom.

She selected one and held out the plastic container. "Want one?"

"Yeah, thanks." He took one and leaned back against the counter. "I talked to Raul today when you were napping."

"What about?"

"I want him to help me design a security system for your house."

"Evan, that's sweet, but this is Cottonwood. As terrifying as the past few days have been, I don't want to start living my life looking over my shoulder all the time."

"Consider this a favor for me, then," Evan said. "Your friends on the police force are for it too. You had us all scared."

"I still can't believe you guys figured out where I was," Tia said.

"Believe me, it was quite the team effort."

"Charlie said you and Raul helped narrow down the search area." Tia finished her cookie and selected a second.

"Raul's better with computers than he let on. If he doesn't end up back on the force, I might snatch him up for my business."

Tia took a bite. "Maybe you should make him an offer."

"I need a business manager first," Evan said. "With my new schedule in Paris, I'll have time to pick up some more jobs, but I have to have someone to deal with contracts, finances, and soliciting business."

"How hard would it be to find someone like that?"

"Well, I'd prefer not to rent office space, so the ideal would be someone who wants to work out of their home but who also has business experience."

Tia saw a light come on next door. "Would someone who has worked finance be able to manage for you?"

"Do you have someone in mind?"

"Yeah." Tia motioned to the bungalow. "Gabrielle."

Evan seemed to consider. "What's her background?"

"Business degree. She majored in marketing but has been working in finance at the high school for the past few years," Tia told him. "The principal has been letting her shift her schedule to bring her daughter to work, but I don't think he'll be able to let her do it for much longer. When we get into postseason for sports, she'll have to be there during the day and pay for a babysitter."

"Maybe I'll talk to her tomorrow." He motioned to the cookies. "Are you done with those?"

"Yeah."

"Are you going to be able to get back to sleep?" Evan asked.

"I don't know."

He put both hands on her shoulders and leaned forward to kiss her forehead. "Come sit with me on the couch. We can watch a movie."

"I don't want to keep you up."

"For days, I've prayed to have the chance to have moments like these with you again," Evan said. "You're worth some lost sleep."

She leaned forward and kissed his cheek. "I'm glad you think so."

"I know so."

* * *

Evan followed Tia down the trail as they made their way through the pines and the occasional barren oak tree. Tia had been home for nearly six weeks, her family finally back in their respective homes. For the first few weekends, Tia's house had been overflowing with friends and family visiting, everyone eager to make sure she received the emotional support necessary to put the trauma behind her.

Evan had enjoyed getting to know her parents and sister better. More importantly, a talk with her father last week had given him the courage to visit a jeweler two days ago. He had nearly gone crazy waiting for the weekend.

"You know what I love the most about hiking?" Tia asked.

"What?"

"I don't have to be on time for anything."

"Do you realize that I have been on time more since I met you than I probably was the rest of my adult life?"

"I find that hard to believe."

"How many times did we talk on the phone, and how often were either of us late?"

"Oh, I don't know. Like never." She reached a clearing beside a small stream.

"Exactly." Evan stepped beside her and took her hand. "No one has ever mattered to me as much as you do."

"I'm honored."

Evan mustered his courage and tugged on her hand so she would stop and face him. "I was hoping I could convince you to be on time for something else too."

"What's that?"

"Our wedding." He could see by the expression on her face that she thought this was another casual mention of marriage. Her eyes grew wide when he dropped down to one knee and drew out the ring box from his pocket. He flipped open the top and asked the most important question of his life. "Tia Parker, I love you so much. Will you marry me?"

Her right hand lifted to her mouth, and her eyes filled. Seconds stretched out and felt like an eternity before she nodded.

"Yes?" Evan asked, straightening to a stand.

"Yes."

He gathered her into his arms, his lips finding hers for a tender kiss. When he pulled back, he stared down at the most amazing woman he had ever known. He slipped the ring on her finger, and everything in his world clicked into place. All that remained now was choosing the date that would start their happily ever after.

ABOUT THE AUTHOR

TRACI HUNTER ABRAMSON WAS BORN in Arizona, where she lived until moving to Venezuela for a study-abroad program. After graduating from Brigham Young University, she worked for the Central Intelligence Agency for several years, eventually resigning in order to raise her family. She credits the CIA with giving her a wealth of ideas as well as the skills needed to survive her children's teenage years. She has gone on to write more than twenty best-selling novels that have consistently been nominated as Whitney Award finalists, and she is a five-time Whitney Award winner. When she's not writing, Traci enjoys spending time with her husband and five children, preferably on a nice, quiet beach somewhere. She also enjoys sports, travel, writing, and coaching high school swimming.